Motorcycle Ride
on the Sea
of Tranquility

- - - - - - - - - - - - - - - - -

PATRICIA SANTANA

UNIVERSITY OF NEW MEXICO PRESS
ALBUQUERQUE

Library of Congress Cataloging-in-Publication Data

Santana, Patricia.
Motorcycle ride on the sea of tranquility / Patricia Santana.
p.　cm.

ISBN 0-8263-2435-5 (cloth : alk. paper)
ISBN 0-8263-2436-3 (paper : alk. paper)
1. Mexican American families—Fiction.
2. Vietnamese Conflict, 1961–1975—Veterans—Fiction.
3. Post-traumatic stress disorder—Fiction.
4. Brothers and sisters—Fiction.
5. Teenage girls—Fiction.
6. San Diego (Calif.)—Fiction.　I. Title.
PS3619.A57 M68 2002
813'.6—dc21
2001004433

1　2　3　4　5　6　7　8　9　10　11　12

Design: Mina Yamashita

In memory of my brother

SERGIO LUIS SANTANA

1947–1996

PART ONE

■ ■ ■ ■ ■ ■ ■ ■ ■ ■ ■ ■ ■

El Arbol Se Conoce Por Su Fruto

The Tree Is Known By Its Fruit

—Popular Spanish Saying

1

When my brother Chuy returned from Vietnam in April of 1969, our sweet peas were in full bloom. Entwined in the fence enclosing our yard, sinewy tendrils and translucent flowers reached up to the heavens, while unruly ones poked out from the worn, picket fence, which had grown lopsided from the weight of bountiful sweet pea vines every spring. It was said not only by our neighbors and those on Citrus Street, but even by people across the railroad tracks on Harris Avenue that you could always tell when spring had arrived in San Diego by checking the Sahagún yard over on Conifer Street. The sweet peas surrounded the whole of our yard, as if our home were in a pastoral state of siege, and the flowers' scent was intoxicating. My best friend Lydia wondered if a person could get high on the smell. Not exactly, I told her. It was a special Sahagún aphrodisiac, its aroma meant to beckon innocent but enormously handsome young men from all over the city to enter this garden of delights. She wanted to know if I was talking about *all* enormously handsome men, or just a certain Francisco Valdivia of Southwest Junior High.

"Don't you see, pendeja," I told her. "The Sahagún Estate sweet peas herald the beginning of spring, of life, of renewal and rebirth, and so it is only fitting that the enormously handsome young men of the city would want to delve into this garden of youth and innocent splendor."

"Please, Doña Shakespeariana," Lydia said. "Spare me your shit load of eloquence and symbolism."

She was helping me wrap sets of plastic forks and knives in a napkin, tying them with orange cellophane ribbon. "Don't tie it so tight," I told her, "otherwise people can't get it off."

"So then what do you do," Lydia asked. "Hide behind the bushes waiting to pounce on these poor, innocent guys?"

"Oh, Lydia, of course not," I said. "How uncouth! You see, the scent enters their skin, into every sexy little pore; it gets into their blood vessels, rushing up to their heart. The moment they set eyes on me, it is love—amor, amor—of the grandest kind."

"For them or for you?" Lydia asked.

"You know, Lydia," I said, "if you're not going to allow me my little fantasy, if you can't cooperate just this once—you know, be romantic and fanciful for once in your life—then just forget it, OK?"

"Is this still too tight?" she asked, showing me a tied napkin and good-naturedly ignoring my last comment. Lydia was my best friend, no doubt about it.

"Yeah, that's better," I said. I had the best part of the task: to curl the ends of the ribbon with the sharp side of the scissors, my ribbon ends obediently twirling and transforming themselves into lively, springy curlicues.

I wondered for a moment whether Chuy would notice these tied ribbons and remember that this was my favorite job for family parties. But he would, I reminded myself, for he was my favorite brother, and I, Yolanda Sahagún, the seventh of nine children by Dolores and Lorenzo Sahagún, was surely his favorite sister.

Each of us had our chores to perform, things to prepare for Chuy's Welcome Home party. Further discussion of the garden, which my parents had diligently grown and nurtured since they arrived from Mexico over twenty years before, would have to wait.

Lydia and I were in the backyard patio organizing the plastic utensils, paper plates, cups, and napkins—while my brother Tony organized the albums and 45s. He was sitting on the floor where he'd set up the stereo hi-fi, the turntable, and speakers. Dozens of albums were scattered around him. Lots of Motown. Already he had Ray Charles singing a lively "Hit the Road, Jack," warming us up for the festivities that lay ahead.

"Oye," Papá called out from the kitchen screen door, "did you find the Javier Solis albums and the Variedad Mariachi?" As always when there was going to be a big family feast, he appointed himself the official food sampler and was now eating a warmed tortilla with beans and rice. "Last time you played too much of that crazy music of yours," he warned. "A little consideration this time for us viejitos, eh?"

Papá didn't seem like a viejito to me. His light blue eyes were too full of fun and fire, too youthful and feisty. Even though he was snacking all the time, Papá was thin and sprightly. He would never grow old. He was Papá, our resident Jarabe Tapatío dancer.

"Hey, do you think your father will make you dance with him this time?" Lydia asked, giggling.

"God, spare me please!" I said. "Don't even mention it— me hechas la sal—are you trying to put a hex on me?"

"Man, if any one of your brothers asked me to dance the Jarabe Tapatío tonight," Lydia said in a low voice just in case my brother Tony could hear her over Ray Charles, "I would in a flash."

"Pobrecita," I said, "don't hold your breath." Poor Lydia and her perpetual crush on my four brothers.

Chuy had come back to the States through the San Francisco airport, spent a night with our Uncle Teodoro, who lived in the Bay area, and was flying down to San Diego today, the day of his homecoming.

I was straightening the living room earlier this afternoon when we got the call from Tío Teodoro.

"But he's all in one piece, isn't he?" Mamá said, speaking into the receiver.

I was all ears, trying to figure out what Tío was saying at the other end of the line. Quickly swiping the dust off with a rag, I set the vase of sweet peas strategically on top of the scar-like crack on the glass coffee table. There, now nobody would notice it. Chuy was probably on his way down now, flying in from Frisco. God, I couldn't wait!

"But of course he's tired, Teodoro," Mamá was saying. "It's a long flight. But he's safe now, bendito sea Dios," and she hung up. She looked distracted, must have been thinking of PSA flight schedules and the quickest way to the San Diego airport to pick up Chuy.

Yes, our Chuy would be home, all in one piece, thanks be to God.

Tito and El Chango arrived at our house early. They had their own stack of favorite albums to contribute to the party.

"Have you talked to him yet?" El Chango asked Tony. El Chango was Chuy's best friend, but he hadn't been drafted into the army because of his polio-afflicted leg. His limp earned him the nickname "El Chango" because he walked like a monkey.

"No," Tony said. "He didn't call when he got to San Francisco. But he's on his way home now. Plane gets in at six thirty."

"What time are people getting here?"

"Around eight or nine."

"Shit, man," El Chango said. "What if he's not in the mood for all this?" El Chango adored Chuy, thought he was the funniest guy in the world, and he always seemed to want to protect Chuy, loved being his straight man when they were up to some new prank, got a kick out of being his partner in crime in their high school mischief—travesuras galore. Chuy and his faithful buddy, El Chango, had earned themselves the much-esteemed reputation of being witty devils.

Tony alternated music, playing some old songs—"Johnny Angel," "It's My Party"—and new songs like "Crimson and Clover" and "Time of the Season."

"Maybe he'll need some rest before the party," El Chango said, still worried about Chuy.

"Yeah, we thought the same, but our uncle up in Frisco told us that when Chuy got there he slept the whole day and woke up fifteen hours later and said he was ready to go home."

He would be ready to come home, yes he would, to us, his eight brothers and sisters who had watched the six o'clock news every night with dreadful anticipation, read the *San Diego Union,* two or three of us at a time awkwardly holding the oversized pages—scanning the national news, local news, international news—wondering if he was in this bombing, or that offensive, knowing that somewhere out there in another world, on that flattened-out map, this very minute our Chuy could be bombed to shreds, exploding bits and pieces of his person scattered on a terrain and in a world we knew nothing about.

April, 1969—our Chuy would soon be home now, all in one piece, bendito sea Dios.

Red, white, and blue streamers hung across the length of the garage. Someone had rescued a scorched American flag from a garbage bin at the San Diego State Campus; cousins in Tijuana had brought us a Mexican flag—both were hanging on the garage wall. The framed picture of the Virgin of Guadalupe was temporarily removed from her usual spot in the living room and now hung between the two flags. Below these, a long table was set for the buffet. The white frosted sheet cake was decorated with two miniature toothpick flags—Mexican and American—and red and blue writing said "Welcome Home, CHUY!"

Mamá stood at the kitchen door. She, along with my older sisters, Carolina and Ana María, had been busy in the kitchen preparing the yummy feast for days, anticipating this moment. Now she looked out at all of us—Lydia and me at the table arranging the tableware, Tony, El Chango, and Tito near us, sorting the albums.

"Buenas tardes, Señora," Tito and El Chango called out to her. Mamá could barely hear their greeting because the music was on full blast. She smiled and waved to them, shaking her head in exaggeration, as if to say they were crazy to listen to that loud racket. Her short curly brown hair crowned her face, her green eyes took in the backyard. It seemed as if she were assessing the fruits of her labor: the beds of begonias, Boston ferns, the birds of paradise. I watched Mamá's eyes caress the healthy guayaba tree, and then the plum tree—still too thin and young to produce. The quince tree. She was sure this fall the membrillos would be as big and tart as they had been two years ago. Maybe now that the family would all be together again the tree would fare better, she must have been thinking as she stepped back into the shadows of the kitchen.

Our Chuy was coming home, gracias a Dios.

Then my oldest brothers, Armando and Octavio, arrived from Tijuana with wooden cases of bottled sodas, tequila and lemons. Although you could buy lemons here in the supermarkets or pluck them from the lemon trees, Papá insisted that the little green Mexican limones tasted better, so my brothers had been sure to make a quick stop at Mercado Hidalgo.

Now they plunked down the cases of sodas and beers, passing out bottles to the few more buddies who had arrived—buddies who always got to our parties early for a head start on the drinking (or maybe for a peek at one of the lovely, ripe Sahagún sisters—Carolina, Ana María or me—I wishfully thought).

"When the moon is in the seventh house, and Jupiter aligns with Mars," the Fifth Dimension sang, the words both haunting and celebratory. Lydia and I, along with my pesky younger sisters, were blowing up the balloons.

"C'mon, mi'ja," my oldest brother Armando said as he led the baby of the family into the middle of the patio and twirled her around to the rhythms of the Fifth Dimension, let her put her tiny feet on his as he danced a kind of Frankenstein step to the beat. Luz giggled and let herself be danced to the middle of the patio where everyone could see her, proud to be dancing with her oldest brother, relieved that no one was telling her to "scramboola" as we sometimes did when she was being a seven-year-old pest. Now Octavio had Monica, second to the last Sahagún, twirling her this way and that to the shouts of "Let the sunshine in!" The music and squeals of delight brought Mamá, Papá, Carolina, and Ana María to the kitchen door, laughing at the mismatched dancing couples.

This is what we were doing, then: singing at the top of our lungs, pretending we were the Fifth Dimension celebrating the Age of Aquarius, all of us snapping our fingers to the beat, clapping and singing "Let the sunshine—Let the sunshine in . . ." when suddenly we stopped in mid-sentence, in mid-harmony, realizing—all of us at the same time—that Chuy was standing before us, quietly staring. His face was stern and disapproving, as if he were a Lieutenant Commander and had just caught his men in outrageous and inappropriate activities. Unruly and disobedient soldiers, all of us. He stood straight, shoulders back, at attention. Impeccable posture. Impossible. Dressed in Army regulation greens, Jesús Manuel Sahagún stared at us as if he were a Martian accidentally alighted on a planet not his own, perhaps not of his liking.

Our Chuy had come home, thanks be to God.

—2

Twilight now. The warm April evening was drizzled with laughter and music, with dancing and good eating. "Blue Angel," "Wah-Watusi," "King of the Road," "Leader of the Pack"—Chuy's favorite songs. Christmas lights in April dangled festively from the guava and quince trees, and the stars were bright and twinkling with happiness or generosity or I didn't know what, but they were up there in some sort of celestial communion. And I thought that this was, indeed, the Age of Aquarius.

Abrazos, kisses, tears—the air was punctuated with sighs of relief, of questions and exclamations. Of love and community. The house, the patio, the yard—cars parked along our Conifer Street and overflowing onto Citrus Street—all were filled with friends and family celebrating Chuy's homecoming.

Papá stood at the front of the house, arms akimbo, relishing his role as the Official Party Greeter.

"Compadre," he called out to Don Epifranio, who tottered toward him with cane in tow. "Now the party can truly begin, eh?"

"Sí, sí," the old man chuckled. "I've arrived, so now the party will get good." They gave each other a robust hug. Don Epifranio was a fixture in Palm City. He'd been here since God only knows when—and was somewhere in his nineties. He refused to reveal his age. "Old enough to know better, and still want more," I often overheard him tell the adults. Once when I asked him how old he was, the old widower explained: "Ah Yoli, if I reveal my age, I may scare away las bellas damas who sneak up to my bedroom window every night at midnight, vying for my love."

Now Papá escorted Don Epifranio to the backyard.

"Where's Chuy?" the old man was asking Papá as they walked down the sidewalk. "I want to see our soldier boy."

Yeah, where was he? That was what I wanted to know, too. Where'd our Chuy gone?

After the initial surprise of seeing him quietly staring at us while we danced, we had rushed to him, engulfing him in hugs and kisses. Mamá threw open the screen door and flew like a crazy angel to Chuy. The guys at the record player charged over, getting in line for their turn to greet him. In the rush, Tony had bumped into the turntable, and you could hear the scratching rip of the record, the Age of Aquarius now repeating itself forever: ". . . sunshine in, sunshine in . . ."

In the backyard, we hugged and kissed Chuy. Monica and Luz, along with their own assortment of best friends and cousins, danced around the adults, skipped and hopped.

Then it was my turn.

"Hi, Chuy," I said, hesitant, shy. Why did it seem he wasn't really looking at me, his favorite sister?

"Yeah, hi," he said, barely touching my hand, a disconnected handshake. He was looking over my head at all the people surrounding him. Annoyed? Angry? Or maybe just tired. Yes, that was it: he was tired. El Chango was right all along in being worried that Chuy might not be in the mood for a Welcome Home party so soon. He was tired, for God's sake, couldn't everyone see that? For God's sake.

And just as quickly, he was on to the next greeter. He

accepted the hugs of the guests as they stood in line to greet him, looking like the groom at a wedding reception, but without a bride, alone in the receiving line. He never once smiled, not really, not the way I knew he could, laughing and grinning, his blue eyes alive and playful. His smile was tight and forced. He was pale and thin.

Now Mamá stood at the kitchen screen door looking out at the party while I heated tortillas at the stove. It occurred to me that she stood there often, the screen from the backyard making her look fuzzy and indecipherable, the silhouette of a guardian angel. I knew what she was thinking: give him big helpings of pozole, a brew of her favorite, most potent herbs. She would check with Rosita, the curandera in Tijuana. If those remedies didn't work, she would give Don Tomás a call in El Grullo, Jalisco, and consult with him. Surely he would have a cure. She would bring him back to normal, Mamá must have been thinking as she looked at her fading war veteran son, my favorite brother, standing amidst all the well-intentioned guests circling him. Her pobre hijo looked lost and distant, as if he had misplaced his soul, and now stood eternally confused.

Tío Teodoro's long-distance call to Mamá had been a waste of his good money. He needn't have troubled himself to warn her. Mamá was no fool. I was sure she knew something was wrong with Chuy in the first months he was in Vietnam. She once mentioned to us that she had had a disturbing dream about Chuy. She must have had these dreams long before the letters stopped coming, long before he was silent in Vietnam. It must have been God's way of warning her: Prepare yourself, Dolores, your son needs to be tended with extra care, like the membrillo tree that has been hit with a mysterious plague. Is that what she was thinking? But no, El Chango was right all along, Chuy was just tired.

"You are one of the lucky ones," Socorrito said to my mother, coming up to stand next to her at the screen door. "Look at the poor Vázquez family. Their oldest son—killed to pieces just a week before his tour of duty was over. Magdalena has never been the same. Pobre mujer, she looks dead herself, just like her son." She shook her head, her foot tapping to the rhythm of the music. In her day she had been a lively dancer, and much as I was sure Socorrito wanted to be out in the middle of the dance floor with those young people, she must have felt it her duty to comfort Mamá, knowing what she must be feeling watching her son who looked bien extraño, not the Chuy she had known since he was a small esquincle of a boy. Socorrito looked doubtful, as if she couldn't quite put her finger on it. What was different about Chuy? Who knew, perhaps it was that dark green uniform, so stiff and official.

"The Conroys lost their boy, too," I could hear Socorrito telling Mamá. "Pobrecito, killed in Vietnam just like Ricky."

"Socorro," Mamá said, turning to her now. "Don't speak to me of the dead right now. Can't you see my heart is with the living?"

Then the music changed completely, rock and roll and Motown making respectful way for our parents' favorite Mexican music. The "Jarabe Tapatío" was playing, and Papá led my sister Carolina out into the middle of the patio and together, as they did at every family gathering, they danced the hat dance.

"Vengan todos," Papá called out to everyone. Many more couples ventured out onto the dance floor—old people, uncles, aunts, and a few silly children. Socorrito, who had grown up with my parents in El Grullo, who just a minute before had been trying to cheer Mamá, was now leading old Don Epifranio carefully out onto the dance floor. Now hopping on the dance floor, kicking out first one heel then the other, Socorrito swished her ballooning skirt flirtatiously, in rhythm with the music.

I left the kitchen and went outside to watch the dancing spectacle. "You would think they knew what they were doing," I said to Lydia who, standing next to me watching the old people dance, ate a second tamal. "They're a bunch of funny-looking grasshoppers, really. Believe you me, Lydia, this is not Ballet Folklórico at its finest. My God, look at Carolina!" My oldest sister was swishing her skirt madly, as if there were no tomorrow. She took her heritage seriously.

We both started laughing, Lydia choking on her spicy tamal. "Ay sí, she's just one hot little dancer, that sister of mine," I said, now turning to Lydia, who was coughing and laughing. "Man, Lydia, can't you stop porking out for just a minute?"

Behind Lydia, I could see Chuy with a crowd of guys surrounding him, all of them talking and gesturing at the same time, vying for his attention. Chuy turned to look from one to the other, nodding slightly, a taut forced smile on his face. At attention.

"Hi, Chuy," I had said, but I might as well have whispered it to myself. He had already turned to greet Monica and Luz, my words lost to him in the confused air. I was afraid, truly afraid, my brother Chuy didn't recognize his favorite sister anymore.

"Do you think he'll lend us his jacket and hat for Halloween?" I heard Luz ask Monica from their spot in the tree. Lydia and I were standing in the grass just beyond the brightly lit patio, next to the pepper tree where Monica and Luz sat high up on a wooden platform, a great spying place.

"If we promise not to get his uniform messy with candy, he might," Monica said.

Ana María was passing a tray of vegetable cut-ups, pausing in front of the older people sitting on the metal folding chairs. She was a beauty with her blue eyes and wild curly black hair, and I was sure she wanted Tito to notice her, even though Tito was supposed to be off limits to Ana María. She and our brother Octavio had gotten into plenty of arguments on the subject of Tito, and Octavio simply ignored her pleas. She was way too young. "Tito's too old for you, Ana," he told her. "He's got a lot of experience with girls. I don't want you to think about him or ever try sneaking around. I know my friends. Stay away from him."

Ana María still managed to give Tito coy bashful looks under her lowered, incredibly long lashes. He managed to get the message, his chest inflating with macho pride. The snug-fitting, red knit blouse outlined the body of a woman, though Ana was only sixteen, and that body promised delicious nights to come. Knowing Tito, he was probably biding his time. Yes, all in due time, he must have been thinking as he watched her from the other side of the garage where he stood with Chuy and the guys. Ana was smiling at something old Don Epifranio was saying as he reached for a soft mushroom, which would be easy on his dentures. All in due time.

When the last of the diehards trudged away, swaggering with a little bit too much to drink, when voices faded and people attempted one last merry but weary good-bye, I was shooed off to sleep along with my older sisters. Monica and Luz had plopped down hours before in the living room and were fast asleep—one on the orange vinyl love seat, the other on the sofa.

I must have dozed off for I don't know how long—a minute, an hour?—but now I was wide awake, my heart beating fast and hard. Was it a nightmare? The night was heavy and still. Everyone else seemed to be in an exhausted sleep. I could hear music playing in the distance, something slow, perhaps mournful, but I couldn't make out the words or the song. The green glow of the alarm clock marked four o'clock in the morning. I quietly got up and made my way to the kitchen. The music became more audible. I peeked out the kitchen window at the patio. The trees and plants were shrouded in darkness; I could only see spidery outlines. A small lamp next to the turntable on the patio gave a feeble bit of light, and I could see someone standing before it. My first thought was that a burglar was stealing the stereo and all our records. I was about to call out to everyone, alert them to the intruder, when I suddenly recognized the song and the person listening: Chuy was standing before the record player listening to "Donna."

He was busy sorting through the records, it seemed. I couldn't tell for sure because his back was to me. When the song ended, he stopped whatever he was doing at the table long enough to play the song again—Ritchie Valens's love song to Donna—the music sounding soft and tender, yearning—a Donna, I supposed, much like Chuy's ex-girlfriend, Donna.

I stepped up to another kitchen window where I could get a better look. Methodically and slowly, he cut the cloth into straight, even strips. Then each strip was laid in a neat pile on top of the one he'd just cut. When he finished, he set the scissors on the table and turned off the record player and then the lamp. Now a shadow in the early morning dimness, he walked to the front and out onto the street.

I tiptoed back to the bedroom and slipped into bed. I felt heavy and old. Tired. Surely I was dreaming.

The next morning we were all awakened by a horrible rumbling. A thunderstorm in San Diego? We ran to the nearest window. The sky was clear blue and it seemed to be the beginning of another warm April morning in San Diego. But that rumbling sound!

He thundered up and down Conifer Street—two, three times—our brother Chuy dressed in his green army uniform, straddled low on a shiny new Harley-Davidson chopper. Mamá and Papá looked horrified, frozen into a confused stupor. Not knowing what to do, they just stood there on the porch, Papá in his thin sleeveless undershirt and boxers, Mamá in her worn, wrinkled, pale blue chenille robe, watching their war veteran son roar up and down Conifer Street on a motorcycle. By the third time, everyone on Conifer Street was either outside on their small front lawns, or fearfully peeking through the windows. The Wiltheims up the street wasted no time in rushing out of their immaculate white stucco house, dressed in their robes and suede house slippers, to see what the ruckus was about. I imagined that this elderly German couple was shaking their head with anger, sure that we, the Sahagún family, wild and unruly Mexicans, had something to do with this noisy *blitzkrieg* now going on up and down the street.

My brothers stood at the side of the street, transfixed with wonder and envy, while my sisters looked startled and worried.

Squinting, I tried not to cry. I rubbed my eyes, cleared my throat, gulped for regular breaths of air.

Then Chuy paused in front of our house, the engine idling with an impatient, raspy noise. He looked at each of his brothers and sisters as if wanting to memorize us. His eyes were a sky blue, immense and impenetrable, and his smile was forced, more of a grimace, but of what—pain, anger, mockery? He looked over at Mamá and Papá standing slightly bent, looking as if they had aged twenty years in that short April morning. Gunning the engine one last time as loudly as he could, he gave them a sharp, clean military salute, and like a bull kept too long in a pen, he broke out and away from Conifer Street.

Stunned, we stood silent a moment, staring at the empty street as if we were expecting Chuy to reappear—or for something more to happen to explain what we had just witnessed.

"Buenos días," Socorrito next door called out, shuffling over to the fence near us.

Her voice awakened us from our trance, from gaping at the silent street. In single file we headed for the backyard to pick up the remains of the party, walking slowly but purposefully, as if we were in a funeral procession, a new kind of grief making us oblivious to our gawking neighbors, oblivious to Socorrito.

She cleared her throat, getting ready to speak. I knew she was tempted to say something, just one more little thing about war veterans, to offer a consoling tidbit of news about Maria García's nephew who had lost both legs. Gangrene.

Vieja chismosa. We ignored the nosy busybody.

We picked up the litter on the grass—crumpled napkins, paper cups. My curlicues were no longer springy. The many scattered ties lay stretched out and worn, as if someone had purposely taken each thin ribbon and pulled it taut, wringing it of life. Nobody entered the patio, though we all immediately spotted the two mountains of cut strips on the table and began to understand where Chuy stood in this strange world of ours. Without a word, then, as if I were disposing of simple party litter, I did for Chuy what no one else could bear to do: I dumped his shredded Mexican and American flags into the garbage can.

—3

"He's probably at the Grand Canyon by now," I said to Lydia as we walked home from school. She was the only one I would discuss the matter with. The bola de chismosas of the neighborhood—gossipy old biddies, all of them—could blab about it all day long, but just not with me.

Lydia wanted to know why he took off so all of a sudden. "Couldn't he have waited a few days," she said, "so he could be with all of you? I mean, how're your parents taking it, you know?"

No, I didn't know, I wanted to scream at Lydia, but instead I said: "Man, when you've been forced into some war like that, I mean, not knowing really what's going on and what you're fighting for, well it stands to reason the first thing you want to do is hit the road. See the world on your own terms."

"Yeah, you've got a point," Lydia said. "Grand Canyon, you think?"

How the hell did I know, really, but it lessened the pain of abandonment I felt, of not knowing the whereabouts of my favorite brother. So there you had it: Chuy was sitting on his Harley, gazing down at that big old canyon, one of the damn wonders of our world—grand and immense.

"But why a *motorcycle*," Lydia asked. "Why not a hot convertible sports car, fire engine red? Why a noisy, weird-looking motorcycle?"

"What are you trying to be, pendeja," I said, "*la* Sherlock Holmes of Palm City? Besides, it's not the same in a car—even in a convertible. Híjole, Lydia, don't you know anything about the feel of freedom?"

"Huh?"

"Never mind," I said. "I gotta get going." I left her at her front yard and quickly walked on across the tracks to my street.

The feel of freedom. Like the time Chuy built that go-cart, a skinny, wobbly contraption. I was eight, skinny and wobbly myself, and since Monica and Luz were way too young to try it out, I was chosen by Chuy to test its speed. That is, I was chosen because I was old enough to manage the steering and reach the gas throttle, but light enough to give the go-cart a chance to show off its speed.

Everyone gathered around me and the contraption—my brothers and sisters, neighborhood kids. There were other kids my age who could've done it, but there you had it: Chuy had chosen me.

"All right, man, everybody move back," Chuy called out to the spectators. They did so immediately, our senior go-cart engineer commanding everyone's instant respect.

He crouched down next to me as I climbed onto the low-lying, insect-looking thing, feeling terrified.

He instructed me on the gas throttle, the brakes, had me practice some steering movements. "Yoli," he said in a low voice so no one could hear him, "just think of the freedom you'll feel with the wind in your face and you in control." He pretended to fidget with some part of the go-cart as he spoke. "I chose you because I know you'll push yourself all the way. *You're* going to make it go. Pretend you're flying and these are your wings. Make her go fast, Yoli, real fast. Hit the road, move with her," he said. "Yoli, you can do it, don't be afraid, OK?"

How old was he then? If I was eight, he must've been

sixteen. Already craving the feel of freedom.

Given a head-start push by my four brothers, I was off, flying down Conifer Street, moving with the machine, screaming a wild, terrified, exhilarated scream. Just me and that machine under me, the vibrations jiggled my every bone and my skin felt tingly and alive; I and only I was commanding the machine to go this way, then that way, a swerve over here, a bump over there. Chuy was right: it was the wind in my face that made me fly and feel free.

Everyone ran after me, but they couldn't keep up. I could hear shouts, all the kids cheering me on, but their words trailed in the wind, and I was way past them. I had hit the road, all right, my hands clenched over the steering wheel, the go-cart charging forward in response to my wishes. Everyone was screaming, "Go, Yoli, faster, faster!" and I did go fast, flooring it with all my eight-year-old might, wanting to make Chuy proud of me. Then I swerved one last time, toward the end of the street, finally crashing into the front tire of a parked car, the go-cart coming to an abrupt, hard stop.

Chuy was the first to reach me. He crouched down and gently lifted me up and out of the contraption, carrying me home in his arms, the bloody gash on my leg a lovely, gory sight for all the envious spectators. I felt on top of the world, a dainty princess who had performed dare-devil stunts for the world and for my brother Chuy. As he carried me home, down Conifer Street, a group of kids in attendance, I nestled my head comfortably, securely against his chest.

Everyone followed behind us, fifteen kids or more. "Hey, Yoli," one of them called out to me, "how did it feel?"

"Did you see the way the whole thing shook, man?" some boy asked.

"Yeah, I thought it was just gonna explode. . . ." Everyone had a story on witnessing the fastest-running go-cart in Palm City.

"You did good, Yoli," Chuy whispered. "Real good." I could tell from the proud grin on his face that he knew I had felt the freedom.

I now made my way across the railroad tracks, toward Conifer. I could see Papá and Armando way over at the other end of the Not-a-Through Street. Their backs were to me as they stood at the chain-link fence, looking, I supposed, at the cars on the freeway.

We lived on a street in south San Diego that was surrounded by tangible symbols of journey. To the east of Conifer Street, below the embankment, was Interstate 5, which began a few miles south of our house at the Mexican border. The interstate wound its way smoothly, evenly, up the length of California, north to Oregon and Washington state. Just past Los Angeles, Interstate 5 was called the Golden State Freeway, as if to impress on the traveler's mind that just ahead, not too far away, were riches to be had—a kind of Yellow Brick Road leading to the Land of Oz. There the highway passed small towns, rolling hills, the San Joaquin Valley. The idea of a pot of gold at the end of the rainbow was translated in my world as this: Somewhere on Interstate 5, acá en el norte, over here in the north, was my parents' legendary El Dorado. But watch out for the big, bad bruja, for lions and tigers and bears. It wasn't going to be an easy road.

If riches were not to be had there, then try the railroad tracks that ran east of Conifer, parallel to Interstate 5. Our small "Not a Through Street" was the line connecting freeway to railroad. Like the middle bar joining the sides of the letter "H," Conifer Street connected the routes. The railroad tracks started north-south at the border, then just beyond our Palm City they began to curve and head east. Union Pacific, Southern Pacific, Santa Fe railroads. The routes followed agricultural paths, branching out up to the San Joaquin Valley, or directly east to the Imperial Valley, touching base with the agricultural packing plants along the way. In concrete terms, then, travel and migration—moving, passing through—were very much a part of my family's world.

Our Conifer Street was an assortment of odds-and-ends kinds of houses, no two looking alike—some boxy, nondescript, a few Spanish colonial, with red-tiled roofs, a two-story Victorian-looking one. For a moment I stopped and surveyed my street, tried to see it with new eyes. I imagined I was Chuy on his chopper entering our hometown. A street like any other in the neighborhood, a house like any other—or no?

I once asked old Don Epifranio about the neighborhood. I was doing a fourth-grade class project on family and community. I wanted the report to seem very scientific and sophisticated, so I interviewed the oldest man in the neighborhood. When I asked him if he knew how this neighborhood had started, he thought about it, didn't say anything for the longest while as I stood attentively before him with my notepad and pencil in hand, ready to jot down his valuable recollections. We were on his front porch where we had a good view of the street. I could hear the cars on the freeway swishing by, sounding like ocean waves.

"Mi'ja," he finally said. "I've heard this was all part of the Swiss dairies. Then somewhere along the line, the city bought it and plunked down a house here, then there—houses moved from some other part of San Diego. Odds and ends, mi'ja." He started laughing. "Just like all of us, eh?"

"What do you mean," I asked.

"Yeah, mi'ja," he said. "Just like us. Look at the Wiltheims up the street—German spies, I bet, and Protestants, too. How about that quiet, very religious Polish family a few doors down? And what do we know about Mr. Lawka? He was probably some famous Swiss watch engineer back in the old country, and now he's just a watch repairman who lives alone in this mish-mash barrio and no one knows anything about him. Walks the four miles to his repair shop in Imperial Beach every morning, bright and early, must wake up with the roosters—or maybe he's a clock himself, has a little despertador in his brain." Don Epifranio laughed, enjoying his own cleverness. "Then there's the rest of us Mexicans—from different parts of Mexico, maybe even different social classes. Odds and ends transplanted from somewhere else, just like our casitas, eh?"

Once Don Epifranio put it that way, I couldn't stop thinking of our street and community in that way, too: odds and ends collected from here and there. And what about Don Epifranio himself—an enigma like the ones he'd just mentioned. Did this revered viejo spend his days sitting on his front porch, conjuring up the lives and secret worlds of his neighbors?

What kind of odds and ends were we? "Odds and ends" made it seem like there was something wrong with us, not quite right. Maybe a little broken. Was our community like the collection of broken watches and orphaned buttons and keys our parents kept in frayed cigar boxes, with the good but never realized intentions of getting them fixed someday, of finding a home for them?

"In their own right," I once blurted out in my American history class, impatient with lectures on Plymouth Rock and the Puritans and all those other brave American pioneers, "my parents, like the covered wagon frontier people of the wild west and the gold rush days of California, were also pioneers of an unfriendly West."

At first some of the students in the class looked confused,

not sure what I meant. A few started laughing at me and shaking their heads. I knew a lot of them thought of me as *La* Miss Head-in-the-Clouds, kind of hippie-ish, kind of Shakespeare-ish, kind of quién-sabe-qué, but they liked me anyway.

Then students started nodding their heads.

"Yeah man, you're right," Ruben had called out to me from the back of the room where he always sat slouched in his seat, reeking of pot. Now he sat up straight. "My jefe came to this country with ten pesos in one pocket and a shriveled up, moldy tortilla in another looking for work at one of the dairy farms," he said. "He couldn't've even afforded a covered wagon if he wanted to. Right on, Yoli, our jefecitos are pioneers, too, esa."

I now came to the end of my street and stood next to Papá and Armando who were in deep conversation and didn't seem to notice my presence.

". . . that's why my brothers and I came up here the first time. Took the train up through Nogales until we made it to Los Angeles," Papá was telling Armando. "The Cristero war was going on and Mamita didn't want us involved in that. We were happy to go. You know, you hear so much about el norte and here we were. God, I was just twenty years old—about the same age as Chuy, todo flaquito, probably didn't weigh more than 120 pounds, ready to discover the world and take it on. Make millions of dólares. I had my dreams. . . ."

Armando listened respectfully, nodding now and then.

I had never heard my father talk this way, saying these

things. I never knew this about Papá.

He started laughing to himself. "Sí, Señor," he said to Armando as both of them stared at the freeway and beyond, "I wanted to come back to El Grullo with my piles of green money and be a professional charro. Travel throughout the country, pues—¿por qué no?—the world. Share with everybody my horseman's skill and daring, the elegant suit. Perform in Saudi Arabia, Austria, la Unión Soviética—dondequiera. Then—and this is the best part, Hijo—I would retire early and raise and train horses on my hacienda."

"Why didn't you do it, Papá?" Armando asked.

"Life, Hijo," Papá said quietly, almost a whisper. "Life got in the way."

It seemed to be the end of the conversation, both of them staring quietly at the cars rushing past on the freeway, as if they understood what that meant.

"Papá," I said, wanting to ask him what he meant by "life," but I stopped. I could tell he wasn't hearing me. He was in a daze, like a zombie. I don't think he even realized I was standing next to him.

I looked closely at him, at his stern set face. Papá's eyes were blue, a crystalline blue, and it was in them that I found Chuy. His blue eyes reflected immensities, untraveled oceans and seas. Although I was sure that as a father he must be worried for his son's well-being, I thought he must also be envious, as I was, of Chuy's dramatic entrance and exit. Especially the exit. Lorenzo Sahagún's eyes recalled the wanderlust spirit he must've been born with, that spirit which had him traveling and searching for his El Dorado, a wife and a pile of kids trailing behind him, that spirit which on this uncertain, confused day yearned to be his son Chuy, taking off.

I turned away, facing Conifer. Looking at my street lined with rickety wooden gates and chain link fences, I wondered if Chuy thought of our neighborhood as "odds and ends." Is that why he just got up and left as soon as he had arrived? Was Chuy right this minute looking for a mythical land of riches and happiness—an El Dorado like the one Mamá and Papá sought when they first moved to the States? Already Chuy had been to lands we'd never even heard of until he was drafted, places whose names we could barely pronounce. Now what road had he taken? I wondered as I kicked at a rock on the street. I hoped Chuy was—at this very instant I was thinking of him—sitting on his Harley looking out at the immense Grand Canyon, feeling the freedom the two of us shared, perhaps had inherited from Papá. I kicked one last time at the stupid, lopsided rock in the street, watching it roll toward somewhere or nowhere.

—4

"God, he was so cute," my sister Carolina was telling Ana María and our neighbor Marisa as I walked into the bedroom.

"He gunned his engine. . . ."

"What kind of car was it?" Ana María asked.

"I think it was a Barracuda. Orange," Carolina said. "Oh, I don't know. I was so busy staring at him and watching for the light to turn green at the same time, I can't remember."

I set my books down and sat at the foot of one of the beds, while little Luz and Monica sat on the floor in a corner like quiet ratoncitos.

"Are you sure you heard him right?" Ana María asked. "What if you go and he's not there to meet you?"

"He said it clearly: MCRD, Saturday," Carolina said, pushing her body back to lean against the wall, extending her legs on the bed. She was clearly the queen for the day, all attention centered on her and her glorious, romantic encounter.

"What's MCRD?" Luz asked.

"I knew he was a Marine the moment I laid eyes on him. Sailor hair's cut a little longer," Carolina said, staring at nothing on the bedroom ceiling. "God, what a papacito."

"But what's the MCRD?"

"Are you *sure* he didn't say *Sunday?*" Ana María asked again. "Because Saturday and Sunday sound alike." Ana María worried about those things, wanted no mess-ups or miscommunications for our oldest sister's romantic rendezvous.

"Oh, I'm absolutely positive he said Saturday," Carolina said. "Man, when we glanced at each other that first moment—híjole—it was like lightning striking us. The telepathy was so strong. Even if he hadn't called out through the open window—'Saturday, MCRD'—I could've read his thoughts." Carolina sounded dreamy and already off in las nubes.

"What's the MC . . . ?"

"Shhh," Ana María said. "Marine Corps Recruit Depot. Now, no more questions or out you go!"

Little Luz and Monica had been allowed to listen in on this romantic turn of events in Carolina's life, but only after being sworn to secrecy. Our parents were strict and we weren't allowed—not even poor Carolina who was already twenty— to go out on dates with guys.

"Let me put it to you this way," Carolina said to Luz and Monica as a way of securing their secrecy. "I'm the oldest sister and so I know that I'm going to have to break the ice, OK? Once Mamá and Papá get used to the idea of boyfriends for me, then it'll be a breeze for you younger ones. They won't be so strict, see?"

"And you won't have to worry about being wrinkly old maids in your seventies before they allow you to date," I added for good measure.

"So just be cool about this. Not a word to anyone," Carolina warned. "Not even to your little friends, OK?"

Luz and Monica, honored to be included in their big sister's secret, nodded solemnly.

"What a papacito," Carolina said, now looking out the bedroom window, as if she were explaining this to some eavesdropper, maybe Socorrito next door, or Don Epifranio—it didn't matter. She seemed to want to share the news with the whole world. "Big, blue eyes. A shy, little boy smile."

We girls were silent, giving Carolina a respectful moment to relish the moment—just fifteen minutes ago—when she fell in love at first sight on Coronado Avenue on a routine drive to the supermarket for a carton of milk and bread. Ten yards away from each other, communicating through the noise of traffic and car horns and car windows stuck half way shut, Carolina was certain that she had met Mr. Right.

This was the plan: Carolina and Ana María were going to tell our parents they were going to Esther's birthday party this Saturday night, but really they were going into downtown San Diego to the Marine Corps Recruit Depot, where Carolina was going to meet up with her Mr. Right of Coronado Avenue.

Somebody knocked at the door. "It's me," Tony said. "Gotta go to the bathroom."

We let him into the girl's room—the bedroom we five sisters shared. Past the bunk beds and the double bed, next to our cream-colored dresser, nineteen-year-old Tony walked, avoiding looking at Marisa, whom he once had had a crush on. Judging from his painful efforts not to look at her, I sensed he still had a crush on her, some tormenting vestiges of feelings for her. He went into the bathroom and closed the door.

I turned to Carolina and whispered, "Yes, Carolina, MCRD

this Saturday," and surveying our cozy circle of young and hopeful women, I pronounced, full of psychic wisdom, "You will meet up with your Mr. Right."

A few minutes later the bathroom door opened again and we were instantly silent as Tony walked past us and out the bedroom door. All of us looked at each other with a smile born of a new importance and responsibility, a conspiratorial circle of young women in the know.

■ ■ ■ ■ ■

Our bedroom—the girls' room—served not only as sleeping quarters for us five sisters, as conference room for the necessary private talks about boys and French kissing and girls whose reputations were lost for going all the way, but it also served as the hallway to the only bathroom in the Sahagún Estate. The girls' room: Grand Central Station, where private, intimate matters were commented on, philosophical discussions argued and pondered over. Tormenting questions: How far was going too far? At what point would a guy lose respect for you? These urgent questions wafted through the air, mixed with the smell of Avon perfume, with bobby pins and empty juice can rollers, with barrettes and hair bands and "Red Coral" lipstick, with the sound of a small, transistor radio playing "OOO Baby, Baby," Smokey Robinson and the Miracles empathetic to our own lovesick hearts. If Francisco Valdivia, for example, knew how much I yearned for him, would he

notice me then? Maybe walk me to homeroom? But if he knew
I *loved* him (yes, I would say it in secret, not even admit it to
Lydia) wouldn't he take advantage of me, use me? How far
was going too far? When did a girl cross the line into dangerous territory? There were times when I was annoyed with Diana
and the Supremes, when I wished she would shout out like
Aretha Franklin and demand R-E-S-P-E-C-T. Oh, why couldn't
I just show him my heart, let him love me as nature intended?
Why did life—*my* life—have to be so complicated, so full of
protocol and caution? Why couldn't I just sing out gloriously
to my Baby Love?

As we pondered the truths and consequences of our feminine behavior, there came the inevitable knock on the door by
one of our brothers who had to go to the bathroom. So the
girls' room once more served as hallway, our sanctuary always temporary and precarious as we retreated into an auto-
matic, practiced silence, as a man—brother, father, cousin—
now entered our sun-filled, feminine domain. Did we sisters
never feel invaded or imposed upon? Or was that a woman's
lot? Were we in some way just a convenient hallway for men
to pass through? Why did all altars seem dominated by men?
I sometimes thought about these things as I watched one of
the guys or Papá confidently walk through our bedroom, into
the bathroom. Oh, but if it be so, that we are but a convenient
hallway for men to pass through, then why, dear God, don't
you let Francisco Valdivia, my love and my life, pass through

me? Let me learn, if I must, to understand a man's psyche and then learn to dance to its rhythms. Was I missing something here, huddled in the girls' room? Were the answers somewhere else, in another domain?

If the girls' room was at the very heart and hub of family life, the boys' room was its antithesis. It stood away from the rest of the house, attached by a bit of wall, yet not really part of hearth and home. Entry to the boys' room was through the yard and patio to a separate entrance. It was never clear whether the design had been done on purpose or whether the small, attached room added onto the rest of the house was an afterthought. No matter. The fact remained that the boys' room was a private domain by virtue of its geographical placement and relation to the rest of the home and seemed to me a symbol of freedom and independence.

So I was drawn to it. First a cautious knock, just in case, and then I let myself in.

Even though the room was dark, with only a single small window facing north, I knew its every piece of furniture and trappings by heart. On top of the one dresser that all four brothers shared sat the wooden case built by Armando in wood shop class. It had glass doors behind which were displayed the many trophies: wrestling, track and field, baseball. A collection of lacy white and blue-ribboned garter belts hung from one of the trophy's bats. I paused to look them over, carefully unhinging the frilliest one in the collection. I slipped it on, up to my thigh just below where my shorts began. Like the can-can girls of *Gunsmoke*'s tavern, I lifted my gartered leg and kicked out a few times, feeling a little naughty. After a minute of this, I reached under Octavio's thin mattress, pulling out a neat stack of *Playboys* and made myself comfortable on his bed, slowly leafing through the magazines.

In a corner were piled high the guys' dirty clothes: gym shorts, t-shirts, socks, a jock strap. The first time I had seen a jock strap—here in this room when I first began visiting it—I hadn't known what it was for. I had asked Lydia about it. She seemed so wise and knew how babies were born way before I had learned. I described the garment-contraption to her.

"It's to hold the guys' huevos so they don't go jiggling all over the place when they're doing sports and stuff."

How funny, I couldn't stop giggling at Lydia's explanation. Huevo-holder, indeed!

"Hey, man, I'm not kidding," she said, annoyed. "It's like a bra, only for guys' balls. If you don't believe me, then ask your brothers. I dare you to."

OK, OK, I believed her.

Now I tried it on for size, wondering what it felt like to have balls. Wasn't it hard to walk with that bulge between your legs? With the lacy blue garter belt wrapped around my thigh and a jockey strap over my shorts, I promenaded down the short length of the guys' room, pretending I was the famous model Twiggy, feeling giddy and free, naughty and perverse.

On the wobbly writing desk sat a clear glass ashtray filled with loose keys of varying sizes, a rabbit's foot key chain, some pennies, nickels, dimes, a pair of gold-colored cuff-links studded with faux diamonds, a matching tie clip. I sorted through the keys, one at a time, wondering what door or car or box these little metal trinkets had the power to lock and unlock. There was the same, familiar smell of the room: dirty gym socks underneath the beds, the morning's urine in the chamber pot not yet emptied, dust balls of hair and woolly stuff, a bottle of Old Spice, the can of Right Guard.

In the distance, I heard my name being called: "Yoli!" Probably Carolina wanting me to help her take down the dried clothes, or maybe bratty Monica demanding to know where I had hidden Barbie and Ken. She'd never find them: I had set them on the highest pepper tree branch I could reach, and naked Ken was right this minute on top of naked Barbie, sucking her pointy boobs.

Quickly, I tossed off the jock strap into the dirty clothes pile, and placed the blue satin and white lace garter back over the miniature bat. A trophy over a trophy, I thought.

For good measure, I closed my eyes and inhaled deeply one last time—my way of feeling close to everything masculine, my attempt at understanding this forbidden world of dark wood, leather and chrome—inhaled deeply, deeply, my private, mysterious incense.

5

"It's a postcard from 'Mickey's Motorcycles' in Mankato, Minnesota," Carolina announced.

We all huddled around her, my other sisters and I. Mamá wiped her wet hands on the dishtowel so she could hold the postcard. Did she feel closer to Chuy that way? The postcard offered Mr. Chuy Sahagún a free oil change next time he was in. Mamá tucked this in her jewelry box, placing it next to her rosary made of rose petals. A week earlier we had received a citation from the Municipal Courthouse of Grand Rapids for time expired at a parking meter on a '69 Harley Davidson, California license plate number 9J3716. By now the citation, sitting in Mamá's jewelry box, probably smelled like roses.

Then came a cryptic postcard of the Liberty Bell addressed to "Chewy Sehaygun" in squiggly, female handwriting: "Come back soon, Baby, you light my FIRE!!!" and signed by a Tania from the city of brotherly love. I took it from Carolina who had fished it from the mailbox. I studied the handwriting—babyish, loopy letters—then flipped it over to the picture of the Liberty Bell, wondering if there was something meaningful about her sending this particular picture. Did Chuy and this Tania girl have some private joke about the bell? Was Chuy's "bell" as big as this one, was that the stupid, private joke? I was glad he left her back there. Love 'em and leave 'em, I thought, looking at that dumb, old bell.

I was hoping Mamá wouldn't want this one so I could hold onto it and show it to Lydia. Already I was conjuring up faces for this Tania—straight, long, blonde hair down to her butt, skinny. Or maybe she had wild curly black hair, wore a skimpy see-through peasant blouse, no bra, some ferns in her hair, maybe a hibiscus flower—if they had hibiscus in Philadelphia. A Love Child itching to get on Chuy's motorcycle and ride away with him.

Mamá tapped me on the shoulder and I had to hand over the card.

"Here's the city," I said, pointing to the map in the "P" volume of the encyclopedia. "Between New York and Washington, D.C." Thin pink lines denoted state boundaries. Thin green lines were major highways. Or was he traveling the back roads? Where were the back roads on this map?

My brother Octavio, reading the paper, his right leg dangling over the arm of the armchair, shook his head. "You know," he said, "he had a couple of friends in Canada. Stevie went AWOL and headed to Vancouver, ¿qué no?"

"But what about the coupon book from South Dakota?" Carolina said, acting as chief investigator in the family. Octavio had all this time been doing a good job of pretending we were all idiots for trying to follow Chuy's trek, but Octavio was the closest brother in age to Chuy and because of this we thought he might understand Chuy. He nonchalantly offered the Canada suggestion. We didn't tease him; we didn't let on that we knew he was just as worried about Chuy as the rest of us.

"Why is there a big dot on Philadelphia and a star by Trenton?" Luz asked. These geography lessons fascinated her.

"Do you think he's doing this on purpose?" I asked.

"What do you mean?" Carolina said.

"Well," I said, "do you think he's purposely leaving his address with these stores and businesses, on mailing lists? He knows they'll be sending junk mail addressed to him here, so maybe this is his way of letting us know he's OK." The idea now seemed so clear and obvious. Yes, Chuy would want to let us know, even in the most cryptic manner, that he was OK. That he was alive and well.

"Shit," said Octavio. "I'd say he was setting up a damn treasure hunt for us. Why doesn't he just pick up the phone and call us? What does he think this is, a game? Has he even considered what the hell this is doing to Mamá and Papá? Why doesn't he cut the crap?"

"This is Chuy being Chuy," said Carolina, who was taking a psychology course at Southwestern College and seemed compelled to analyze and comment on our psyches any chance she got. "Don't you remember the time he . . ."

Now a part of me wanted to cover my ears and not hear what was about to commence. It seemed that ever since Chuy took off on his motorcycle our conversations were dominated by talk of this or that thing Chuy once did, our talk always beginning with "Remember when Chuy . . ." as if we were reminiscing about some long gone, dead person. He isn't dead, you stupid idiots! I wanted to shout at them. Stop talking as if he were dead. He wasn't dead, no, but he was somewhere in limbo. So I never covered my ears when people reminisced about Chuy, because I wondered if maybe this was the right thing to do after all: Did we need to look to the past, to our family history, to Chuy's history, as one would look to a map for directions? If we were going to journey with Chuy, was it necessary that we speak of the past to prepare to set foot on unknown territory in the future? Damn treasure hunt, was that it?

So we remembered the old Chuy: One time when we were playing hide-and-seek out in the front yard under a full moon, Carolina was It and had to seek fifteen kids, including most of us brothers and sisters. She found all of us or else we made our way safely back to base, except for Chuy. He was nowhere to be found. I was about nine at the time and so he must have been about seventeen. We all wanted to get going with another round of hide-and-seek, but first Chuy had to be found. Frustrated, Carolina gave up, and we all called out his name.

"Chuuuuy," we shouted as we wandered about looking in all the usual hiding spots: behind bushes, fences, fire hydrant.

"He's doing this on purpose," Carolina, a year younger than her brother, said. "He just wants to let everyone know he won. He just wants to make a big point of it. Damn him, he's just trying to make me look stupid."

Then from out of nowhere, an apricot hit Carolina on her shoulder.

"It's him," she said. "He's up in the apricot tree." By now she was beside herself with rage. "Let's get him, you guys, and pull down his pants." Everyone ran from the street over to George O'Blander's apricot tree next door. But he wasn't there.

"Damn him, I'm going to get him for this." Carolina seemed to be spitting fire.

We went back out to the middle of the street, everyone surrounding Carolina, full of rage and good ideas for revenge. "We'll pull his pants down and make him walk around in his calzones for the rest of the game."

Then again, out of nowhere, peppercorns from the tree in the empty lot were being shot at Carolina. The eerie thing was that only she was getting hit by them, even though there were about fifteen of us standing with her.

She screamed bloody murder and charged over to the empty lot, all of us running behind her.

He wasn't there.

"He's in the trees," she shouted to all of us. "Find a tree and catch him."

For a minute I stared at Carolina. She reminded me of the Wicked Witch from the *Wizard of Oz* with her monkey soldiers. Now all her soldiers scattered, each assigned to look for Chuy in one of the nearby trees. I was exhilarated: my favorite brother Chuy was some magical tree urchin being pursued by the Wicked Witch of the West and her monkey soldiers.

Carolina would not let him get the better of her. I could tell she wanted to cry or go in and tell Mamá and Papá how Chuy had ruined everything. But that's when she got hit by a pinecone on the back of her head and now there was no stopping her: she would kill him for this.

No sign of him in any of the trees, Carolina's monkey soldiers returned for further instructions.

Standing again in the middle of the street, we all stared at the apricot, the pink peppercorns, and the pinecone as if these held vital clues. I was sure all of us were in awe of his trickery.

That's when we saw him, strolling up to us from down the street, easy and slow, as if he were the King of Palm City now approaching his humble subjects. He came up to us, directly over to Carolina. He held something cupped in his hands.

"Here hermanita," he said to Carolina, handing her a cluster of jacaranda blossoms—lilac, bell-shaped flowers. "With my apologies." She stood still, looked stunned and unprepared for this, eyed him suspiciously, as if this were just another one of his tricks.

"But wasn't this a whole lot more fun than a regular, old game of hide-n-seek?" He smiled at her, mischievous, monkeyish. "I got the fire going in you, ¿qué no, hermanita?"

—6

The screech of burning rubber, then the inevitable hard crash of metal colliding with metal. The first one on Conifer Street to hear these sounds and make it to the telephone dialed "0" for the operator and shouted: "Crash on 5 North between Palm Avenue and Main Street." Most of the neighbors on Conifer Street were already congregated at the end of the block, standing by the chain link fence at the embankment, observing the bashed up cars below. Any passerby would have thought it was a block party.

"Is anybody hurt? Can you tell?" Carolina asked our neighbor, Marisa.

"No, it doesn't seem so, but I can't tell. The crash is over by the Big Sky Drive-in," she said. Marisa looked past Carolina's shoulder, over toward our house. I was sure she was wondering if our gorgeous brother Octavio, whom she had loved probably her whole life, might come out of the house to see the accident, too. I bet she was hoping.

Socorrito, who seemed to live in her fluffy blue mules and Hawaiian-print shift, shuffled over to where Mamá stood. "This is very strange, Dolores," she said in a whisper, but loud enough for my antennae ears to hear. "Have you noticed how many car accidents we've had in just these past months? At least four a week."

Mamá was silent, shielding her eyes from the sun, which

was slowly falling in the west. Her face was stern, the kind of expression I was used to seeing on her when she was studying the monthly bills or watching Walter Cronkite. Her green eyes were now dark and worried. I knew what she must be thinking, because I was thinking the same: so many car crashes since Chuy had left.

"What do you make of these plane crashes, too," Socorrito said. "The one in Venezuela, that Arab one and then one in Monterrey, wasn't it? I have a cousin who lives there. His wife is an espiritualista, you know, but just practices on Fridays. She's Catholic the rest of the week."

Mamá turned to Socorrito, now giving her full attention.

"Well, this wife of my cousin says these are signs. All these crashes," Socorrito said. "What do you think, Dolores? Here on the freeway and in the air, what kind of signs?"

The sirens were wailing now, approaching the scene of the accident. A familiar sound—especially lately.

"Mamá," Monica called out, expertly latched on to the chain link fence as if she were a graceful spider on her web. "Can we go down to the fields to get a better look? The girls said it was OK with them. They'll watch us."

Distracted by something Socorrito was saying, Mamá nodded her "yes." We hopped off the fence and scurried down the embankment into the field, headed for the Big Sky Drive-In.

"Wait, here comes Octavio," our friend Marisa shouted. "Let's wait for him."

Octavio came sauntering toward us, a proud macho swagger. I could understand why Marisa loved him. Who wouldn't? He had a sexy stride, his abdomen thrust slightly forward. He was confident, knowing perfectly well that Marisa was crazy about him, always had been since they were little kids. I was proud to be his sister.

We bounded out into the brush, the sour grass. Carolina, Ana María, Monica, Luz, Octavio, Marisa, an assortment of other kids from Citrus Street. We scattered and whooped with joy, running wild, hopping over sagebrush, some pieces of rusty barbed wire, a dented hubcap, a rotting bike tire. The car crash was the last thing on our minds: we only wanted an excuse to hike down into what had years ago been a dairy farm owned by Swiss immigrants, the Kastlungers' field.

Ana María had wandered off to pick a bouquet of wild-flowers, daydreaming about Tito, no doubt.

Octavio, who had been saying something to poor lovesick Marisa, suddenly turned to us and called over to Carolina, "Hey, let's go into the culvert."

Carolina didn't say anything at first. She looked over to where the giant drainage pipe ran under the freeway. "But what about the kids? We can't take them with us."

"Why not?" Octavio said, walking over to Carolina, Marisa close at his side. "They wouldn't understand the graffiti."

"But Mamá and Papá have said they never want to catch us over there."

"So, ¿y qué? How many hundreds of times have we been there? What's the big deal? I'll take responsibility if they find out." It was obvious to us sisters that Octavio was showing off for Marisa, acting real grown up and in charge. We loved him too much to want to ruin his show.

So we gathered Monica and Luz, and Ana María, Octavio, Marisa, Carolina, and I walked across the field toward the freeway and the culvert, leaving the other neighborhood kids behind.

I could see the Conifer Street neighbors above and beyond us, all seemingly huddled together. I couldn't hear their words, which were drowned by the whoosh of the cars gliding down the freeway, but for a moment I hesitated, wanting so badly to run back up Conifer Street and be in the secure hubbub of their conversation. Mamá and Socorrito were standing next to each other, talking seriously about something, while Mrs. Wiltheim directed her binoculars toward the Big Sky Drive-In, immersed in the gory vivid details of the accident, no doubt. There were many people congregated at the end of Conifer Street. Car crashes, it seemed, were becoming the main reason for our impromptu neighborhood meetings. Once we had determined the gravity of the accident and had sent the victims speeding on their way in the ambulance, and after the fire engines sprayed clean any spilt gasoline on the road, our neighborhood remained standing at the end of the block, by the chain link fence. Doña Abundia kept close tabs on the soap operas, never missing an episode. So if Mamá was too busy on any given day to watch a segment of *La Cruz de Marisa Cruces,* then Doña Abundia, at these spontaneous, end-of-the-street meetings, was happy to fill her in on the missing segment.

I turned my gaze from the cozy familiar scene on Conifer Street and looked toward the culvert. I was trembling, maybe because of the sudden cool gust of wind or maybe because I was excited and nervous: I had never been inside it.

Octavio led the way. "There's a lot of mud and crap, so watch out," he said. "And remember, you all swore you wouldn't tell Mamá about this."

The drainage pipe looked like a monstrous, concrete hair curler and ran the width—east and west—of the freeway. The traffic just above us seemed to roar and reverberate in our heads. I felt as if I were Jonah entering the bowels of the whale.

Although it was dim in the pipe, I could make out the uneven, angry graffiti: MAKE LOVE, NOT WAR! FUCK YOU. KISS MY DICK. U.S. OUT OF VIETNAM. FUCK THE GOOKS.

The stench was putrid—dank and humid, smelling of urine and vomit and shit. Green slime outlined the stagnant water running the length of the culvert.

"Uuuuuuuy," Octavio spookily said, his ghost-call echoing against the concrete walls.

"Let's go home," seven-year-old Luz said, whimpering. "I want to go home."

"Ay, mi'ja," Octavio said, "it was only me. I didn't mean to scare you." He picked her up and carried her in his arms. "Come on, we're going to the other end and then back. Then home, OK?" Safe in her brother's arms, Luz nodded her OK.

At the end of the tunnel, the round bit of light seemed years away.

In those moments, I wished I could be Luz, that I could be carried protectively in my brother's or sister's arms. I was feeling frightened, uneasy. There was about the whole place, this cold gray tube of concrete with its angry, defiant graffiti, a sense of doom. I felt imprisoned and lost in the stinking, bloody entrails of a monster.

We walked to the other end of the culvert, the west end, and peered out. Not much could be seen, just the same overgrown brush as on the east end.

"Hey, look," Monica said, "whose are those?" Lying nearby was a brown, raggedy sweater, a pair of black muddied men's shoes and grocery bags set out as ground covering amongst the bushes.

"Probably some wetbacks camping out," Octavio said. "They camp out here all the time before going on to L.A. Come on, let's go back."

"What's a 'wetback'?" Luz asked Octavio as we all entered the culvert, heading back.

"It's those people who sneak across the border illegally from Mexico."

"Why do they sneak across?" Now ten-year-old Monica wanted to know.

"Because they shouldn't be in this country," Octavio explained. "So they sneak in."

"Why are they called 'wetbacks'?" Luz asked.

"God, Octavio, that's a hell of a way to explain it to them," Carolina said. "How insensitive."

"OK, Miss College Girl, you explain it to them."

"Well, mi'jas," she said, "first of all you've got to understand that there are a lot of poor people in Mexico with no jobs, no money, no food. So they come to the United States to find jobs and get paid for their work. . . ."

"So then they sneak in," Luz said, " I know that part. Did Mami and Papi sneak in, too, when they came from Mexico?"

"Shit, Carolina, now look what you've done," Octavio said, laughing. "You've opened a great can of worms."

"No, they didn't," Carolina said, giving Octavio a look. "I'll explain it to you when we get home. Look at this shit. We've got it all over our shoes. Now how're we going to explain this to Mamá?"

"Don't worry," Octavio said. "I'll handle it."

We made our way back through the stench and the mud, surrounded by rude words and epithets on the hard, thick concrete. The excitement of this adventure had died out. We were quiet, concentrating on avoiding the dank spillage that made a stream in the center, walking with legs as spread out as possible, waddling.

There were secrets here I knew nothing about, echoes that reverberated from the cold hard walls and into my soul. The graffiti itself hid messages I read over and over. At some point these messages were impenetrable and yet begged to be understood. Who wrote them and when? In the late night? In broad daylight? The clothing strewn on the ground—who was the owner and why was he living here in the bowels of this subterranean freeway giant? If Lydia were here right now, I was sure we could come up with some good explanation.

"Wait, I want to look at something," Octavio called out to us. "Go ahead, you girls." And to Marisa he said: "Come here, I want to show you something." He put Luz down, and she ran over to me. Holding hands, we cautiously walked to the east end, trying to avoid stepping in the muck. Everyone was too busy keeping her shoes clean and out of the stream of sewage to take much notice of Octavio and Marisa, who lagged behind.

"Ouch," I said, my ankle twisted. I crouched down to ease the pain and at the same time turned to look back at the other end of the long pipe where we'd just been. Octavio was kissing Marisa, grabbing at the front of her blouse. I quickly looked away, feeling hot in my face. I knew Octavio didn't really care for Marisa; he had other girls who made his heart go wild, but not poor Marisa. I felt sick to my stomach.

Once out of the tube and in the fresh air, my stomach was

in convulsions, and I vomited on the field, a few feet away from our busy Interstate 5.

The spring air had grown cold in the twilight, and I shivered all the way home.

"You OK, Yoli?" Everybody kept asking me.

I nodded, too confused and hurt to look anyone straight in the eyes, except for Marisa. She was sad. She, too, knew what Octavio's sexual advances had meant: They meant everything and nothing. Just a quick thrill for him. How would our brother Octavio feel if some guy did that to one of us sisters? How would he feel if Tito manhandled Ana María that way? Was that why he didn't want our sister dating Tito—because Tito was just like him?

Make love, not war, I wanted to shout. I felt dizzy and weak. Fuck you, I wanted to answer.

We slowly climbed up the embankment to our street, all of us exhausted. The informal neighborhood meeting had long dispersed. The street was silent, empty, except for the sound of our slow shuffling feet.

We paused in front of Marisa's house and waved good-by. Then past Socorrito's. I imagined her on the phone this very moment, reporting to her comadres the strange phenomenon: so many car crashes ever since Chuy Sahagún took off on that noisy motorcycle. Unnatural phenomenon: shooting stars colliding. The "German Spies" were probably in their neat, organized home commenting on the many car accidents since

April. Did they, also, think of Chuy Sahagún?

I was certain Mamá was this very moment in the back yard watering her rows of tomatoes and squash, the gladioli. Carolina need not have worried what Mamá would say about our muddy shoes, what excuse or little lie to think up to explain why we were so late in coming home. No need for explanations, I thought sadly. Mamá would not notice the dirty shoes, nor our getting home after dark. Her only pre-occupation in those days when Chuy was missing was to make sure her plants and flowers were growing, growing, growing.

Already lights inside the houses had been turned on, entic-ing us to walk a little faster toward home and warmth and family. Out of the cool spring night, into the smells of tortillas and beans, to quick baths and Crema Nivea, a dollop of Dep for our hair about to be set on empty frozen juice cans for the straight-hair look. Secure in the soft light of the living room, soon we would be sitting together watching *The Beverly Hillbillies* and *Gilligan's Island*. The freeway cars rushing by sounded like waves, and the Santa Fe 8:38 train wailed its lonely call. We families were not alone on a desert island. We could afford to laugh at poor Gilligan and his friends in their futile attempts to be rescued; we could love Granny who continued to be Granny even as she sat transplanted in a mansion in Beverly Hills—such a sumptuous house. How we would love to be Granny! Each one of us dreamt our own dreams of sudden fortune and mansions, swimming pools, and movies stars. Such unattainable wealth, but oh, could we ever dream!

I could now smell the light fragrance of our sweet peas. By the time we waved good-bye to Georgie from Citrus Street, and made our way to our familiar rickety fence, night had set in.

—7

The Sahagún Estate was founded four years before I was born. Back then Papá worked with a crew that demolished old buildings or moved them to new locations. He was sent to Conifer Street to check the new site of a house about to be moved there. This was how he always told it: the eucalyptus trees were waving to him while the bushy pepper trees quivered with anticipation. The wind softly called to him: "Lorenzo, ven acá—over here—dear, hardworking father of six children, someday nine children. Come here," the wind whispered, beckoning Papá over.

"Was your father trying to be poetic?" Lydia asked when I recounted Papá's rendition of our history in Palm City.

"Yes, ¿y qué?" I said. "We're a family of mad poets, if you don't mind, Miss Run-of-the-Mill."

At the end of this Not-a-Through-Street, Papá stood before a lot with a shelter which might have been a chicken coop or a large tool shed. Now it stood empty and abandoned, a "For Sale" sign in front of it. It was April 1951 when Papá surveyed Conifer Street, when the spring breeze whispered enticements to him. He walked, as if in a trance—

"You're going a bit far, Yoli," Lydia said. "I can take just so much shit, OK?"

—over to the canyon that led to the Kastlungers' field. He looked down at the sour grass with its yellow blooms blanketing the canyon, looked up at the cool friendly trees. Two fat date palms in the distance. Most of Conifer Street already had houses, and he could hear children's laughter and squeals of merriment, of affectionate roughhousing. And the breeze spoke to him and said that this would be his home and soon he would have one more child, and another and another. And the one named "Yolanda" would grow to be a beautiful, passionate, intense, indomitable, wild woman with an army of innocent but enormously handsome young men at her beck and call, men she could delight and torment as she wished.

"You know, I was with you there for awhile," Lydia said. "I was even beginning to *hear* your father actually tell the story, but you just blew it, pendeja. Too many adjectives. You are so full of shit. . . ."

"Palm City," he whispered to himself, over and over, the "palm" sounding like a gentle mantra, "city" giving it a staccato closure. He had lived in Solana Beach, Ramona, Lemon Grove—moving, moving, moving—from one odd job to another. Pobre Dolores looked tired and worn out, traveling from one place to another with five children, then six, another on the way.

"Híjole, your poor mom," Lydia said. "What a drag."

Then and there, with encouragement from the enticing whispers of the breeze, Lorenzo Sahagún decided he was going to find a way to borrow some money and buy that little plot of land and fix up that chicken coop into a cozy casita. And so it was that the last of the Sahagún children—first Ana María, followed by the charming and brilliant Yolanda, then Monica, and Luz—were born. And so it was that the Sahagún Estate was founded.

It wasn't a total embellishment. There was something about Conifer Street and its surroundings that led one astray, into dreaminess and reverie and soulful pondering. There was something about the canyon across from our house that whispered to me, beckoned me to its secret crevices and corners and offered itself to me as my very own pastoral sanctuary.

And so tell me, Dearest Diary, why does he torment me so? Why does his glance, ever so slight and indifferent, make me quiver and lose focus, the world a helpless blur to my being? When will this end? If I can't have him, then vanish him from my mind and my heart. I'm only fourteen years of age, an innocent child of the universe. If he is not for me, then Dearest Diary, why am I mocked? Why does this heart of mine pitter-patter even now, in these moments of extreme anguish? If he is not meant for me, then I beseech you to have me be done with this torment and fire in my heart and soul: Francisco, my love and my life! Oh, indeed, indeed, you are nothing more than a horrid, pinche cabrón! Why do I even bother to write your name, to waste these drops of ink in my ballpoint pen; how dare you grace the pages of my diary, you wretched, ungrateful, gorgeous cabrón!

There were some things I couldn't share even with Lydia, and so I took refuge in the canyon with my diary in tow. Only in my diary could I make a complete ass of myself; only my diary could see all my dimensions. From my perch on some old wooden steps built behind someone's backyard leading to the canyon, I had a full view of Interstate 5 just beyond the Kastlungers' field. I spent long afternoons in this pastoral sanctuary. My big family, my sharing a bedroom with four other sisters—all this compelled me to scratch out a little cubbyhole for myself, a peaceful retreat from the constant talking, laughter, or shouting, from the radio blaring non-stop. Ever since I was a little girl, as long as I could remember, I visited my canyon every day—my diary and a new book in hand, sometimes Barbie and Ken—sitting in the green and yellow sour grass field in April, or among dry, scratchy tumbleweed in November, all the while staring at my perfect, unobstructed view of the freeway with its cars flashing by. Only there, in the privacy of my pastoral sanctuary, could I admit how scared I always was for my brother Chuy. It was as if somehow we were bound to each other by more than just our blood relation; as if due to a genetic anomaly, I were his twin spirit and could feel the reverberations of his life.

I was nine years old at the time. We sisters sat huddled as usual in the living room at night watching *The Twilight Zone,* with its bizarre twists and ironies, forever forcing us to see life through different angles. Chuy suddenly staggered in through the front door. El Chango was supporting him, trying to keep Chuy from stumbling and falling.

"Hey, help us out," El Chango said in an urgent whisper, so as not to awaken our parents who went to sleep right after *Bonanza.*

Our eyes, for so long transfixed on the spooky screen where Rod Serling had been leading us down a labyrinth of unknown corners and dimensions, turned to look at Chuy who was gasping for breath, blood striping his face in rivulets. He stumbled into the room, leaning heavily on El Chango.

Carolina and Ana María rushed over.

"Oh, my God, what happened? Here, take him to the bathroom. Shhh, Mamá's going to hear us." The blood splotched Carolina's hands as she and Ana María helped El Chango lead Chuy to the bathroom. Monica and I sat petrified, scrunched up on the orange love seat, unable to move, unable to breathe. All that blood! Maybe we should wake our parents, I thought. Call the police.

Then suddenly a burst of low, masculine laughter, some feminine shouts. "You stupid idiots, you'll be sorry." Carolina and Ana María came storming out of the bathroom and into the living room, not caring if our parents did wake up now, they were that angry. Chuy and his pranks: fake Halloween Dracula blood. He'd be sorry for this, my sisters said, promising to get back at him with their own prank. Monica, only four at the time, started to cry, scared to death. Stupid idiots.

Chuy and El Chango followed the girls out of the bathroom and into the living room, had a good laugh, congratulating each other on their gag. Then Chuy caught my eye as I sat still, numb, unable to laugh, unable to cry—somewhere in between, as usual.

He immediately stopped laughing. "It was just a joke, Yoli," he said, coming over to me. He knelt down in front of me so I could get a good look at him. "See, mi'ja, no one's hurt, OK?"

I turned away from him and stared at the TV screen. Rod Serling had left and *The Twilight Zone* was over for the night.

▬8

My period came to me at the same time I discovered Diana Ross and the Supremes. "Baby Love" caused me wrenching, heartbreaking hysteria as never before. Quickly slipping into the bathroom where no one could see me, I sobbed and gulped and stared at the hideous reflection in the mirror. Why, why, my God, was I so ugly? Look at these cursed pimples all over my face. Why me? Why couldn't I look like Annette

Funicello in *Beach Blanket Bingo,* or any one of the actresses in their shapely, bikinied bodies, their beautiful complexions? Why the pimples and the boobs and the broad hips? For an answer, the muffled pleading strains of Diana, in the bedroom just beyond the bathroom, begged Baby Love not to break up with her.

"Mountain face" is what Alfonso Zuñiga called me whenever he was feeling especially cruel. Ana María assured me he only teased me like that, called me "mountain face" because he had a crush on me. Carolina, not yet in college at the time of my pimples' first appearance, but already sounding like our resident psychologist, said that Alfonso Zuñiga was really referring to my nicely shaped breasts, but he couldn't bring himself to admit it.

"It's a subconscious thing. He likes you and your boobs, but he's a confused pre-adolescent and so gets boobs mixed up with pimples. He'll say any stupid thing just to get your attention, so ignore him."

I was only eleven years old when they first appeared, these horrid little zits, and already I could tell this would be the cross I would bear for years to come. It was an aesthetic demise for me, the beginning of the end: the beautiful duckling was turning into an ugly swan. And nobody in the world, nobody at all, seemed to understand my agony, except for my brother Chuy.

I stood before the dresser mirror, so close my breathing

kept fogging the glass, studying my pimples: three white heads at the side of my nostrils, four and a half angry red ones on my forehead, my chin and jaw line under a mountain range so dramatic it could easily have challenged the Himalayas. I'd start with the white heads by my nose and work my way down.

"No, Yoli," Chuy said, "don't pop them." He was suddenly standing next to me and looking at my face in the mirror.

"But they look so gross," I said, blushing furiously. It was embarrassing to be caught picking my pimples.

"Nah," he said. "They aren't that bad. Only to you do they seem really ugly. But anyway, here," he said handing me a short round jar. "I got you this. I use it now and then when I have a flare-up."

"Yeah, but this is a fire burning out of control," I said, staring at my wretched miserable zits. Could I ever really zap them for good?

"Watch how I do it," he said. Opening the jar he took out a round, paper-thin pad. "See this pimple I have on my chin? Just rub it, like you're cleaning it, but not too hard. Don't scrub or anything, OK?" He was looking at himself in the mirror and so I looked at him in the mirror, too. There we were, brother and sister—I was eleven and he was nineteen—staring into the mirror, sharing pimples and moistened, medicated pads. How serious and concerned he seemed. I blushed, my zits now redder than ever. I felt like hugging Chuy,

'Thank you, thank you, hermano tan lindo' is what I wanted to say. 'You understand me, don't you?'

"If you rub it too hard, you'll irritate the skin," he was saying. "I read that in my health book. Here, try it," he said, handing me one.

As if receiving Holy Communion, I accepted the host-like gauze from my brother.

"Let me know when you run out," he said. "I'll get you some more."

"Thank you, Chuy," I mumbled into the mirror.

When I finished using the first batch, I kept the jar for good luck, filling it with a collection of my favorite odd-colored stones. It was my way of honoring the fact that Chuy understood.

Even now at the age of fourteen—some years after that first fateful moment when I became a "young lady," yes, even at the age of fourteen, already a seasoned menstruating woman—I oftentimes couldn't bare to look at my reflection in a full-length mirror.

"You know, Yoli," Ana María said to me as I watched her wet the thin brush with her tongue, dab it in the caked receptacle before applying it to her top eyelid, "someday you're going to thank God you have big boobs."

"That'll be the day," I said, buttoning every single button on my sweater, even though it was a warm May day. "Where are you going, getting all dolled up like that?" I asked, noticing that Ana María was already applying "Red Coral" lipstick to her mouth.

She was silent a moment, concentrating on her lip line. "I'll tell you if you swear to keep a secret," she said. She looked at me in the mirror.

"Cross my heart, and hope to die, stick a hundred needles in my eye," I said.

"Well," she said importantly as she checked her teeth for smudges. "I'm going to Silver Wing Park."

"And?" I said.

She was wearing the yellow skirt that was easy to roll up at the waistline once she was past our parents' strict, observant eyes.

"Tito's going to meet me there. And just remember," she said, "you swore you wouldn't tell."

"OK, OK," I said, "But I don't know, Ana. Isn't he too old for you? Isn't he around twenty-five, like Octavio?"

"Yes, ¿y qué? I'm very mature for my age, don't forget. And anyway, it's better to have an older man. Women are always more mature than their male peers. So what do you think, how do I look?"

She twirled around for my benefit, posed as if she were the famous model Twiggy, but unlike Twiggy, Ana María had curves, beautiful curves, in all the right places, and a complexion that was flawless, long eyelashes, blue eyes, black curly wild hair past her shoulder. She looked like a magical Queen of the Gypsies—an exemplary specimen of a woman blessed with Beauty, while I stood next to her cursed with Ugliness. Ha, ha, Yolanda, God must have said in a mean moment, take that thunderbolt of hideousness!

"Wish me luck," she said to me, winking and giving herself one final inspection in the mirror. Then Ana María bounded out of the house and onto Conifer Street, headed for Silver Wing Park, although for permission's sake and for an alibi, she pretended to be going over to Esther's house on Harris Avenue. I watched her from the safety of the bedroom window, and for no good reason that I could think of—I just did—I said a Hail Mary for her.

Even then, in those moments when I buttoned my thick sweater on hot summer days, I knew I wouldn't be doing this for long. Even then I could feel a weird wetness—not my period, not my urine—dampening my underpants. I tried to be clinical about these secretions. I sneaked Carolina's booklet *Sex and the Teenager,* which she thought she kept safely hidden under her mattress. Hiding it between the covers of my copy of *Wuthering Heights,* I slipped out of the house to the safety of my canyon where I read portions of the forbidden booklet as quickly and thoroughly as I could, always with a cautious eye behind me, alert to possible intruders. As clinical and impersonal as I tried to force myself to be, my romantic, blissful, fantastical longings had a greater hold. I was, after all, crazy about Francisco Valdivia—my own "dark-skinned gypsy" Heathcliff—and I longed for the day he would slide his hands up my blouse, grab hold of my breasts and have me.

What of my brothers and their loves? Who were their girlfriends, and what did they do with them? It seemed impossible to penetrate a man's world. The meaningful glances and chuckles, a certain posturing with the abdomen—all difficult to decode. Then one day my brother Armando offered me a job: a dollar fifty a week to clean the guys' room, make the beds, sweep, mop and empty the chamber pot.

What a deal! Little did my brother know what doors he was giving me permission to enter. What a world! And to be paid a dollar fifty a week for this entrance—with no more sneaking in—yes, what luck!

So I walked into their room once a week, feeling like a sexy little chambermaid entering the masculine domain, ready to discover manly secrets. But for all the snooping and prying, lifting up of mattresses, poking through drawers of underwear and t-shirts, I was still unable to find the answers to my questions—answers that I was certain could either make or break a woman: How far was going "too far" with a guy? If you went "too far," your reputation was ruined and, marriage out of the question, you would need to resign yourself to either being a piruja or dressing saints like all the old maids for the rest of your life. A kiss seemed acceptable, but what about French kissing, the tongues swirling around, bumping into each other? And the guy's groping—waist up,

OK? Waist down, bad, bad, bad, the young woman now hope-lessly falling into an abyss of "loose," "slutty," and—worst of all—"cheap and easy." And what was the reward for the good girl, for the girl who controlled herself and her man? What was our goal, pray tell, when all was said and—my God—done? The goal was to marry a guy and live happily ever after. No loose, cheap and easy slut could ever hope for that kind of blissful destiny—or could she?

This called for constant discourse with Lydia on the topic of Men:

"His frown is kind of rough and mean. It makes it a great challenge for a woman to soften him up, loosen him up," Lydia was telling me as we sat on the metal patio chairs in the front yard. Armando was washing his car, far from hearing range, but close enough for field observations by Lydia. "He always seems so worried, preocupado-like. It must be because he's the oldest of the clan, huh? He's the second man of the house," Lydia said, as if she were carrying on a dialogue with herself. "But then suddenly he'll be joking and teasing Monica and Luz, twirling your little sister around and he's all tenderness. God, what a gorgeous mystery he is," Lydia said, sighing.

She came over to my house way too often in the summer, in the hopes of catching a glimpse of one of my brothers. She made it a personal mission, as if she were working on a summer project titled "Observations on the Sahagún Brothers." I didn't mind that Lydia constantly talked about my brothers, made her little observations of their sexiness. I felt the same way, my heart inflating with proud love for my four handsome brothers. It was a good feeling to know that I was the sister of four gorgeous, sought-after men. Had they not been my brothers, I would have married any one of them in a heartbeat.

Our next-door neighbor Marisa had probably been secretly in love with Octavio since her elementary school days. His blue eyes sparkled and danced, teased and flirted relentlessly. Forever electric, magnetic, hypnotizing women with his sexy stride (according to my own field notes), and his little-boy pout at just the right moment, Octavio was Frankie Avalon, James Dean and Elvis Presley rolled up into one heart-throbbing lover, and he knew it. He had at least a hundred girlfriends, or so it seemed from all the phone calls he received.

"What is it with these girls chasing Octavio, acting so loose and cheap, begging to know when Octavio will be home?" my older sisters often said. "Stupid gringas, don't they know that if Octavio wanted to talk to them, he would call them back?"

"How do you know they're gringas?" I asked.

"Of course they're gringas," Ana María said. "Mexican girls don't go falling all over guys like that. Uy, chale, we've got our dignity, man."

In light of my recent plan of going up to Francisco Valdivia in the hallway before homeroom and giving him a big fat kiss on the lips, just like that, just to get his attention, let him know what's what, I wasn't so sure about Ana María's comment about Mexican girls' dignity. It was something I had been seriously contemplating doing by this Friday. Ana María's comment about loose gringas made me pause and reconsider.

But if I was willing to do that for Francisco Valdivia, I couldn't blame the gringas for chasing Octavio. Even my Francisco wasn't that handsome.

Secretly in love with our neighbor Marisa who was secretly in love with Octavio, Tony remained shy. Miss Psychologist Carolina said it was a defense mechanism in this world of aggressive men and women, of wars and slogans and political agendas that left him confused and dizzy. He listened intently to everything and everyone around him. And Ray Charles's music brought him comfort. His blue-green eyes were tentative. When he talked with someone, he rarely looked them in the eyes, seeming to concentrate better looking away to the side or just beyond. Lydia and I often commented that if only Tony aggressively proclaimed his love for Marisa (say, go up to her and give her a big fat kiss on the lips, just like that, let her know what's what), Marisa would surely fall gratefully into his tender shy arms for protection against Latin Lover Heartbreakers like Octavio.

Then there was Chuy.

The amazing thing was not that he had passed his high school courses without studying, but that he had passed them with top scores. He listened to the teacher's lecture only as far as it would interest him, and when it became too dull for his liking, Chuy diverted his attention to showing off in front of his classmates, tossing outrageous, flirtatious notes to Donna, who adored him as everyone else did. He was not a mere class clown: Jesús Manuel Sahagún *was* the class. A dose of Chuy-A-Day kept the doctor away, or so all the students at Mar Vista High thought.

What I knew of Chuy's loves came from conversations—some clearly reported, others in whispers and half-phrases—that Carolina and Ana María had with their girlfriends. I secretly listened in from the inside of the bathroom, pretending that I had to go Number Two. Given all the times I took cover in the bathroom, rushing in as I saw my sisters' girlfriends coming over for a gossip session, I was surprised they never wondered if I had some sort of bowel disorder. Or maybe they knew the truth, that I was hiding out in the bathroom listening in on their Top Secret conversations, and accepted my sneakiness as a kind of initiation into the wonderful world of feminine secrets, opinions and final judgments.

"She hangs all over him and sometimes they'll be kissing right in the middle of the hallway! Carolina calls her 'chicle' because she's stuck on Chuy like a piece of gum."

"Sometimes I feel like stomping on her as if she was a piece of gum!"

"Just make sure you don't stomp on her in front of Chuy.

It'd piss him off if he knew we called her 'Chicle,' his querida little Donna."

"You know, every time that song comes on the radio, I change the station so quick. Man, I want to throw up when I hear it. How can Chuy be so blind? She's so easy. . . ."

"What do you expect, eh?"

All of them were silent a moment, knowing what each was thinking: what did you expect from a gringa?

The Christmas Eve just before Chuy was sent off to boot camp at Fort Ord, he had invited Donna to our house. She walked in, Chuy behind her, his hand touching her back, proudly guiding her into the Sahagún household. She looked nervous, she did, what with all those people—Chuy's whole family gaping at her—but she also made the little angel at the top of our scraggly Christmas tree look like a pitiful, droopy imitation of what a real angel must be. As she shyly shook hands with Mamá and Papá, I took in every particular of this live angel, memorizing each detail of her in order to report to Lydia the next day.

She wore a white, virgin wool sweater—I was sure it was virgin—with a matching red, white, and green plaid skirt—most certainly imported from Scotland. Black patent leather shoes graced her dainty feet. Her red velvet hair band crowned golden hair in soft waves all the way down to her waist. Her blue eyes nervously looked into Chuy's blue eyes for reassurance. Chuy was not blind, no siree, and I could easily understand his letting Donna stick to him like chicle.

After the initial, all around introductions, I was the first to approach her. "May I offer you something to drink?" I asked this golden angel. I made certain I used the proper "may"— surely this would impress her, convince her that I was genteel enough to be a part of her entourage. "Coke, 7 Up?" I was ready to be her apprentice. The idea of curtseying was not far off on my list of proper things I should do when in the presence of royalty. My thinking was that if I hung around her, say, was her slave, offered to do errands for her, some of her beauty would rub off on me. She, my mentor, I, her protégée. "Perhaps a glass of our delightful wine?" I asked.

My family stared at me a moment, annoyed and unimpressed with my finesse. Barbarians, the whole lot of them!

She politely accepted the cup of atole Mamá served her.

As we all sat down to dinner, a few of us on the couch, another four at the kitchen table, the little ones on their knees at the coffee table, I made sure that the orange vinyl love seat was reserved for Donna and Chuy, giving Tony the evil eye and quickly glancing Donna's way as he was about to plop himself down on it. He immediately got back up, understanding my look to mean that the seat was reserved for My Lady.

We were all discreetly staring at her, each of us brothers and sisters sitting somewhere in the living room or the kitchen or wherever we could find a comfortable enough spot to balance our Christmas dinner plates of tamales. I'm sure we were all thinking the same thing: this beautiful Scottish lass in fine wool apparel had never tasted atole in her life—maybe not even tamales. No matter. That Christmas Eve I feasted my eyes on a real live angel: Chuy's Donna.

After eating our Christmas Eve dinner—it'd never been so quiet and orderly like that Christmas Eve—we settled in for a couple of rounds of lotería, Luz and Monica in charge of passing out the illustrated bingo cards and the uncooked pinto beans for markers.

Chuy and Donna snuggled up next to each other on the orange love seat, bingo cards on their laps.

I got to be the Caller the first time around. "El Nopal," I called out, showing the card to everyone, pausing in front of Donna so she could get a good look at the cactus since she probably didn't know how to read in Spanish. In my round of calling, I was very patient, calling out each object three or four times, pausing and gently hovering over her just to make sure she didn't miss something on her lotería card. My brothers and sisters looked at me, perhaps annoyed over my slowness in getting to the next card, surely envious of my meticulous enunciation. Unhappy brutes, all of them!

"El Diablito," I called out at the same time Donna giggled and pointed to Chuy—the little devil!

Then, "La Sirena," and I paused a little more than I had for the other cards, feeling suddenly tripped up, disoriented, wondering in that moment, there on the spot, as I held up the card, was Donna a kind of Homeric, evil siren or an innocent mermaid—or both?

Chuy had his arm around her, now and then gently, lovingly stroking her blond, sleek hair. They were in love, all right, in some kind of a trance, love-zombies smiling at each other whenever they both had the same item on their card, Chuy putting a bean on her square and his.

Was she really an angel—or was she a devil? Was she the kind of girl we were raised not to be, the kind of girl we talked about in secret?

"Hurry up, Yoli," Monica called out to me. "I just need two more to win."

"La Dama," I called out quickly, impatiently now.

I wondered if every Mexican guy had a "Donna" somewhere in his life. I imagined Ritchie Valens's Donna—blonde, golden, perfect—part of the El Dorado of his impossible dreams.

"*LOTERÍA,*" Chuy shouted, victorious, laughing and leaning over to give his Christmas angel a kiss on the forehead, the beans on his card now spilling to the vinyl floor, making a clickety-tapping noise. Annoying. Confounding.

9

Our household was not built on democratic, egalitarian principles. The Women's Liberation Movement was as far away from our parents' consciousness as the moon. The "feminine mystique" was just that: something mystical and powerful that Papá felt obligated to preserve and rein in. Having grown up on a ranch, Papá raised his children much as he had raised and tended ranch animals. We five daughters were his fillies, and he wasn't about to let us wander off and start reproducing at the first sign of heat.

So the first rumblings in our house were not caused by the San Andreas fault, but by Carolina's request for permission to invite Tom over to the house to meet our parents. She approached Mamá first.

"Absolutely not," was her answer. "What kind of parents do you think we would be to allow such a thing? I'm not an alcahueta, some busybody matchmaker. Don't even think of asking your father." Case closed, Mamá instructed Carolina to take down the clothes from the clothesline.

"I don't care what they do," Carolina said. "I'm going to invite Tom over to meet the family. And if they don't like it, they can throw us both out!"

"God, Carolina, where will you go?" All of us sisters sat huddled in the girls' room in an emergency conference.

"Yes, do it," I said, wanting to let out a whoop of sheer excitement. "This is so romantic. And besides, it's for a good cause, remember? You'll be breaking the ice for us, you'll be paving the way. Carolina Sahagún, your name will go down in history. Oh yes, do it!"

Luz and Monica stared at us three older sisters.

"But where will you go and live when they throw you out?" Monica's voice trembled.

"I'll miss you so much," seven-year-old Luz said, beginning to cry.

"Oh, mi'ja, don't you worry," Carolina said, gathering them into her arms for a tight hug. "Every night, no matter where I am, I'll sneak in through this window and come and hug you good-night."

We all sat quiet a moment as we imagined Carolina climbing through the window into the girls' room, hugging us goodnight before quickly climbing back out into the hostile black night.

■ ■ ■ ■ ■

On a warm evening in late May of 1969, Carolina's true love knocked on the Sahagún front door for the first time. We had just eaten dinner and Papá was dozing in the green velvet armchair with Tijuana's *El Mexicano* newspaper draped over his lap. All of us were in our rehearsed positions: Ana María and I sat on the orange vinyl love seat pretending to read, while Luz and Monica pretended to play quietly with their paper dolls on the coffee table. We had planned it for an evening when all our brothers were working, so they wouldn't be home and band with Papá in beating up the poor, unsuspecting guy.

When she heard the knock at the door, Mamá froze. Just

an hour earlier, Carolina had simply announced to her: "Mamá, I'm going to do it the American way. No secret notes, no meeting at the corner. These are modern times, Mamá, and I am a modern woman of the sixties." And she planted a kiss on our speechless mother's cheek and went to the room to freshen up her make-up.

So Carolina was now walking up to the front door, her long brown hair smooth and shiny, her chin up, feeling self-assured, ready for battle, it seemed. I noticed her hand was trembling as she turned the doorknob.

There he was, standing tall and handsome at the doorway, Carolina's man, dressed in his Marine uniform. (Carolina had asked him to dress this way, hoping it might impress our parents, make him look extra clean-cut and responsible; Carolina was wise that way.)

"Hi, Tom, come in." Carolina sounded chipper, except to us sisters who, in the know, could detect the tremble in her voice.

We all stared at our father who sat with his mouth slightly open, snoring.

"Papá," I called out. "Papá, we have company. Despierta."

"¿Qué? Hum?" he opened his eyes, rubbed them sleepily.

Carolina stood next to Tom, and in a crisp, clear voice she announced to our father: "Papá, I would like you to meet my . . . my . . . good friend, Tom."

He stared. That's what he did, he stared. First at his oldest daughter and then at this strange young gringo man in his house. He stared.

Carolina was brave that night. She stood her ground as our father jumped to his feet, letting the *El Mexicano* fall, pages scattering all over the floor.

"Get out," he said to Tom, pointing to the front door. "Get out this instant."

"Papá, if you make him leave, then I'll leave, too."

"What?!" he shouted. "What did you just dare say to your father?" His face was red, his blue eyes looked dark, almost purple.

"I want you to meet Tom. I want you to know who I'm dating. . . ."

"Dating? You are dating, you say? Who gave you permission to date? Your mother?"

We all turned to look at Mamá, who hadn't moved, still frozen at the kitchen doorway with the dish towel in her hand.

"No, Papá," Carolina said. "I gave myself permission. I'm twenty years old, Papá, for God's sake."

"Ah, so now you use God's name in vain, on top of everything else," he said. His body was beginning to stiffen, we could see the rage rising from his toes to his feet, up his legs and torso, to his face.

"Papá, I want to do this the proper way. I want you to meet my friends, to approve."

"The 'proper way,' you say. Who told you what the 'proper

way' was? How dare you think you know the proper way, chamaca ingrata. How dare you go against my rules!" he shouted. "You bring this guy into my house without my permission. Then fine, vete, just go."

Silence. Nobody moved, nobody breathed.

"Lorenzo, por favor," our mother called out.

Tom stood in the same spot. Too stunned to say anything at first, still he held his ground.

"Mr. Sahagún," he began. "I would like your permission to date your daughter. . . ."

"Get out, both of you," Papá shouted. "What insolence! Todos, todos, váyanse al diablo. You are no longer my daughter, you ungrateful child." And he stormed out of the living room, slamming the front door behind him.

It was a heroic stand, nevertheless. Carolina Sahagún held her chin up proudly as she packed an overnight suitcase with cold cream, pajamas and underwear. She was going to spend the night at Esther's house over on Harris Avenue.

We surrounded her, Luz and Monica crying, Ana María and I pale as we envisioned the day we also would be packing our things.

"Mi'ja, look what you've done," our mother said. She was confused, her allegiance now divided. "How could you have done such a thing?"

Carolina paused in her packing, looking up at Mamá.

"Mamá," she said, "how could I *not* have done this?"

Mamá was pensive, silent. Then she nodded and said: "You're right, Corazón. How could you *not* have done this." Getting up to leave, she kissed Carolina on her cheek, and then walked out of the bedroom, softly closing the door behind her.

It occurred to me that maybe Carolina had made a mistake in advising Tom to wear his dress greens, that when Papá set his sleepy eyes on Tom dressed in his Marine uniform, he must have felt tricked, as though a sick practical joke had been played on him. Yes, that must've been it, why he reacted the way he did: tricked into thinking the young man standing before him in a military uniform was Chuy, his missing veteran son now home again. Deceived, cruelly tricked.

When Armando returned home from work later that night, he entered the abnormally silent house and walked into the kitchen to reheat some late dinner. He found our mother sitting at the table, her elbows propped on it, her hands covering her face.

"¿Qué pasa, Mamá?" he asked. "What is it? Chuy?"

"No," she said. "Carolina brought a boyfriend over for your father to meet."

She told Armando the story, how our father stormed out of the house in a rage. God only knew where he had gone, and Carolina was spending the night at Esther's.

"I'll handle it, Mamá," Armando said.

"No, mi'jo," she said. "Stay out of it."

The front door opened and closed. Papá walked into the kitchen, giving Armando and Mamá a glance that said, I know you two have been talking about what just happened and I don't care a bit; just leave me alone. He opened the refrigerator, whistling to himself, ignoring them, it seemed to me, as I stood huddled with my sisters at the kitchen doorway within hearing distance, taking turns peeking in, in anticipation of something.

"Papá," Armando began. "We need to talk."

"Buenas noches to you, too," our father said. "Or have you forgotten that's how you're supposed to greet your elders?"

In silence our father heated himself a tortilla and filled it with refried beans. He served himself a large glass of milk and then pulled up a chair at the table where Armando and our mother sat, watching him.

"So what is it that you're in such a need to talk about? Are you and Sonia finally going to get married?" He took a bite of his tortilla. Sonia was Armando's longtime girlfriend.

"No, Papá," Armando said. "It's not about me. It's about Carolina. She's twenty years old, and I think it's time you let her have a boyfriend."

Our father stopped chewing a moment. "Ah, is that so?" he said. "Who are you to say when she can start dating? Since when are you the one who makes the rules in this house?"

"Papá," Armando said. "She's a woman now, for God's

sake, and it's only natural she should go out with guys."

"'For God's sake, Papá, for God's sake, Papá,'" our father said, now pushing the kitchen chair away and suddenly on his feet shouting. "Why is it you children have to have God enter into this whenever you please, as if God were just a toy whose name could be tossed around without its due respect?"

"Lorenzo, por favor," our mother said, now standing. "You're out of control. Cálmate."

"I am not out of control," he shouted, his veins about to pop. His face was red and sweating under the bright kitchen light. "This is my house and I make the rules, do you understand?" he shouted at Armando.

"Papá, you are being so unreasonable. . . ."

"Ay, tú, 'so unreasonable,' eh?" our father said. "Come on then. Let's see who's the boss. Come on, let's see you try to punch your father." Our father crouched, his fists ready to swing a punch at Armando who looked pale and miserable.

"Lorenzo, for the love of God, stop this," our mother shouted. "You're making a fool out of yourself."

"Come on, just one good punch. Let's see if you can hit your old man one good punch, just try it." Papá's eyes were blazing—spitting fire, it seemed to us four sisters huddled at the doorway.

Then Luz let out a shriek so high and powerful that it made us all freeze, the hairs on the back of our neck rising and leaving us cold. She began to cry and wail uncontrollably, her whole body trembling.

Startled out of his fierce trance, our father came running over to Luz and scooped her up into his arms and held her.

"Mi'ja," he whispered soothingly in her ear as he cuddled her in his arms. "Shhhshhh . . . está bien, Corazón. It's OK, don't be afraid. Everything's OK."

The next day Papá called Esther's house and ordered his daughter back home where she belonged. Punto. Period.

It seemed to me that we did a lot more praying than usual that summer of 1969. I had to remind myself that Lent was over, but it didn't seem so. It was as if our parents had decided to extend the spring Lenten season into summer. We prayed the rosary every evening after dinner, our mother and father, all of us brothers and sisters—minus Chuy, for whom we were praying. We knelt before the fake fireplace and the Sacred Heart of Jesus, there in the living room where just a week before Carolina had tried to proclaim her freedom or at least exercise her American Civil Liberties—her efforts prematurely terminated by our father's wrath.

This June evening was especially hot, and it seemed a cruel penance to have to be kneeling in the tiny living room, one right next to the other like cloistered nuns and monks, praying the rosary. But our parents were relentless on the subject of God and Mass and Holy Days of Obligation, and so with only a rickety old fan that seemed to be gasping for breath, we surrendered ourselves to the *Padre Nuestros* and the *Dios te salve, Marías* and to a litany of chants that on hot summer days seemed interminable.

Although trapped for fifteen minutes of forced reflection and prayer in the Sahagún household, we made the best of our time. Ana María, checking for chipped nail polish on her fingers, was not once off beat with "ahora y en la hora de nuestra muerte, Amen," while Carolina caught sight of another split end to attack. Maybe popping that new little white head by my nose and praying the rosary at the same time would give God the hint. Yes, why not? Maybe tomorrow I would be pimple-free and beautiful? A good reason to pray—but suddenly an angry "cruzen los brazos!" from our father brought us back to the real task at hand, and with our arms obediently crossed, we temporarily abandoned thoughts of split ends, chipped nail polish and pimples.

So when someone knocked at the door, we were eager for any interesting distraction. Armando, kneeling nearest the door, got up and opened it.

"Hi, Tom," he said. "Come on in."

Carolina's Tom walked in, all ten pairs of eyes staring at him in disbelief. This was his second visit, and I thought he was either a masochist of the worst kind or very much in love with Carolina. I prayed it was the latter.

Papá stood up, faltered, unable to speak.

"May I join you?" Tom asked, looking directly at our father.

Our father stared. Hesitated. He must have been thinking that the world was coming to an end, or that this was a test from God. Who knows what he was thinking in those crucial seconds?

"Yes," he finally said. "There's room over there by Octavio."

Tom knelt down, Papá knelt down, and turning to look at the Sacred Heart of Jesus, I prayed the remaining Hail Marys and Our Fathers with such fervor and gratitude I thought I was going to burst.

—10

I refused to believe that that's how it was; what Alan Jensen in sixth period always chanted when a girl passed by: "Wham! Bam! Thank you, Ma'am." I refused to believe that the world was full of Alan Jensens who saw love and the act of love as this crude, insensitive slogan. I knew there was more—much more—to lovemaking than this. There were men out there who were brave and gallant like Carolina's Tom; there were men who were sensitive and romantic. Men like my brother Chuy.

Just before he was drafted, sent off to Fort Ord boot camp, Chuy had planned a surprise birthday party for his Donna. I was in charge of tying cellophane spaghetti-thin ribbon around napkin, fork and knife, creating curlicues with the scissors. Chuy's little-boy excitement over putting on this party for Donna had impressed even my sisters when they observed him opening the oven and pulling out his slightly lopsided chocolate cake, vanilla frosting still on his upper lip from licking the spatula a few minutes earlier. So even Carolina and Ana María—who usually regarded my brothers' gringa girlfriends with disdain—had offered to help out with the party decorations.

Crepe paper was looped from one corner of the patio to the next, and green and gold balloons, Mar Vista High's colors and Donna and Chuy's colors, were everywhere. Mamá lent a hand, creating floral table arrangements with whatever flowers we had in bloom in September—daisies, lilies, gardenias—and plastic Virgo symbols on sticks propped in the center of each flower arrangement.

The plan was this: Chuy would take Donna out for an early dinner and then make some excuse to get her to our house. (Luz's suggestion: "My mother wants us to drop by because she has a gift for you and wants to give you a birthday hug"; or mine: "Oh, Man, I forgot your gift. Let's stop off at my house. I left it on the coffee table, it'll just take a minute"; or El Chango's contribution: "Hey, I gotta take a shit. Mind if we stop off at my house? I'm particular about where I go caca.")

Now El Chango was honking his car horn, waiting for Chuy so they could go to Tijuana and buy sodas and stuff for the party. It was Saturday afternoon. Plenty of time. Chuy passed through the festive patio, pausing long enough to plant a kiss on Mamá's forehead, winking at me and giving Luz—silly, goofy baby sister—one last good twirl in the air. Wheeee! And then he was taking off with El Chango at the wheel.

Around seven o'clock, people started to arrive—mostly Donna's friends and some of Chuy's. Because Chuy and El Chango hadn't yet returned from Tijuana with the sodas, around six o'clock we had made a quick trip to Brown's Market, figuring the guys must have gotten stuck in the border traffic and that Chuy probably had gone directly to Donna's.

But what about El Chango? my sisters wondered. The guys were in his car, so wouldn't he be here by now? Mamá and Carolina and Ana María gave each other secretive, worried looks, but I wasn't worried. I knew Chuy would come through. Things must have just taken a little detour.

I was proud of our party decorations. Donna's girlfriends— three of them on the Mariners' cheering squad—ooh'd and ahh'd over Mamá's floral arrangements, said our house looked like a "cute little cottage."

"I think they're pushing it, don't you?" Lydia whispered to me when she and I overheard the girls say this to Mamá.

Well, yes, maybe, but I felt flattered that Donna's friends— the most popular girls at Mar Vista High—felt the need to kissy-up to Chuy's mom.

There were about forty people milling around, talking and laughing, catching up on some good gossip. My other brothers wandered in, although Armando was getting ready to go to work, and Tony and Octavio had hot plans of their own for the night.

Around seven thirty we got a call from Donna: Where was Chuy? He was supposed to pick her up at seven.

That's when we all got worried, figuring something had happened to the guys in Tijuana. Carolina suggested she come on over to our house and wait for him, reassured her that he probably got stuck in some horrendous border traffic. Why not wait over here?

Sometimes Carolina could be pretty neat. How wise of her to figure Donna could still have a surprise party—the show must go on!—whether Chuy was at her side or not. She probably figured Donna might as well be here with her friends till we heard from the guys.

Where were they? In truth, they should have been home hours ago—border traffic or no border traffic.

Soon, Donna was knocking at our front door. With us standing in the living room, scrunched—shhh!—holding our breath, Carolina opened the front door.

"Surprise!" we shouted in unison, and then laughter.

She was tickled pink that Chuy had planned this for her. His lopsided cake with eighteen white, unlit candles in a circle, a good-luck nineteenth in the middle, and the letters

"HAPPY BIRTHDAY, DONNA" sliding down the vanilla frosting hill was the cutest thing. She had no idea, didn't suspect a single thing, that clever rascal!

The party came and the party went. Chuy never showed up. We had gotten a call from El Chango around nine o'clock in the night as we all waited, subdued, quietly drinking Brown's Market sodas and eating potato chips, wondering—or worrying—what had happened to Chuy and El Chango.

They were still in Tijuana, El Chango reported on the phone, his voice sounding too loud, a little slurred. It was hard for Carolina to understand him. Something about stopping off at "Mike's A-Go-Go" for a couple of drinks. Yahoo, he said, cracking up. El Chango sounded drunk, wished us a Happy New Year in September, told us not to wait up. Nightynight, sleep tight and don't let the bedbugs bite. Chuy? Very well, thank you. Then he hung up.

After the phone call, Donna's friends, her best girlfriends, quietly, politely got up, thanked Mamá for the food, diplomatically said, "Oh well, boys will be boys"—but really were thinking "Poor Donna" and left.

Donna stayed behind a little bit, helping us pick up. She had been crying, you could tell, though she pretended to be busy throwing out paper cups and crumpled napkins. The birthday cake remained untouched.

Mamá apologized for Chuy, Donna thanked all of us, and then left.

I waited for him on the front porch. I could hear the sound of the TV, my older sisters still up watching some late show. My parents were in bed. It was growing cold, and I was shivering there in the dark. I pulled my knees up and held them tight with my arms. I should've put a sweater on at least, but I didn't want to move from my spot, not even for a minute. I wanted to be the first to confront him, to pound on his chest and scream at him: "How could you hurt her so?! How could you do this to Donna!" How could he do this to *me*?

Around midnight, he drove up alone in El Chango's car. He cut the ignition and opened the door. The front porch light bulb was bright enough for me to see him from the driveway, to notice any drunken swagger; perhaps he would clumsily trip over himself, now on his knees, a stupid, dopey grin on his face. Boys will be boys.

But this was not the case. He walked toward the porch, his shoulders hunched, looking tired and sad. Defeated.

"Chuy," I said, now all the anger dissipating in the cold thin air, "what happened?"

He sat down, staring miserably at the dark street in front of us. "You can't believe the shit I just went through today," he said. He rubbed his face, tired and disgusted. "*I* can't fucking believe what I went through. . . ."

It *was* incredible: They had started out fine, plenty of time. But as soon as they crossed the border things took on an almost surreal tone. Now, looking back, it seemed like a comedy caper with a tragic ending.

They stopped off for a bite to eat at their favorite torta restaurant. This Saturday, though, the place was jam-packed with people and it took the guys longer than usual to get their orders.

It was five o'clock when they finally headed back to the car. El Chango was driving, insisting on stopping at his favorite liquor store, insisting that they had the best prices in T.J. He rolled through a four-way stop sign, all the while arguing with Chuy who wanted to go to "Licores AS" because his uncle owned the chain, and that's where they always went, and Chuy was paying for the drinks anyway, so what did it matter to El Chango?

Before long there's a Tijuana cop right on their tail, red light flashing, siren letting out a quick shrill cry for good measure. The guys pull over to the side of the road. Oh, shit.

Didn't the Señor see the stop sign back there? Did they think that because they were in Mexico they could disrespect the signs?

Yeah, yeah, let's just get to the mordida. How much do you want? El Chango is impatient and not in the mood for this shit.

What? The police officer looks at him, feigning insult. What do you mean by "mordida," Señor? Are you trying to bribe me?

He calls for back up and soon three police cars show

up and lead them to the station.

In the meantime, Chuy's looking at his watch, trying to remember what time the jewelry store Joyería La Perla closes on Saturday. It's almost six o'clock.

At the station the bureaucratic paper work—what is your name? mother's maiden name? date of birth? address? car insurance policy number?—has El Chango fuming. What is it with this shit? What happened to the good old mordida? How about a fucking little traffic ticket? Who the hell do they think they are jerking us around like this? Tell them you're about to go to Vietnam and save the fucking world.

"Why was El Chango acting like that?" I asked Chuy.

"I don't know," Chuy said. "Ever since he knew I was being drafted and he wasn't because of his leg, he's been acting stupid. I don't know, just angry and shit."

Chuy pulls him aside and tells him to behave. Keep his goddamned mouth shut and maybe they'd get out of there in time.

In time? In time for what, El Chango wants to know. In time for the Chinese New Year? In time for breakfast at Tiffany's tomorrow? El Chango is slowly but surely losing it, and there isn't much Chuy can do but ignore him and hope the jewelry store doesn't close early on Saturdays.

It's seven thirty before they can finally strike a deal with the kind gentlemen oficiales. By then Chuy is ready to explode. He should have been at Donna's by now, walking up to her parents' front door, giving her a birthday hug, escorting her to the car and on to a romantic dinner at "La Nena's." Instead, he asks the police officers how to get to Boulevard Agua Caliente from here. He's praying that Joyería La Perla is still open. He could try and get ahold of Donna, call her from some public phone, let her know he'll be a little late. . . .

Now El Chango is getting into the driver's seat in the police station parking lot. No fucking way, Chuy says, grabbing El Chango's arm and insisting on driving himself. El Chango's gotten them into enough trouble with his driving.

Boulevard Agua Caliente. Where the hell is it from the police station? The officer's directions were twisty and winding. Perverse. Chuy's not sure he trusts them anyway. He looks at his watch. 7:45. God, please be open, please be open.

El Chango wants to know where the hell they're going. They've passed at least fifty liquor stores—including his precious "Licores AS."

They're going to Joyería La Perla.

Oh, for Christ's sake, El Chango is moaning, a fucking *jewelry* store? He needs a traguito, just one good stiff drink after all this T.J. police shit. "Mike's A-Go-Go," he instructs Chuy. Just leave him off at "Mike's" while Chuy goes to his goddamned jewelry store.

Chuy ignores him, heading straight to Boulevard Agua Caliente and Joyería La Perla. He looks at his watch. Eight o'clock.

Sure enough—Chuy's not surprised, given the way the day is turning out so far—the jewelry store is closed.

He bangs on the door anyway. And again and again. By now he's ready to scream, to kill someone or something. Break down the goddamned door.

A light goes on on the second floor of the building. A man— it's el Señor Lepe, the jeweler—peers out the window.

Chuy calls up to him, his voice sounding desperate. He identifies himself, and Lepe pauses, thinking a moment— although to Chuy it seems like a hundred years. Then the jeweler nods, now remembering him. He tells him to wait, he'll be down in a minute.

Once the blue velvet box is in his hand, Chuy jumps back into the car and is hightailing it to the border.

"Why didn't you call home and let us know what was happening?" I asked, shivering on the cold porch.

He did. Or rather, he had El Chango call.

Since he still insists on going to "Mike's," El Chango tells Chuy he can take the car so he can get home to his Donna; he doesn't feel like going to anybody's birthday party. El Chango needed to get good and drunk, and besides, there was this cute chiquitita who hung out at "Mike's." Don't worry so much, he tells Chuy. He can find his way back home when he's good and ready, thank you very much.

He drops El Chango off at the bar, telling him to get ahold of a phone and call home immediately—right now, before he gets smashed—and let them know what happened, have his sisters call Donna. In the meantime, Chuy doesn't want to waste another moment and heads for the border.

"You can imagine the rest of the story," Chuy said, looking like he was about to cry. "I thought it might take me about an hour and a half to get across. It took me three and a half fucking hours. Jesus Christ," he said, shaking his head. "This was supposed to be the most important night of my life."

"What do you mean?" I asked.

He searched in his pant pocket and brought out the blue velvet box.

"This," he said, handing it to me. "I wanted to give her this before I went to boot camp."

I opened the small box. Inside, snuggled on a white satiny interior, was a diamond ring. An engagement ring.

For a moment, I didn't say anything. I was speechless. A thousand emotions ran through me: relief, frustration, sadness, and sheer, unexplainable happiness. You would have thought the ring was for me.

"Go to her, Chuy," I said. "Now."

"Are you kidding?" he said. "She'll probably shoot first, then ask questions."

"No she won't," I said, now laughing, ecstatic. "Go now. Don't waste another moment."

I playfully tugged at his arm, trying to pull him up off the porch chair, giggling.

"Yeah?" he said, slowly getting up, doubtful. "You think it's OK? Maybe I should wait till tomorrow. It's almost one in the morning."

"Oh, no. Go now, Chuy," I said. "I'm sure her parents won't mind once they realize why you've come. And besides, true love and romance can't wait."

"OK, Hermanita," he said, laughing. "If you say so."

Yes, yes, I do say so, I thought, smiling to myself, watching as he made his way back to the car. "Hey," I called out to him. "Don't forget this." I quickly ran down the three porch steps and handed him the blue velvet box.

"Right on, Yoli," he had said, planting a kiss on my forehead. "True love and romance can't wait."

—11

We drove to Tijuana every Sunday as regularly as taking vitamins—as if our parents needed a weekly dose of Mexico. I barely understood this routine. It seemed nothing less than a way to torment us children, piled in the Chevy station wagon, "Radio Ranchito" blasting norteña music. Now that our brothers were older and held jobs, they weren't required to go on Sunday outings with us to Tijuana to visit relatives. When Papá started the car, I was always shocked to see Armando or Octavio—any one of my brothers—get in at the last minute with the rest of us, with no obligation to do so.

Our summers were mild here in southern California in comparison to most parts of the U.S., but something about crossing the border, ten minutes away from our home, something about Tijuana itself, seemed to intensify everything: the heat, the dust, our hugs with our cousins, the laughter. Even the Coca Cola in the short bottles seemed sweeter, darker.

We were just about there, up the dirt street of the hill where Colonia Libertad sat, Mamá and Papá in the front seat, the radio full blast, the accordion and polka-like music twangy and silly to me. Since we drove to Tijuana every Sunday, there was nothing new to us in its sights, but ten-year-old Monica picked this Sunday to wax philosophical and ask probing sociological questions.

"Why are there so many poor people here? Did you see that little boy selling Chiclets and how his face was full of mocos? And all dirty and raggedy . . ."

"Sssshhh, Monica, don't talk that way. How mean," Carolina said. "It's like you're making fun of Mexico or something."

"She isn't making fun," I said. "She's just asking an honest question. Don't tell me you don't notice all the beggars and poor people."

"If Mamá and Papá hear you, they're going to be real mad," Carolina said. "This is their country and you're criticizing it. Mexico has a lot of beauty to it, and you just have to learn to focus on the beautifulness all around."

"The *beautifulness?*" I said. "God, Carolina, are you ever

on planet Jupiter. What beauty? Seems to me, I see—and so do you, but you don't want to admit it—a lot of sad things like shacks for houses and raggedy people all over Tijuana."

"Well, you can see whatever you want, Yolanda. I see beauty and warmth here. I see my roots and my rich heritage," Carolina said. "And like I say, see whatever you want, but just make sure you don't go telling your gringo friends about poor people in Tijuana. That's all we need, to have Americans think we're all poor on top of being lazy and dumb."

"Hey, wait a minute. I didn't say anything about Mexicans being lazy and dumb. . . ."

"No, you didn't. But I'm just telling you what's being said about us. Now that I'm in college, I'm learning a lot about negative stereotypes and how the Anglos have kept us down all these generations."

"But aren't we gringos, too?" asked Monica, who seemed to have been pushed aside in this philosophical argument even though she was the one to bring it up.

Ana María and Tony didn't say anything, but you could tell they were listening carefully, waiting for Carolina's answer, wondering the same thing.

"No, not me anyway," Carolina said. "I was born in Tijuana, so I'm a Mexican."

"So why do you live in the United States, Miss Mexicana?" I asked her.

"You know, Miss Coconut, if you weren't so sarcastic we

might someday be able to have an intelligent conversation."

"Coconut?" Monica giggled. "Why do you call Yolanda a coconut?"

"Because she's brown on the outside and white on the inside. . . ."

"Eat shit, Carolina," I said.

"Uyyy, get down, hermanas," Ana María said, shaking her head. "Why don't you two lay off each other? What is it with you guys?"

"You know, Carolina, you've got a lot of damn nerve to call me a coconut. You're the one that's seeing a gringo, not me. Or have you forgotten about your honeycito, Tom?"

"Tom isn't a gringo, not really," Carolina said. "His grandparents are Italian and French Canadian with some Native American blood. . . ."

"Uyyy, qué la fregada. A real half-breed," Ana María said, now taking out her nail file and checking her fingernails. She wasn't really interested in the polemics of our discussion. She just liked seeing Carolina and me go at it.

"We're all half-breeds, pendeja," Carolina said, now turning to Ana María. "What do you think you are? You're a mestiza. Look at your black hair and blue eyes. Jesus, Ana, you better start getting wise. Get past the make-up and nail polish, woman. Get ready for college and the world out there. Be prepared to defend yourself, arm yourself with knowledge."

"Uyyy, you sound like a drill sergeant, Carolina," Ana

María said, now giggling. "Did you go to boot camp with Chuy or something?"

One mention of Chuy and nobody said another word. We could use God's name in vain—our conversations forever punctuated with "for God's sake," "Jesus Christ," "goddamned"—but mention of Chuy, who had been absent now for two months, made us quiver, grow sad and lonely and afraid. We had gone too far, we all felt it. The feisty discussion was over and each of us solemnly looked out the car window.

We saw stuccoed buildings with uneven, brightly painted letters on the wall, people on rickety bikes most probably salvaged from American dump yards, women holding straw bags filled with grocery staples, walking briskly down the rough dirt paths. Having taken a verbal detour into the realm of identity, we were now back in Tijuana, on our way to our relatives' house in Colonia Libertad.

So this is a tale of two colonias: Colonia Libertad and Colonia Chapultepec. Located on an incline leading to the Tijuana airport, Colonia Libertad had no sidewalks, no asphalt for roads, only a lot of dirt and dust and holes on the streets, which the people of this poor colonia did not seem to notice. Colonia Libertad—freedom from what, I often wondered. On a mound of dirt in a lot full of rubble, broken glass, dented hubcaps, skeletal remains of an old Chevy, children were playing. It made me think of our own playground in Palm City, the Kastlungers' field across the street from us.

Our aunt and uncle and cousins in Colonia Libertad always received us warmly. They seemed even grateful to us—the relatives who lived "al otro lado" and honored them with our visit to their humble home. These Sunday visits to our relatives' house in poor Colonia Libertad made me feel like royalty, that even though we didn't have much more than they, we did have a beautiful oak china cabinet next to our green Formica kitchen table. At least we had that.

"Pasen, pasen, por favor," our aunt greeted us with hugs and kisses. Our cousins ran into the kitchen to bring out the short bottles of cold Coca-Cola for each of us.

"¿No ven cartones?" Luz asked our cousins.

"'¿Cartones?'" our cousins asked, not having any idea what we were talking about.

"Sí, cartones," Luz said. "Like 'Popeye'. . . ."

"Ah," our little cousin said. "Yes, if you would like, we can watch caricaturas. There are many cartoons on this day," she said in Spanish.

That was the beauty of visiting these cousins from Colonia Libertad: We could feel safe in our minds knowing that even though our Spanish wasn't perfect, these cousins would not make fun of us, would correct us in kind, diplomatic ways. We didn't feel less than they, even though our Spanish was unreliable, often pronounced and punctuated with black holes, filled suddenly with words and phrases rediscovered at the last minute.

Sundays in Tijuana went well when we spent them with our cousins in Colonia Libertad. But on some Sundays we were forced to spend the afternoon with our other cousins in Colonia Chapultepec, the rich section of Tijuana, where cement sidewalks were lined with jacaranda and olive trees shading large pink or gray modern, box-like houses.

Torture. Humiliation. We were considered the "pochos," who lived "al otro lado" and spoke a mishmash language—not completely English, not completely Spanish. Our rich cousins from Colonia Chapultepec who lived in a house with marble floors and crystal chandeliers, a collection of Lladró figurines in a teak china cabinet, laughed at Luz when she suggested they watch "cartones."

"What size box of carton would you like to watch?" our smarty-pants rich cousins asked Luz.

"Cartones," Luz repeated, looking confused. "You know, like 'Popeye'. . . ."

"'Cartones,'" the cousins laughed, running down the long marbled hallway of their rich house in Colonia Chapultepec in Tijuana. "Ay, ¡qué pocha!"

I hated them as they must have hated us—we the poor cousins living "al otro lado." So where was the pot of gold for the asking? they must have been snickering to themselves. Yes, go you dummies, al otro lado and find your El Dorado, and while you're looking for your gringo riches, make pochos out of your children. Have them grow up not knowing what they are: Mexican? American? When the question is asked, what is your ethnic background, look for a category called "Pocho." Think twice, you foolish cousins who live al otro lado, filled with ridiculous American dreams in your head. Laughter and derision echoed on a marble floor and sorely hurt my ears. Stabbed deep into my pride.

"You know why your mother and I make you come with us to Tijuana every Sunday?" Papá said every Sunday afternoon as we headed back to the famous línea—the busiest port of entry in the world. "You need to practice your Spanish, be proud of your roots."

On the dashboard was the daily *El Mexicano,* from which we were forced to read portions out loud, each of us taking turns, every Sunday afternoon.

With a vengeance, I clutched the *El Mexicano* and read my portion out loud to everyone. I listened carefully to my father correct my pronunciation. I rolled those "rr's" with the gusto of an angry lion. I would prove to them who was king of the jungle. Pochos, indeed! You smarty-pants, rich cousins from Colonia Chapultepec.

"Look, quick, Lorenzo," Mamá said, pointing out the window. "There's a new lane opening up."

The chase was on: a mad, angry, horn-blowing contest to cut in, to figure out which was the shortest line, the quickest way across the border. For me, the border crossing back to San Diego meant hot, dusty waits scrunched in the car smelling Tony's farts or exhaust fumes, watching over-heated radiators steaming dangerously close to our own car. But for my parents, there was no border, just something referred to as "la línea"—a line on the map we crossed over time and again. But to which side of the line did we belong? We seemed to be somewhere between the two sets of relatives, somewhere between dirt-ridden, dusty Colonia Libertad and cement sidewalk, jacaranda-tree-lined Colonia Chapultepec; somewhere between cartoons and cartones.

But once a year, on Father's Day, we didn't go to either relatives' home. Instead, the whole family was obliged to go for our professional family photo sitting. In all my life, we had only missed the two years Chuy was on his tour of duty in Vietnam. Papá had postponed our photo session until he returned. Now he was back from Vietnam but not back with us. Papá gathered his troops and made us get dressed up.

"But Chuy's not here," Ana María said.

"It's Father's Day, right?" Papá said. "And I am your father and so we do what I want to do on Father's Day, right?" The truth was we did whatever Papá wanted to do whenever he wanted to do it—Father's Day or no Father's Day, but nobody, not even Carolina, dared remind him of this.

It was clear to us what Papá meant: It was one thing to be away at war, another thing to abandon your family by taking off without permission or any explanation. Unpardonable.

We would be a family, with or without Chuy. Punto. Period.

We went in two cars, Armando driving one and Papá driving the other in order to fit us all in.

"Fuchi, that was a stinker," Carolina said to Tony. "So help me if you lay one more fart, I'm going to tell Papá. It's hot enough already without your stinky pedos."

"Relax, man," Tony said, laughing, "the window's open and we're getting some fresh air."

"Yeah, well let's keep it that way."

It was a warm and bright June day. We were wearing our Sunday best for the photo session: Sons in suits and ties, daughters in this past Easter's dresses. Little Luz and Monica wore matching yellow taffeta dresses, their light brown hair in bucles—little, turd-like ringlets. Now that she was going to the community college and taking psychology courses, Carolina refused to wear matching dresses with Ana María and me. "You're suppressing our individuality," she immediately said in protest. Mamá didn't insist with Miss Freudiana, but she did with the rest of us: Ana María and I wore our Easter suits, light yellow skirt and matching jacket top.

We parked the cars at a pay parking lot and walked the couple of blocks to Jalisco Studio. We were Papá's little army, walking single file at the cross streets. We were a handsome family, I knew this even without noticing the looks we got from people passing by us. And it seemed we always ran into one of Mamá and Papá's compadres or long lost friends. How could anyone not recognize this handsome couple—no matter how many years had gone by? Papá's sprightly body, fiery clear blue eyes and Mamá's curly brown hair and green eyes, a softness in her face which spoke of patience and tranquility.

Immediately the barrage of introductions, as if Papá, the director, were describing the cast of his play, promoting his obra de arte. His introductions seemed almost to be the play itself, with at least one editorial remark for each of his children. No matter where we were—at home, at a wedding, or in the middle of Avenida Constitución in Tijuana—Papá insisted on introducing us with a kind of importance and loftiness that was, in truth, embarrassing to us children. But we loved Papá and so endured his grandiose introductions.

Stepping to the side of the busy street, people pushing past as the clanging of the church bells summoned them to ten o'clock mass, Papá made the ritualistic introductions to his friends:

"Armando here is the oldest and takes care of his little sisters. Octavio is our mujeriego. Breaks women's hearts all the time." There was pride in Papá's voice when he said this.

He used to introduce us in chronological order: first Armando, then Octavio, Chuy, Tony, Carolina, Ana María, me, Monica and Luz. But since the day Chuy took off on his motorcycle, Papá seemed to have forgotten his children's age order, as if chronology were out of whack, family sequence in quiet chaos.

"Ana María is our teenager, and we keep a good eye on her, eh Ana?" he said, winking at her. Ana María rolled her eyes up to the heavens. I wondered if Papá had any idea what was going on between her and Tito.

Turning now to the youngest of the boys, to Tony, he said, "Antonio is our Ray Charles expert. I'm trying to get him to appreciate Javier Solís and Agustín Lara. Now there's some talent." Tony nodded slightly, letting his overgrown bangs hide his shy eyes in the hustle and bustle of handshakes.

"Carolina is our college girl. She's getting a degree so she can educate all of us, ¿sí mi'ja?" Carolina nodded with a smile, happy to oblige.

"These are my cachorros—cutest puppies you've ever seen, ¿qué no?"

"Ay, Papi," Luz and Monica giggled while timidly shaking hands with Mamá and Papá's long lost friend or compadre.

"Yolanda is our dreamer, en las nubes. Maybe she'll be the first one in this family to travel to the moon." I smiled, gave the courteous "Mucho gusto, Yolanda Sahagún Ramos, a sus órdenes."

Papá gave each of us an appreciative nod, his "thank you" to us.

Then he added: "My son Jesús is off on a journey right now," he said. "Who knows, maybe he's beaten Yolanda to the moon."

Mamá and Papá presented us to their friends with the same

sort of pride that a member of the American Rose Society has when showing off his garden of roses: "Mr. Lincoln is a hybrid tea, usually tall, one rose per stem, opens quickly from bud to flower; the Lanvin stays in full bloom for a long time; the French Lace, delicate and creamy with a pink edge, has a short stage of production but with an average of five flowers per stem. . . ."

So this garden of flowers, the fruits of our parents' labor, stood before the camera at Jalisco Studio, all of us in various stages of bloom and maturation. Smiles on our faces now, smiles that ignored a hundred other emotions. For this one moment, then, we set aside worries about how to ask for a raise at Brown's Market, what blouse to wear to the Sun n' Sea Festival, or whether Clearasil was going to perform miracles. The photographer arranged us in the same pose we struck every year. Only this time we felt awkward. With Chuy absent from his usual spot between Octavio and Tony, we shuffled, uncertain, all of us aware that something—someone—was missing. Then finally, settling into some sort of family pose, we smiled for the camera, smiled for ourselves: a kind of curtseying and bowing in honor of us as a family. Yes, we smiled, but with Chuy missing, it was a gap-toothed smile.

PART TWO

- - - - - - - - - - - - -

In the midst of the conflict,

the heroes, I stood,

Or pass'd with slow step through

the wounded and dying.

—From "The Return of the Heroes"
by Walt Whitman

—12

By July the sweet peas were spent and Mamá wasted no time in clearing away the dried up vines and blossoms, leaving our picket fence looking bald and lonely. It was July 20th, and everyone was home, near the TV. Even Papá had taken off early from his gardening job to be with us for the moon walk— one of the rare times we'd all be home together, except for Chuy who was still out God knows where on his motorcycle.

Monica was looking through the "M" volume of the encyclopedia. She was playing teacher to five-year-old Luz, her solitary but enthusiastic student.

"See?" she said. "The moon's surface has different names. For example, the Sea of Serenity. That one sounds real pretty. The Sea of Tranquility. Luz, are you listening to me?" She tapped the yardstick against the kitchen wall.

Luz giggled. What a strict teacher Monica was turning out to be!

I was listening to them as I chopped an onion, my sunglasses on.

Carolina, now sautéing the rice, gave me one of her Oh Brother looks, shaking her head. "Is this some sort of attention-getting device?" Miss Future Psychologist asked me. "Am I supposed to be full of curiosity and wonder about why the sunglasses indoors?"

"Aha! You *are* full of curiosity and wonder, aren't you?" I said. "OK, I'll appease that small, but curious mind of yours. It's simple: I saw Gidget do it on TV once while she was chopping onions. With the glasses on she didn't cry."

"Jesus, Yoli," Carolina said. "You shouldn't believe everything you see on TV."

"Oh, so maybe this moon landing we're about to see is all bullshit?" I said.

Monica and Luz were suddenly quiet, listening to our conversation.

"Oh, for God's sake, Yoli," Carolina said, now adding the boiling chicken broth to the translucent rice. "*Gidget* was a TV show. Fiction, nonreality, a little surfer fairy tale."

"Ay, tú," I said. "Who said you were the expert on reality?"

"Look," Carolina said. "You don't have to get defensive about it. I know you've had a very natural adolescent crush on your Sally 'Gidget' Field. Ever since you were in the fifth grade and you wrote her that fan letter, I've seen you standing in front of the mirror practicing the same faces she would make, scrunching your nose, pouting this way and that. And I notice you still have her photo taped to your notebook: 'Hi to you from me, Sally "Gidget" Field,'" Carolina said in an exaggerated baby voice.

"Oh bug off, Carolina," I said. "You're just jealous I look like her and you don't."

"Have you forgotten that she went from being the top

surfer girl to a flying nun? Now there's a thought, Little Miss Chicana Gidget," Carolina said, laughing. "Why don't you become a nun like her. . . . Stop it!"

I was throwing a few kernels of chopped onion at her, to see if maybe I could make Miss-Know-It-All cry.

"Oh get *thee* to a nunnery," I said. "But I mean, really, what if the only reality is no reality? Surfer fairy tales, moon walk fairy tales. What if we are—this very minute—living in the twilight zone?"

Monica had closed the "M" encyclopedia and now sat quietly at the green Formica kitchen table, staring at us. Luz, too.

"Are you entering some sort of adolescent *angst*, is that it?" Carolina asked. "Because if you are, don't expect me to put up with you, OK?"

"Eat shit, Carolina," I whispered as I spotted Mamá coming into the kitchen.

Mamá served herself and Papá some wine in the juice glasses. She did this on special occasions. She didn't say anything to us about our arguing, although I was certain she could hear us from the living room where she and Ana María were setting up the TV trays. She was wise that way, didn't get into our squabbles as long as they weren't carried out blatantly in front of her. She had more important things occupying her mind, like wondering where Chuy might be. I'd overheard her talking about it with Socorrito the other day. Mamá was defending Chuy, defending the fact that he'd just up and left us right after his welcome home party. I wondered how she was going to defend that, knowing she must've been pretty hurt and pissed by it herself. So I had to eavesdrop on her conversation with Socorrito.

"It's only natural he'd want to get away. Perderse, you know," she was saying to Socorrito while cutting plump roses next to Socorrito's fence. "Lose himself in a way that makes him feel free. After all that time being forced to be somewhere, taking orders. Vaya," she said, clipping a thick velvety one, "es lo más lógico. Do you know how many times I've dreamed of just getting up and going, leaving all my kids behind and just hopping on a motorcycle of my own and heading out to God knows where? Anywhere."

"Dolores," Socorrito said. "I can't believe you're saying these things. Abandon your children? Ay, Mujer, ¿estás loca también?"

"If you think it's crazy to want to escape—at least for a little while—nine children, the laundry, the cooking, the housecleaning and then more laundry, and the grocery shopping and more cooking for eleven mouths to feed. If you think it's crazy for me to want to hop on a noisy, wild motorcycle and ride anywhere—even to la casa de la chingada—then yes, Socorrito, I must be the craziest woman alive."

I'd never in all my life heard my mother say a bad word. It must have been that "también" at the end of Socorrito's question that riled Mamá up. What was Socorrito meaning by asking if Mamá was crazy *also*? It was one thing for us, the family, to have our doubts and suspicions about a fellow member of the family, but who the hell was Socorrito to insinuate someone in our family was crazy?

Judging from Socorrito's expression, I guessed she'd never heard my mother say a bad word, either.

"Well, Dolores," Socorrito said, pausing, eyeing my mom suspiciously. "What can I say to that . . . I mean, Mujer, you needn't be rude, I mean, we've known each other . . . I thought we knew each other. . . . "

Mamá gathered her rose clippings and left Socorrito to bumble with incompetent words and thoughts.

Yes, this gossipy old biddy must have been thinking, these Sahagúns, they're all going insane, familia loca, the whole lot of them.

I never felt so proud of Mamá as on that wonderful afternoon.

I watched her as she now took the glasses of wine out to the living room, setting them on her TV tray and Papá's. Did Mamá really feel like that? Was she capable of just one day— like Chuy—getting on a motorcycle of her own and taking off? Was Carolina wrong in thinking Mamá was just another traditional, passive woman? There was something in her eyes when she said that to Socorrito, in the tone of her voice that made me think, yes, she could do it, just get on a

Harley and take off, wave "goodbye" to all of us. "Take care of my garden and make sure your father prunes the roses in January," she'd call out to us. Then she would blow us a motherly kiss and be off, any further domestic instructions drowned out by the Harley's roar. Why not? Chuy was her son just as much as he was Papá's son. Maybe Chuy was, in some way, fulfilling both of our parents' secret dreams.

Once the rice was done, we got in line at the stove, served ourselves and headed back to the living room to watch the news special, the moon walk.

One small step for man, one giant leap for mankind.

We were silent, speechless. A fork suspended midway to the mouth, grains of rice falling back onto her plate, Mamá looked away from the TV screen over to the Sacred Heart of Jesus. Her green eyes filled with tears. It reminded me of the time I came home from third grade and found her crying in front of the TV, the day President Kennedy was shot. Perhaps Mamá was crying now because she felt something again was lost. Perhaps she was remembering when she was a young maiden in love with the idea of a romantic moon and an evening in the blooming jardín and dreams and illusions somehow mixed up and stirred with a bit of moon rays. Hopes and aspirations, love and passion. What was one to think of the moon now?

My sisters followed her glance, quietly praying a Hail Mary for good measure, all of us still too young to understand the kind of faith a woman like Dolores Ramos de Sahagún put into the moon. Behold, the moon's rays still shone and we could only hope it wouldn't deny us—we who were still young and dreaming—the brightness of romantic musings.

Papá, just returned from his gardening job at the other end of town, must have been thinking back to his days growing up on a small ranch in Mexico where cars were an extravagance, almost unheard of, and the possibility of journeying to the moon was nothing more than a fairy tale fantasy. Papá, who prided himself on having traveled up the Mexican Pacific coast as if he were the Caballo Blanco of the popular ballad, the last of the frontiersmen, was now witnessing an even greater trek. Would that he could be a part of that new frontier, he must have been thinking, be up there exploring new realms, perhaps hostile terrain—lighting out into new territory. He quickly wiped his wet eyes.

Armando, Octavio and Tony stared at the TV, looking anxious or excited. Was the man on the moon not made of cheese, after all? What clever, romantic things to make up now for their girlfriends?

This was when we heard the thundering sound of a Harley, way over on Hollister Street, the sound of a hungry giant growling its way toward Conifer Street.

"It's Chuy!" Octavio called out to all of us.

He needn't have bothered. We were already springing to action, piling out the front door in a frenzy.

"Who is it? Who did he say it was?" little Luz called out.

"Hurry, mi'ja," Carolina said. "It's Chuy."

In a instant we were all outside—all ten of us—waiting for him to drive down the length of Conifer Street to its end, where we lived.

It was warm that day, the air felt electrical and impossible. A man on the moon—my God! And here was my brother Chuy setting foot on home territory. His hair was down to his shoulders, brown and unkempt, and he now had a bushy beard—no sight of the clipped, immaculate soldier whom we met back in April. His was a metamorphosis from skinny green insect to wild, groovy, love child. My mother and father took one long look at their Vietnam veteran son and must have thought that the world was coming to an end.

For me, life was just beginning. Chuy had come home again.

Big smile. Even with his bushy beard you could see the grin from ear to ear. "Hey, Mrs. Sahagún," he called out to Mamá. "What's there to eat?"

He swung his leg up and around his chopper, his cowboy boots dusty and worn. Then he sauntered over to all us open-mouthed brothers and sisters, shaking hands with each of us, as if he were an international emissary, the guest of honor just arrived.

"I haven't had a friggin' good meal in months," he said. "Got any pozole?" He marched right into the house, the rest of us, stunned and confused, following silently behind him.

Once in the living room, Chuy looked around at the TV trays, noticed the TV on.

"So," Papá said, clearing his throat. "Where have you been, mi'jo? Your mother and I . . ."

"What're you guys watching?" Chuy asked, ignoring Papá's question.

For a moment, no one answered, as if we had to pause and recollect: What had we been watching? Something about space? *Lost in Space? The Twilight Zone?*

"Is this all you have to say for yourself?" Papá began again. I could tell from the tone of his voice that he was trying very hard to control himself. "You mysteriously leave for four months without a word, worry your mother half to death, and this is all you have to say for yourself?"

"I'm hungry," Chuy said. He made it sound like an explanation, as if that were all we needed to hear and that in itself—"I'm hungry"—would make us go about our business. He stared out the front window.

"Did you hear what I just said?" Papá asked him. We all held our breaths.

"Yeah," Chuy said, still staring out the window at something or nothing. "Did you hear what I just said? I'm friggin' hungry."

Mamá stepped in just then, right when Papá was about to open his mouth, his face already red and angry. "Yes, of course you're hungry, Chuy." She turned to Papá. "We'll leave the talking for later," she said.

The talking never came.

While we all settled back down to our places in front of the TV, Chuy went into the kitchen and Mamá heated some tortillas for him.

"Dolores," Papá called out to her. "Come and watch with us."

"In a minute," she called back, although it was plain to Papá and all of us that she had no intention of leaving Chuy alone in the kitchen.

And why should she come out? There was nothing left to watch. Now the newscasters were commenting on this and that about space and technology and things that in that moment seemed irrelevant to our lives, irrelevant to my life. We squirmed in our seats. My brothers and sisters kept glancing over at the kitchen door, probably straining, like me, to hear some conversation between Mamá and Chuy. Papá was the only one who seemed to refuse to look that way, staring, instead, at the TV in a way that seemed forced. Yet how could he not be wondering what, if anything, was being said between Dolores and Chuy? Because the real news for us was this: July 20, 1969 was Chuy's second coming home.

Some rattling of dishes being put in the sink to wash, and then Chuy sauntered out to the living room, sized us up, a big dopey grin on his face. He headed for the front door.

"Oye, tú," Papá called out to him. "Where do you think you're going? You have some explaining to do."

"This is so fucking full of shit," Chuy was saying to himself now. "Men on the fucking moon . . . what a damn hoax . . . fucking gooks, all of them." He laughed a private, little laugh under his breath, feeling very clever with himself.

Papá bolted out of his chair, but Mamá was right next to him and held his arm. "Déjalo," she said. "Let him be."

Surprisingly, Papá obeyed her.

The front door slammed behind Chuy.

For a moment I had the impulse to stand up and call out to everyone, to run over to the TV and turn it off, demanding everyone's attention. Say: Atención, todos. Something's not right here. It's Chuy, we need to help Chuy. Maybe we need to examine this more closely, think about the shredded flags he left us back in April; figure out something here. Because I realized he wasn't really with us that July 20th sharing in the excitement and incredulity of a man on the moon. No, Chuy was somewhere else, doing his own traveling, on a road all his own.

There are roads one should never take, I had been cautioned my whole life. In mass every Sunday, silvery-haired Father Stadler, standing at the podium, spoke vehemently of the need to follow the right path. I often asked myself which was the "right path," where was the "high road?" Sitting in

St. Charles Church on any given Sunday, I looked around me at the congregation, the women with scarves on their bowed heads, engrossed in prayer, while husbands with paunchy stomachs dozed comfortably during the sermon. For instance, Socorrito, who always sat in the first pew, the one closest to the altar, went to confession every Saturday. I knew this because I went to catechism every Saturday morning and so I'd see her pop into the confessional. She stayed in there a good twenty minutes. How many sins could she have committed in a week's time that should merit a whole twenty minutes in the confessional?

Bless me, Father, for I have sinned. It has been a week since my last confession. These are my sins: I covet my dear friend Dolores's husband, but not being able to have this handsome güero and father of nine beautiful children, I make wild love to any other man who walks down Conifer Street and will have these old bones of mine—this I have done three times this week. Or Lydia's version of Socorrito's confession: *Father, I have committed adultery with three men this week and the greatest sin was in forgetting to take off my raggedy, stinky night slippers as I made wild love to these men.* I had to hand it to Lydia; she could be funny now and then. Or this version: *Father, I have sinned only one time this week, having made wild love to the Southern Pacific train conductor, and because we went overtime, the poor man was late in getting to his next stop and was fired. He will no longer be blowing his whistle for me at eight twenty-three.* What, what could she possibly be saying to Father Stadler for twenty minutes in the confessional each week? Was Socorrito trying to atone for hidden sins of her childhood? Were there dark secrets somewhere in her young life? Had she once taken the wrong road?

When I was a little girl, I often took Mamá's catechism book with me down the canyon. The pages were yellowing, thin and brittle, and although I could not read all the Spanish writing—I was six or seven years old then—the etchings were eerie and fearsome. Wonderful. The incessant swoosh-swoosh of the traffic nearby lulled me into a hypnotic trance, engrossed as I was in the illustrations before me. And there was that sketch, my favorite, of two paths—one to heaven and one to hell. The first road was bordered with voluptuous, fat roses. Who wouldn't want to go down that road? And yet—wait!—there at the end of the road beckoned the evil Devil with horns and spear-tipped tail, the end of the road engulfed in flames. The other path was bordered with thick bushes of sharp thorns, an entanglement of brambles, and its pathway looked mean and uninviting, but at the end of that trail rose billowy clouds, a rainbow and the Archangel extending his hand to you. The two juxtaposed etchings— the road to hell and the road to heaven—instilled in me deep religious anguish. What if I accidentally took the wrong road? The roses looked enticing and beautiful. Even as a child, then, when I could barely read, I knew that the high road, the righteous road, was a difficult one.

So I wondered now: Had Chuy taken the wrong road? Had he already been to hell and back?

—13

"Leave him alone" was Carolina's advice, and since she was the one taking the Intro to Psychology course at the community college, we listened to her. Even me. "Let him find himself and us on his own terms," she explained.

He kept us at arm's length, mumbled "buenos días" to Mamá and Papá, but that was about it. The rest of us brothers and sisters seemed oblivious to him. My other brothers had their own lives, so if their brother Chuy needed to unwind without a lot of talking and chitchat, well, they would, as Carolina had instructed, just leave him alone. Sometimes he seemed not even to realize we were in the same room as he, and if he did notice us, he usually looked annoyed with our chatter, his mouth twisted in aggravation or disgust or something I couldn't quite make out. In these instances, he'd eat as fast as he could, gulp down his oatmeal, glass of milk, orange juice, dry cereal, and a couple of tortillas with last night's refried beans. He had a voracious appetite—como un monstruo insaciable—I'm sure nosey ol' Socorrito must have been reporting to Don Epifranio and anyone else who would listen. He'd spend the rest of the morning polishing his already-sparkling chopper. But one odd thing about that: he allowed—no, *expected*—me to help him polish the chrome on his motorcycle.

"Did you see a lot of dead bodies in the war?" Seven-year-old Luz, riding her bike up to us, asked Chuy as he and I polished the chrome on his motorcycle out on the street.

"Dead bodies? What are you talking about?" he said. "You want to see dead bodies, go over to Humphrey's Mortuary."

"But you were in a war fighting the communists," Luz said. "Didn't you kill a bunch of commies?"

Chuy handed me some more chrome polish and pointed to a spot I had missed.

"Luz, I think Mamá's calling you," I said, trying to catch her eye, give her a warning signal.

"No she isn't," she said. "I didn't hear anything."

"There are no dead bodies, Luz," Chuy said quietly, not looking up from his polishing. "And I don't know what war you're talking about and what communists you're talking about. Maybe you watch too much fantasy TV and shit, so why don't you just scramboola."

I nodded when he said this, not so much in agreement as in support of whatever—no matter how wrong—my brother Chuy had to say.

Luz stared at us a moment and then got back on her bicycle and rode away.

When she was out of hearing distance, I looked up from my polishing, stealing a glance at Chuy. I was afraid to look him in the eyes.

"Chuy," I asked, rubbing an already shiny spot. "Chuy, why'd you say that to her?"

"Because it's nobody's goddamn business, Yoli, that's why. Especially not Luz's business to be thinking about dead bodies and shit," he said. "What the hell does she need to be thinking about those things? Man, she's just a baby. And what am I supposed to tell her? Should I give her some war hero shit so that when she grows up and has boyfriends she'll remember some fantasy story her brother cooked up when she was little, and she'll be happy to send her boyfriend off to the war?"

"But you were fighting in a war," I said, now looking for other dull spots.

"Yeah, it was a war with a lot of shit and no heroes, should I tell her that?"

"It's only natural she should ask," I said. "But maybe you should talk to *someone* about it, you know, about fighting in a war and all."

"I wasn't fighting in a war, Yoli. What the hell are you talking about?" he said, putting the lid on the can of chrome polish. "I've gotta go," he said, tossing me his polishing rag.

He quickly straddled his motorcycle, started it—the engine deafening as I stood right next to him. "Nothing the fuck's natural, Yoli," he said, and he took off.

Chuy's motorcycle sat low and shiny, like a slinky, sexy woman of the night. It knew a part of Chuy we didn't, would probably never know. The rumbling, powerful machine had been to places with him that we, his family, had never been. To me, his motorcycle symbolized freedom and recklessness, an I-don't-give-a-shit-what-you-think attitude, and so I was happy to help him polish it.

Every morning before taking off for the day, he parked his chopper in the middle of the driveway and shined the chrome, checked the oil, the engine, the brakes, tinkered lovingly with his baby. I stole glances at him, wondering a lot of things, thinking back to his four-month trek across the country. I imagined he probably even talked to his machine at times, shared with her his anger and fear about his future, about his past, about whatever happened to him in Vietnam. Lydia and I, forever creating scenarios for every situation possible, were at a standstill when it came to picturing in our minds the war in Vietnam. We couldn't penetrate those jungles, all that rain Chuy mentioned in his Vietnam letters. Some things we were smart enough not to even attempt to visualize; some things we knew were forbidden territory.

El Chango wasted no time in coming to see his favorite buddy. He must've wanted to hear all about it—everything—how it'd been in the war, if he'd seen a lot of action. Like Luz, he was probably wondering if Chuy had seen a lot of dead bodies, killed a lot of commies.

"Hey, Chu," El Chango called out to him. We were in our regular spots, doing the daily bike polishing. "What's happening, Brother? When did you get back?" El Chango, with his polio-afflicted leg, limped over to us, smiling, glad to see his favorite carnal.

Chuy didn't say anything, just kept on polishing his already spic and span motorcycle.

El Chango hesitated, looked over my way as if to say "what's with him?" I shook my head, kept on polishing.

"Hey, Chu, what's happening, man?"

"Nothing," Chuy finally said. "Nothing's happening. Why do you think anything's happening? What do you want to happen, huh? If you'd gone to Vietnam, you would've known what was happening."

Silence. In the distance, somewhere on the freeway, I could hear a siren wailing. That darn spot, I just couldn't get it to sparkle.

"Hey, Chuy," El Chango said quietly. "You know I couldn't go. My leg, remember? Why're you saying that? You know I wanted to go with you, be there fighting in the trenches with you, man. Why are you saying that?"

Nothing from Chuy.

"Remember the Mohawks just before you went to Fort Ord?" El Chango said. "Remember that, man?"

The day before Chuy was sent to boot camp at Fort Ord, El Chango and Chuy had walked into our house with freshly styled Mohawk haircuts. Mamá, just coming out of the kitchen into the living room, let out a startled scream. "Ay, por Dios, muchachos, what've you done?"

The rest of us squealed with delight and laughter, surrounding the two guys for a closer look.

"They're going to chop it all off tomorrow anyway," Chuy said to Mamá, smiling and putting his arm around her. "Thought we'd have us some fun before things got too serious."

Carolina insisted on taking a snapshot. El Chango and Chuy posed with arms around each other, looking like proud twins, looking as if they had just taken part in a blood brother ritual, the Mohawk haircuts binding them forever.

"Hey, Chu, what's the matter with you, what's going on? It's me, El Chango, Brother," he said. "Why are you talking that way?"

"You want to know what's happening?" Chuy said to him, finally looking him square in the face. "Then go to Nam, man, kill yourself some goddamn gooks and fuck yourself while you're at it. Pinche chango, man. That's all you are, all right. Go climb a tree and eat your bananas and then fuck yourself for good measure," Chuy said, chuckling as if he were too clever even for himself. "Yeah, cabrón, eat your pinche banana and swing your dick from the trees."

I watched as El Chango limped away, walked down Conifer Street, away from us, his shoulders hunched, now a ninety-year-old viejito in less than a minute's time. I continued to watch as he made his way to the end of the street and turned on Hollister and then disappeared.

"There's a spot over there, Yoli," Chuy said, pointing to somewhere on the bike.

I didn't turn to see where he was pointing. I kept looking down the street where El Chango had disappeared. Then I set the rag on the bike's seat and went inside.

When school rolled around in September at Southwest Junior High, Lydia and I along with other Palm City kids walked on the railroad tracks the two miles to school. Even though I was now in the ninth grade, and the summer should have ripened me and made me feel sure of myself, confident—alas!— nothing had changed: I was still hopelessly in love with Francisco Valdivia whom I hadn't seen all summer because he lived in San Ysidro and went to Mt. Carmel Church. Once when I suggested to Mamá that we try that church out for mass, just to see what other churches were like for Sunday mass, she looked at me as if I had turned into a wretched traitor. St. Charles Church and Father Stadler were just fine, her look told me. And besides, talk had it that a new priest from Spain was going to come to this parish. Mass in Spanish was just around the corner. So there you had it, no glimpse of Francisco Valdivia all summer long.

"Hey, isn't that Chuy up ahead?" Lydia asked. "What's he doing just sitting there?"

We arrived the back way, over by the baseball field. Sure enough, Chuy was sitting on his chopper just outside the school's chain link fence, looking over at us kids as we trudged to lockers and homeroom.

"Wow, look at that thing," one kid called out.

Pretty soon Chuy had a group of kids, mostly guys, surrounding him as they checked out his chopper, asking a hundred questions. How fast did it go? How much did it cost? He rode around the United States on it? I came up to them, though I stood a little behind all the guys. Then one boy asked him if he could someday have a ride on the bike.

"No fucking way," Chuy said quietly. The tone of his voice spooked them, made them look him nervously in the eye. The crowd now backed away from that voice. So did I, leaving him there alone on his chopper, staring at us on the other side of the chain link fence.

Although Chuy didn't get a job right away, as our parents had hoped, they were patient with him, having heard that war veterans could come back like this, a little lost and confused. Socorrito, next door, was quick to document case after case of these kinds of situations—and she assured Mamá it wasn't just happening to our muchachos. Gringos were coming back a little strange, too. So Mamá and Papá were willing to give him time to recuperate and get his bearings. They didn't complain about his going off early in the morning on his motorcycle, not to be heard of again until late in the night when he reheated some dinner for himself alone at the kitchen table, one or two in the morning. My sleep became restless. Without wanting to, I waited up for him as I lay in bed and, not until I heard his chopper roar up the driveway, followed by the front door opening and shutting and his quiet steps in the kitchen, the sound of the refrigerator door opening and shutting, could I fall into a fitful sleep.

It never occurred to me to mention to my parents that most mornings Chuy hung out just outside my junior high. When I walked past him every morning and said "Hi, Chuy," he simply nodded at me. I never thought twice about Marisa's comment one day to my sisters that she'd seen Chuy just outside of Mar Vista High around the time school was letting out. I never wondered what it meant, or why he might be doing that, hanging around his old junior high and high schools. Chuy rarely spoke more than a word or two, didn't seem to hang around with anyone, not even his old buddies, and he never took anyone for a ride on his motorcycle.

Later, when we started getting visits from the police, when there were whispers in the kitchen where Mamá and Papá and my older sisters and brothers assembled in a kind of family conference—Monica, Luz, and I were not asked to come in—I began to understand things were worse than they seemed, and these secretive things had something to do with Chuy. A part of me wanted to deny this, to at least pretend whenever I could that there was nothing wrong with Chuy. I was, as everyone in my family claimed, somewhere in the clouds, always daydreaming. But what could one expect of a fourteen-year-old? I was eager to be reckless and independent, eager to be against my family and upbringing—those old-fashioned Mexican values that stunted one's growth, one's sexuality, one's individuality. Like the heroes of the movies of 1969, I wanted to be an Easy Rider.

■ ■ ■ ■ ■

That's all I want. His gentle hands inching their way from my waist, up under my warm sweater, finding my heaving virginal breasts. Yours! Yours! Yours! And then grasping and rubbing and fondling them for dear life. His! His! His! I can't breathe, my dear diary, my eyes are out of focus. Francisco Valdivia, my love and my life—I am yours!

I took a deep breath. My pen in my hand was shaky, the diary on my lap slightly wobbling. I wondered if this was a sin. Would I have to confess to Father Stadler these lustful thoughts, tell him about my damp underwear, too? Would he then demand to know the name of the recipient of these sinful fantasies? What if he insisted, as penance, that I reveal my diaries not only to him but also to my family? Could

I live with myself after such shame? I thought of poor Hester Prynne with her embroidered scarlet letter "A"—adulteress! Would I also be a disgrace to my family, banished from the community? Would they cast me out to that dark shack in the empty lot at the end of the street? Would I be condemned to live there the rest of my adult life, alone, withering into an old spinster? To all these fearful questions I had but one answer: I would have to find a foolproof hiding place for my diary.

The eucalyptus and pepper trees that lined the bottom of my canyon had a tranquil effect on me. I sat on the wooden steps and stared out at Kastlungers' field, over to Interstate 5. From where I sat, I could see the culvert we had ventured into last summer. I had no desire to visit it again. It seemed odd to me that summer was already over, and that now I was in my last year of junior high. September was here, all right, and I could smell autumn as only a native southern Californian can smell autumn in subtle but distinct ways. The bushy pepper trees seemed quieter, as if tired from a summer of children romping about and climbing up them. The eucalyptus seemed to perk up, its fresh, medicinal smell more pungent with the early morning dew. The green of the canyon had begun to fade and patches of brown cropped up like Armando's five o'clock shadow. As usual with every coming of autumn here in my Palm City, I felt nostalgic and emotional.

I give you my body for your pleasure, dear Francisco. What I ask for in return is a glimpse into your soul, a small loving portion of your heart. My legs and my thighs and my breasts and my lips—all of it, all of it, is yours for the asking . . .

I stopped in mid-sentence, feeling my hands and fingers trembling. Perhaps I was going too far. I felt frightened by my own thoughts. Hail Marys and Our Fathers now seemed to be suddenly, ominously swirling in my mind, my guilty conscience making me feel weak and ugly, dirty and tainted.

I could hear Monica and Luz up above on the street playing ball. The days were getting cooler and darker earlier, another sign of autumn settling in. I quickly closed my diary, put it back into my vinyl backpack, and hid it under the steps. Feeling overwhelmed by my thoughts, I climbed up the embankment, running over to see what was up with my little sisters. Later I would come back for my diary and confront my sinful thoughts.

"Damn it," I shouted at my sisters. "Watch where you throw that stupid ball." I grabbed the ball as it hit me on the arm. I threw it back, making sure it went in a direction far from either of them, glumly, grumpily satisfied that they would have to run after it.

That was when I heard Chuy's motorcycle up the street, the rumbling closely approaching. I was surprised he should be home at this time of day, since he usually didn't come home to eat until way past my bedtime. Monica and Luz, running to catch the ball while yelling something or other about me being a stupid idiot, turned their heads toward the noise.

He paused in front of the house, gunning his engine a couple of times.

"Hi, Chuy," I said, the same as when I passed him in the morning under the pepper tree, just outside my school.

He looked at us sisters a moment, seemed to be studying us or considering something. Monica and Luz, about to retrieve the ball, had now stopped in mid-track, staring at Chuy. And then he looked my way.

"You want a ride?" he asked me quietly, almost a whisper.

For a minute I thought I hadn't heard him right, that maybe he was just talking to himself, but then I saw he had moved a little bit forward on his low-sitting black leather seat to make room for me.

He didn't have to ask a second time. I hopped on and Chuy made a U-turn, now facing the street going out. As the force of the machine lurched me forward, I glanced back at Conifer Street: The small, irregular houses sat still, quiet; the telephone poles with mysterious wires and lines hung overhead, like threads in a half-finished embroidered street scene. The slender eucalyptus, the lacy pepper trees, a few fat date palms—trees that had enticed Papá to move here, trees I had known all my life, had grown up with—now stood mute and firm, like loyal sentries on duty, guarding something. But what?—my neighborhood? my street? my family?—and from whom?

The chain link fence at the end of the street defined our boundaries, the crisscrossed pattern of the links a constant backdrop to games of tag, hide-and-seek, and baseball, to hopscotch and bicycle riding—all part of the cross-stitches that made up our lives.

Monica and Luz stood in the middle of the street staring at us as we took off, their mouths open, gaping and stunned. Already they were embedded in that backdrop I was leaving behind, racing past: Two young girls frozen, suspended for the moment, while their red ball bounced away from them. People and houses, trees and fences remained motionless in the tapestry, while only the ball, like our planet Earth, continued revolving.

—14

If you were to ask me what routes we took, what avenues and lanes we whizzed past, I would think of shimmering colors and blurs of neon lights strung together in festive streaks. I would be hard put to recall whether it was Hollister Street we glided through or Palm Avenue, whether we swerved and scooped and turned or whether we were actually flying overhead, seeing San Diego as might a graceful, lovely swallow. I only knew this for sure: that my stomach was doing a series of breathless cartwheels while my heart soon fled its proper place and now stood wrapped around Chuy's waist, hugging my brother for dear life.

My God, this was the life! No wonder Chuy got on his Harley one day and just kept going. No wonder he didn't stop. What freedom, wild, lovely abandon, to ride on a huge motorcycle, to feel its humming, its vibrations run through your body, you and the motorcycle one powerful piece of machinery, all the while casting your cares to the wind.

People we zipped past stared at us, looking startled, perhaps afraid of the long-haired hippie and his girlfriend sitting straddled behind him, her hands in his green and white letterman's jacket pockets, hair flying every which way. We were untamed and dangerous creatures. God, if only Francisco Valdivia could see me now—stupid Francisco Valdivia who probably had the hots for blonde, clear-complexioned Susy Johnston. Chuy and I would zoom past him laughing as we whizzed by, our laughter lingering in the wind, forever haunting shocked and dumb-struck, stupid Francisco Valdivia. There was no end to my passionate fantasies in this exhilarating moment of flight.

Just like that, we were in places I had never been, going north toward downtown San Diego. Had I ever been here? I couldn't remember, and certainly not in the night on a Harley-Davidson chopper. It was dark already, with a magical sprinkling of city lights around us and bright stars above us, an evening that wrapped itself softly and seductively around me in a kind of conspiracy. I welcomed the September night into my being, wanting to absorb it, wanting the evening to lift and carry us away into the mysterious, wild darkness.

Then I saw it, startled, my breath catching: The newly constructed San Diego–Coronado Bay bridge loomed before us, splendid and grand. The blue steel bridge connected downtown San Diego to the small peninsula of Coronado. I had seen shots of it on TV when it was completed last month, the grand hoopla that attended its inauguration. There were those who felt the bridge symbolized progress, that the ferry boat with all its obvious charm, now retired, signaled the end of an era, while the bridge heralded a new age, a fast-paced, highly technological way of life. Many Coronado residents were resentful of the bridge, feeling intruded upon, feeling a sense of trespass into their private, small-town domain. Ahead of us loomed the completed controversial structure, a force to be reckoned with, a magnificent blue bride inviting us with outstretched arms into new territory. In a dash, Chuy and I were on it, riding it, accepting its invitation.

San Diego was behind, Coronado lay ahead, and the water below. The docked war ships were toy boats—small and insignificant. In the cool night of September in the Year of the Men on the Moon, Chuy and I took off on our own moon, above and beyond glittering, light-speckled San Diego, heading west toward Coronado, past knobby palm trees, a town square park, trim and lonely in the night. We could have been heading farther west, right into the Pacific Ocean, it didn't matter. I was ready to go on, over the edge, to travel with my most wonderful Chuy. Let him lead, I would follow. I rested my head against his back, feeling protected and shielded from the wind, against anything that might harm me.

We rode quickly in and out of the center of Coronado's town. It lay quiet, seemingly deserted. We passed the famous Hotel Del Coronado, regal and proud. Zooming down the Silver Strand, that strip of land connecting the island to the mainland, the bay was to our left, the ocean to our right, and our refreshed and invigorated faces were to the south.

At the end of the Strand, Chuy slowed down, now entering the mainland, driving expertly on Imperial Beach Boulevard. We rode past First Street, Second Street and soon he slowed the bike and gracefully veered to the right to the faculty parking lot of Mar Vista High, onto the campus, slowly cruising between school buildings, down the walkways, past the lunch compound. He revved the engine and in the empty stuccoed halls of the outdoor campus, the motorcycle's engine echoed, sounding ten times louder, as if there were a hundred lions roaring angrily, hungrily, in Mar Vista High's lunch compound.

Passing the classrooms, Chuy picked up speed as he headed toward the football field. He drove over the grass and onto the track where he sped around—one time, two times, three times—each round going faster and faster. The black night enveloped us and I was shivering.

Then he suddenly swerved off the track, off the school grounds and headed back to Imperial Beach Boulevard, toward the sea. He turned right on Second Street, slowly cruising down a residential area of tidy, box-like homes. He stopped in front of a yellow house with a white picket fence. He lay low in his seat, silently studying the house.

Then my brother shouted with all the fury and strength he could muster, "Doonnaaaaa."

I began to shake uncontrollably.

When Chuy had left for Vietnam, they were still going steady. At the airport to see him off, she clung to him as if to dear life itself. Her pretty blue eyes were red and puffy from all her crying, and I heard her whisper to him, "I'll wait for you." She was proudly wearing the engagement ring he had just bought her at Joyería La Perla. Then a long, luscious kiss, there in front of our mother and father, Monica and Luz, Carolina and Ana María, Armando, Tony and Octavio, and me—the whole family witnessing their passionate kiss.

But she did not wait for him, and after six months of peppy funny Vietnam letters from Chuy, we suddenly heard nothing from him. This silence made us stay glued to the TV, listening to the statistics, the war casualties, wondering if maybe . . . but no, we refused to think our Chuy was dead or missing in action. We prayed the rosary every night. This was at the same time Donna was seen hanging around with another guy at Mar Vista High. She got pregnant, we soon found out, and took off with the guy to another state. And Carolina and Ana María let me in on this bit of information, told me they had always known it: Donna was a cheap slut.

Again he shouted—"Donnaaaaa"—and I was afraid his lungs would burst, that his insides would explode in agony.

No one came out. I looked around and soon realized the house was vacant.

Then he started to howl. At first I couldn't believe it. I thought it was my imagination, maybe a neighborhood dog. I looked around me. But no, it was Chuy, howling a long, deep woeful howl.

Just to the side of the house was a jacaranda tree. Through its dark, spidery branches, I could see the moon. It wasn't even a full moon, but a sharp sickle of a moon, not yet the full harvest moon of September. Although I was sitting behind him, shielded from the sudden cool air, my hands still tucked into the pockets of his letterman's jacket, my body was shaking uncontrollably, and I bit my lips to keep them from quivering.

Then he howled again. His howl was long and eerie and piercing. And I thought he must be howling for all the men in his infantry who cried a thousand tears in wet, gloomy, putrid tents in a dark, labyrinthine country they knew nothing about. He howled for all the men who had ever received "Dear John" letters in the middle of a confused war, and I sat behind him, trembling and thinking that the end of the world must be near, and knowing that for me it was just beginning, that the world was now slowly revolving within my reach, making itself more palpable, and I was starting to take off to distant worlds, unknown terrain.

So I, too, began to howl. A small, feminine howl, but there you had it: in chorus, then, we wailed and grieved together.

Lights came on in neighboring windows and porches, some heads peeked out, fearfully watching us from the safety of their homes. I was sure they saw a drug-crazed, long-haired hippie and his girlfriend atop a low-lying, dangerous chopper, insanely howling, howling, howling at the moon. No one dared come out.

This was what happened, my glimpse of Chuy's planet, his loneliness. In that night of the Year of the Men on the Moon, we zipped past red, yellow, purple neon lights. Car headlights shone on our faces, then passed. Our thoughts and feelings crossed paths in the night breeze, in the motorcycle-swept wind.

We turned onto Palm Avenue, over to Hollister, and then Conifer Street.

Instead of going up the driveway, Chuy stopped in front of the house, the motor idling.

"Go ahead and get off here," he said to me. "I'm not coming home yet."

I hopped off and he revved the engine.

"Thank you, Chuy," I said.

He nodded and took off.

The first thing I noticed when I entered the house was that the TV wasn't on. Carolina, Ana María, Monica and Luz were sitting in the living room, whispering. When I entered, they immediately stopped talking. They looked at me as if my death sentence had just been pronounced.

"Mamá has been sick with worry," Carolina said to me. "How could you have been so stupid?"

"What are you talking about?" I asked her, glancing at my other sisters. They all looked pale and scared to death.

"Chuy, you idiot. How could you have gone on a motor-cycle ride with him? Don't you know he's dangerous? He's been loitering at the junior highs, at Mar Vista, making passes at the girls, hanging out at the compound during lunch. Carmen told me he even tried grabbing her boobs, right there in front of everyone. He doesn't care. Don't you see something's wrong with him? These war veterans come back all messed up, they can't cope with this reality. We're trying to get him interned, get him into some mental hospital. . . ."

"What the hell are you talking about? Chuy's not that way."

"You idiot, you just don't know what's happening. You go off to the canyon and escape into your own little world. . . ."

"Why don't you just shut up, Carolina?" I said.

From Mamá's bedroom, I heard a weak, hoarse voice call me.

"Boy, are you ever a pendeja," Carolina said, as I walked into our mother's room.

I was not surprised to find the votive candle lit below the Virgen de Guadalupe, the bedroom dark except for the quivering light of the fat candle.

Papá, who had a nighttime job as a bus boy at the Hotel San Diego, was not home and my three brothers, who so often acted as surrogate fathers, were also not around, so I was spared their reactions. I was, instead, faced with something worse: Mamá's agony and worry.

She was lying in bed in the dark.

"Are you OK?" she asked. I could tell from her hoarse voice that she had been crying. "Did he do anything to you?"

"No," I said weakly, fighting back the tears. "No, he didn't do anything to me."

"You're so much alike," she said in a whisper, more to herself than to me.

"What?" I asked, wanting her to speak up, to tell me what was going on. Help me understand.

"Yolanda," she said. "Don't ever go anywhere alone with Chuy. Don't ever go on another motorcycle ride with him."

I wanted her to slap me or punch me in the stomach—anything—so I could be angry at her, at all of them, for not understanding. But my mother didn't punish me, and I realized, a sick and scared feeling now in my stomach, that I didn't—couldn't—understand the depths of my mother's immense grief for her lost and confused child.

—15

Our garden was magnificent.

"It has to do with the moon, eh Dolores?" Our neighbor Socorrito prodded our mother. "You work with the moon's cycle, is that it? Your sweet peas are always taller and better perfumed than mine, in June your roses are . . . are . . . monstrosos. What is your secret? Do you sneak out in the middle of the night of a full moon to do your gardening? I've heard of people going on moon diets, all this talk of the power of the moon. Oye, comadre, be nice and tell me your secret."

Mamá laughed. How I loved to see her laugh, her moon-shaped face, her green eyes looking greener and richer, her tentative smile now wide and almost carefree. Short curly hair crowned her face and in the sun the frizzy curls made a soft halo. Proud and secretive she was about her gardening. I thought it must give her a girlish glee to be able to stump Socorrito, to keep her guessing.

They were standing in the front yard, talking from their respective sides of the garden, Socorrito and Mamá, while Lydia and I were sitting at the patio table on the front lawn going over some algebra homework.

Mamá tended her garden in the same manner she tended her children, I felt like telling Socorrito. She's not some busy-body chismosa like you who's so busy sticking her nose into other people's gardens, she doesn't have time to take care of her own.

"So do you have the answer to this problem?" Lydia asked.

"What?" I asked. "Oh, that one. No, not yet."

"Pendeja, you're not even paying attention," Lydia said. "I'm warning you, I'm not going to end up solving all the problems like last time."

Chuy came out of the house, slamming the door behind him. We all turned to look.

"Hey, old lady wetback," he called to Socorrito. "Why don't you go back to Mexico where you belong? Go to the Coahuila in Tijuana," he said, chuckling to himself. "Offer your services." He came down the walk, headed for his motorcycle. We all stared.

"Jesús Manuel Sahagún," my mother called out to him. "How dare you speak that way. Who do you think you are?"

"Oye, mocoso," Socorro shouted at him. "Who are you calling a wetback? I've been a citizen of this country for over thirty years. . . ."

"Damn wetbacks, all of you," he muttered. "Goddamn gooks is what you are. Go back to Vietnam and kill yourself some commies, you fucking wetbacks."

He was on his motorcycle now. "Hey, Lady," he called out

to our mother. "My name isn't Jesús Manuel Sahagún. No fucking way," he said. "It's Jesse Mitchell Sahaygun, so don't forget that, OK?" He started the engine, and then took off, the loud rumbling leaving us lost in the stormy, startled air.

I looked up at the September afternoon sky. Clear, clean and bright blue, not a speck of a cloud anywhere near. Yet I felt that there should have been a thousand clouds racing in fast motion, charging and growling, darkening the day. In the moment Chuy walked out of the house, there should have been an eclipse, the moon imposing herself on the sun, all God's creatures rattled and confounded over sudden night during the day. But no, it was a perfectly beautiful day, and neither Mamá nor Socorrito, Lydia nor I knew what to do with this kind of day.

He had dressed my wound that time. I was the Queen of the Go-Carts and he was my admiring, attentive knight. Mamá ran to the medicine cabinet, got the alcohol, bandages, cotton swabs, but Chuy had said to her, "Let me do it. I'll be careful, I promise." He was. He cleaned the sticky, bloody gash, gently dabbing peroxide on it, blowing on the fizzing white bubbles. If Mamá had been doing it, I would have cried out, but I didn't dare cry out in front of Chuy; I wanted to seem stoic and brave to him. A few kids were still straggling along, until they got bored watching my wound get cleaned, when there was no more blood. Then Chuy and I were the only ones there.

"It'll probably leave a little scar," he said. "You should get stitches, but this is OK. This is kind of like a war wound, Yoli," fourteen-year-old Chuy had said, smiling. "You can point to this scar and say this was the price you paid for the feel of freedom on that go-cart. And you can be real proud."

I was silent, in awe of my brother, and ever so grateful for his attention.

Then he dressed the gash with some gauze, made a square of white tape on all four sides, the dressing now looking like a package, a gift.

Could I do the same for him now? Could I dress the wounds he suffered, make them not hurt, make them heal?

It was Socorrito who told on Chuy, gossipy tattle-taler Socorrito. Mamá would never have said a word. Papá was just getting home, getting some of his tools out of the back of the truck. Socorrito wasted no time in coming out of her house, slamming her front screen door with much pomp and importance.

Lydia and I were still sitting at the patio table working on the last of our algebra problems.

"Oye, Compadre," Socorrito called out to Papá. "Did you know your son is anti-Mexican? Un racista de primeras, ¿eh?"

Lydia and I looked up instantly from what we were doing. I couldn't at first believe Socorrito would tattle on Chuy. Ever since Chuy had returned from Vietnam, she'd been supplying

Mamá with statistics about war veterans so that Mamá wouldn't feel it was only happening to Chuy—Socorrito's morbid but typical way of comforting Dolores. But I figured Socorrito had quickly come to her limits of goodness and when it came to being personally attacked by Chuy, she couldn't resist getting back at him.

"What are you talking about?" Papá asked Socorrito as he shuffled through the gardening tools. He was hunched over, his work shirt soiled and worn thin by the sun, some stripes of grass stains on his jeans.

"Yes, indeed," she said. "He called me and your wife and daughter and Lydia there, yes, called us, um, yes, he called us fucking wetbacks, yes, he did."

Papá stopped what he was doing, straightened himself up and looked at Socorrito.

"What did you say?" he asked her quietly.

"Yes, he did," she said, now looking over at Lydia and me. "Didn't he, muchachas? Called us 'fucking wetbacks,' just like that. To his own mother, too."

Papá looked over at me. "Yoli, is this true?"

I looked him straight in the eye. "I don't know what she's talking about."

"She's lying," Socorrito said. "Of course she's going to say that. Look who you're talking to. She'll cover up for that crazy brother of hers any time."

"Lydia," he said, now turning to my friend. "Did he say that?"

Lydia glanced at me and then at my father.

"We, you know, Mr. Sahagún, Yoli and I, we were doing our homework," she said. "Lots of formulas, you know. I, no, I was here busy. I wasn't paying attention."

"Are you going to believe them or me?" Socorrito said, now screaming, taking a house slipper off and hitting the chain link fence with it. "Lorenzo Sahagún, how dare you doubt my word. . . ."

Papá jumped off the back of the truck and quickly went inside, slamming the screen door behind him.

Within seconds he was shouting, I could hear him from way out in the front yard. So could Socorrito who, the more she heard him shout, the calmer she became, putting her slipper back on, finding her much-needed vindication in Lorenzo Sahagún's wrath.

"'Leave him alone,' 'leave him alone,' you all say," he was shouting at Mamá. "But look at him, Dolores. Our son is making us the laughingstock of the neighborhood. He's a spoiled brat, laughing at us. I'm sure of it. He's pretending to be crazy, but he's the one having the last laugh. Wait till I get my hands on him. . . ."

I couldn't hear Mamá's response from where we sat in the front yard, though Lydia and I were straining to hear what she had to say.

"This is the last straw, making fun of Mexicans, calling us 'damn wetbacks.' Insulting our heritage, our people . . ."

Something was being said by Mamá.

"If he dares to say it once more, te lo juro, Dolores—I swear by the Virgen of Guadalupe—I will kill that boy or have him put away for the rest of his life if he doesn't stop with this mierda. . . ."

"Lydia," I said, "Let's go."

We closed our textbooks and walked out onto the street. We didn't say anything to each other until we were close to Hollister Street and far from hearing distance of my house.

"Thanks, Lydia," I said.

"It's OK, Yoli," she said. "Socorrito is just a pinche vieja chismosa with nothing better to do than get people riled up for no reason."

"Yeah," I said, feeling thick and old. "Yeah, I know."

"Yoli, I gotta get home now," Lydia said. "Are you gonna be OK?"

"Yeah," I said. "I'm going over to Brown's Market for a soda. See you tomorrow."

I watched her cross Hollister Street, then the train tracks. I stood there for a minute or so, not knowing what to do.

I could see Don Epifranio sitting on his front porch a couple of doors from my house. I wondered if he could hear Papá's shouting. Don Epifranio, our local historian, could he supply me with some history that might explain what was going on now? Did Chuy's hurt have to do with the origins of man, of bacteria, the history of Mexico and the United States, the fall of the Roman Empire? Should I have paid better attention in my World Geography class? Or was this just some sort of life puzzle for us to put together—a cruel, sadistic game meant only to confound all its players?

I walked over to Don Epifranio's, never really meaning to go to Brown's Market for soda in the first place, just wanting to go somewhere other than home.

He watched me as I made my way up his walk, then the three steps to his front porch.

He nodded his hello, pointing with his cane to the patio chair in the corner. I pulled it up next to him and sat down. Both of us were silent as we stared across the street at Kastlungers' field, at the cars rushing past on Interstate 5, at a plane droning above, until finally the shouting in the distance subsided.

—16

"I'm going to do it, and I don't care how forward I look," I said to Lydia one morning on our way to homeroom. "All last year I waited and waited, and the idiot didn't make a move."

"What are you going to do?" Lydia asked.

"I'm going to write him a note and tell him that I lov—like him a lot, and you know, something like that. Kind of declare myself to him."

"Híjole, Yoli, I don't know. That's like throwing yourself

at him, falling all over him," Lydia said. "What if he doesn't go for it? God, that'll be so embarrassing."

"No, not really," I said. "What have I got to lose, anyway?"

"What have you got to lose?" Lydia said. "How about your self-respect, your good name, your reputation? Gee, I don't know. . . ."

"The hell with my reputation. What has that got me? I'm going to be fifteen and I haven't even gotten kissed by a guy. God, Lydia, I might turn eighty and still not have been kissed by a guy. I've got to take action, woman. That's all there is to it."

The bell rang for homeroom.

"Well, look," Lydia said. "I promise to always be your friend, even when the talking and snickering behind your back starts. When word gets around that you threw yourself at Francisco Valdivia and made a complete ass out of yourself, I'll stand by your side and pick up the pieces. Loyal to the end."

"Thanks for nothing, Lydia."

I decided to first consult with one of my older sisters—or both of them—before doing anything too impulsive, although in my mind the decision to go forward with my plan was set.

That night I hung around Ana María, since Carolina was on a "date" out in the living room with Tom, who now had official permission to sit on the couch with Carolina and watch *The Beverly Hillbillies, Gunsmoke,* and *The Twilight Zone,* with Mamá and Papá, Monica and Luz as attentive chaperones.

"Where are you going?" I asked Ana María, who was

getting dressed in the girls' room. I sat on the top bunk watching her put on a pair of blue bell-bottoms my mother had made and then a sleeveless shell top.

"Esther and I are working on a history presentation together and so Tony's going to drop me off at her house for a few hours."

"They gave you permission to go at this hour?" The alarm clock on the dresser said eight-thirty.

"Yeah," Ana María said. "This is a real important report."

I watched her dab some perfume on her neck and then on her ankles.

"It's Tito, isn't it?" I asked. "Is Tony in on this?"

Ana María stopped brushing her hair and looked at me in the mirror.

"I know you've got a crush on Francisco Valdivia, and I can give you some good advice on how to catch him. . . ."

"It *is* Tito you're gonna see, isn't it?"

"Look, Yoli," Ana María said. "Tony isn't in on this. Nobody is. Tito and I love each other a lot. We can't stand being apart. It's something really heavy and good. It's like your crush on Francisco, but about ten times more powerful. You know what I mean?"

"How are you arranging this little rendezvous if nobody's in on it?"

"Well, Esther knows. And now you know," Ana María said. "Please, Yoli, I know I can trust you. I'll give you some tips on how to catch Francisco. You can wear my lipstick whenever you want, yeah, take it to school sometimes, but swear you won't fink, please swear to the Virgin Mary and the Father, Son and Holy Ghost, please swear it. . . ."

I swore. I swore to the blessed Virgin Mary and to the Father, Son, and Holy Ghost that I would not tell on Ana María and her secret love Tito. I swore a lot of things that night: I swore that I loved my family and wanted them to be all right. I wanted Carolina and Tom to hurry up and get married, break the ice so then Ana María wouldn't have to sneak around with Tito and could, instead, date him in our living room watching *The Beverly Hillbillies* in a proper, no-sneaky way. I swore to her that I would help in her quest for true love. And when I confessed to her about the love note I was planning to give Francisco Valdivia, she had me promise I wouldn't do it just yet. She had a lot of good, effective tips to give me on how to catch my man, and so I promised I would hold off on the love note.

Tony banged on the bedroom door. "Hurry up if you want that ride to Esther's. I'm going to be late for work."

"Yoli, you're the best sister anyone could ever have," Ana María said. "I love you, Hermanita." Then she ran out of the girls' room, leaving me there on the top bunk bed, my legs dangling as I stared at the mascara, the lipstick and bobby pins and perfume on the dresser. What did all this female paraphernalia mean? For whom were we taking risks and at what price? I swear I just wanted to start crying and I wasn't sure why.

Before the morning bell rang for homeroom, I stood at the entrance to the locker hall. I was wearing a tight-fitting yellow and orange shell top and an orange skirt now hastily rolled up to mini proportions. Wearing Ana María's favorite lipstick, my brown hair down to my shoulders, feeling good, looking good, I waited for Francisco Valdivia to come by.

Ana María had instructed me the day before on how to catch my man. "Put this on," she had said, pointing to those clothes he would find sexy (I was wearing them now); how to do my hair (straight, part in the middle, bangs); and—for the grand finale—she handed me her "Red Coral" lipstick for me to take to school for repeated applications as the day wore on. Then she instructed me on Step One in the magical nuances and techniques of man-catching: The Look.

Standing before the dresser mirror, we both practiced The Look.

"See," she said, "your eyes meet. Just an instant, not longer. Then quickly look down like to say 'oops, I didn't mean for you to catch me looking at you.' Don't do this more than once a day."

On the third day when this quick, self-conscious meeting of the eyes occurred, I was to go on to the second part. After casting down my eyes with my long eyelashes (Ana María had agreed to lend me her mascara so this eye communication could have more dramatic appeal), I was to follow up with a quick, stealthy glance at him again, only this time I was to let my glance linger an instant longer for the opportunity of heightened intensity.

"Not a stare, exactly. That's too much. You give away too much with a stare," Ana María warned. "Besides, it'll make you look like a boba. Just let your eyes lock with his for a second more. Yoli, remember, timing is everything."

"What about accidentally dropping my books in front of him?" I asked. I didn't let on this was a tip I'd read in my hidden copy of *Sex and the Teenager.*

"Drop your books in front of him?" Ana María stared at me as if she had just received news that I was named Boba of the Year and she hadn't known I was such a dummy, even though she was my sister. "You know, Yoli, this isn't a Gidget movie. Maybe gringas do those stupid things, but not us. Besides that being an obvious and old trick, you don't want him to think you're a clod on top of being a boba." She shook her head and sighed. "No, Yoli, trust me. It's all in The Look. And timing is of the essence in The Look."

Then what, I wanted to know, what was the next step? A note? A "hello"—what?

"Then you wait, tonta," she said, looking at me in the mirror. "See those eyes of yours, pretty blue eyes, Yoli. Use them, Hermanita, use them. And remember, it's all in The Look."

How about a smile? I wondered.

"Week one, you stick with The Look. The Smile is Step

Two—next week."

I stared at her. A whole week of just The Look?

With both hands, she directed my face toward the mirror and said, "Practice The Look, boba."

Here I was waiting for Francisco Valdivia to enter the locker hall so I could cast him The Look. I was disappointed that Ana María hadn't considered dropping-the-books-in-front-of-him a worthy strategy. Still, I waited patiently for him to come, casting my eyes this way and that as a warm up exercise. So busy was I in rehearsing The Look, I almost missed him walking in my direction with three other guys. Francisco Valdivia, my love and my life.

I never said Francisco Valdivia was gorgeous, I never claimed that, but he was a Looker—handsome in his own way. He was dark—very moreno—and this in itself was exciting. What a striking couple we would make: He, moreno, dark-eyed, black hair slicked back, while I stood next to him, his girl—no, his woman—light-skinned, light-eyed, soft brown hair. His arm would be around me, protecting me, because I was his woman and he was my man. Sitting in the lunch compound together, sharing a bologna sandwich, taking turns sucking on the plastic pouch of tamarindo paste so tart and sweet, that's what we'd be doing, my man and me.

What happened next was against all the laws of gravity and romance and true love. What happened next was that

Francisco Valdivia and his three buddies came up to me and started laughing.

"Hey, Yolanda," one of them said, "what's with the bright orange? You look like a naranja, mind if I have a juicy taste?"

"Aren't you a little early for Halloween?" another said.

"Sí, esa, what's with the Agent Orange costume?"

More laughter.

Francisco smiled at their comments, but he didn't say anything. Other people rushing by to get to homeroom on time suddenly slowed down to listen in on their remarks.

I stared at them in naked embarrassment. In that short time—how long, fifteen seconds? fifteen hours?—I thought about all the care that had gone into this preparation, how sure and true Ana María had been in her advice. How I'd rushed to school early that morning, prepared myself in the bathroom, brushing my hair, checking for smeared lipstick on my teeth, not even having time to put my stack of textbooks in my locker for fear I would miss Francisco's arrival. So here I was standing in front of these imbeciles— pinches idiotas, children, little baby boys undeserving of my attention—lugging a stack of heavy textbooks, a fat notebook binder, while my backpack held my compact powder, blush, foundation, eyelash curler, mascara, cake eyeliner, lipstick, hair spray, brush and comb, and bobby pins and Ana María's favorite, most treasured perfume that she lent me for just this occasion.

So I did what any respectable, proud, and humiliated woman would do: I took the top book from my stack and flung it at the closest idiota. Then the next book, and the next. Just started throwing those books at them as if I were some Queen of the Javelin throwers. I flung those heavy books at them with all my might, and they backed away real quick, but not before being hit here and there, and what sweet revenge I felt. Next came my heavy three-ring binder full of hundreds of sheets of college-ruled notebook paper, a pencil case filled with ten pencils, five pens, a fat eraser, a pack of spearmint gum—and I threw the binder at them in the hopes of erasing the whole pinche lot of them. I was breathing hard and fast and full of vengeful savagery, and it felt so good and tart and sweet to see them backing up real quick, covering their faces, fearing my potentially lethal flying weapons: *History of Western Civilization, First Year Algebra, America in Literature, World Geography, Beginning French*—wonderful friends of mine, these textbooks now coming to my rescue. Damn these pinches cabrones, I was thinking, but I was too out of breath to shout it.

"Orale, Yolanda, do it, yes, right on esa," I heard a girl call out to me, and then I saw another girl pick up my *World Geography* and throw it at the guys again. People started laughing. The homeroom bell had rung, but nobody was budging. They all crowded around to watch the Queen of the Javelin throwers break fantastic records, aiming high and far, right on the mark.

Francisco and his buddies were trying to stroll away from

the scene with dignity, trying not to walk too fast so as not to seem like they were hightailing it away from the Queen, but not cruising their easy, everyday cool stride either.

Then a girl with red hair picked up one of my books and threw it at Mr. Agent Orange Commentator and *America in Literature* whacked him on the lower lip.

Everyone was cheering and clapping for us. I was sweaty and itchy in my knit top and out of breath, panting with such delicious ecstasy, and thinking that this must be a whole lot more satisfying than making out.

And when the pinches cabrones finally walked past me, silent and embarrassed, not knowing what kind of walk to walk, Francisco's eyes and mine met, and I gave him The Look.

—17

Because I knew by heart every single object in my brothers' room—meticulous snoop that I was—I immediately spotted the new item in the bottom drawer of their desk. Tucked way in the back was a lacquered black box about the size of my hand, a red and gold dragon painted on the lid. I opened it. Inside, a stack of neatly folded Chinese cookie fortunes filled the box. *A mysterious person will soon come into your life*, one read. *Perseverance will bring desired results. Happy news is on its way to you. Opportunity knocks on your door every day—answer it. The current year will bring you much happiness.* The skinny slips of paper were portentous, but hopeful. On the back, dates had been penciled in. I checked a few of them. May 22, 1969. 5/4/69. May 15, 1969. May '68. There was a pile more for June and July. These must be Chuy's, I thought to myself as I read each fortune.

The box looked like something he might have bought in Japan, like the souvenirs he'd bought us, while on his R & R. Souvenirs he'd bought us, including a Sony reel-to-reel tape recorder for me, just before we stopped getting letters from him, when suddenly all communication broke down and we heard nothing from him for a couple of months—the same time Donna had broken up with him. Now here was a pile of fortunes Chuy must have collected while on his motorcycle trip. Had Chuy been desperately buying Chinese fortune cookies every chance he got, gobbling down the cookies for extra luck? Was he hoping they'd come true, hoping Donna'd come back to him?

He must have been carrying this box around with him on his motorcycle trek. Now home, Chuy probably thought he could safely hide it away in the bottom drawer, knowing that our brothers rarely used the desk except to toss on top of it everything from dirty socks to girls' barrettes and crumpled pieces of papers with phone numbers.

A good position and a comfortable salary will be yours, another one read. *You will be awarded some great honor.* How cruel and teasing these messages seemed.

As I picked up the last fortune, I noticed four pills underneath the piece of paper. Medicine? Did Chuy have a cold, allergies? Why were they hidden in this box?

Just then I heard whispers in the patio, coming toward the room. I quickly put the pills in my pocket, stuffed the fortunes in the box, shut it and put it back in the bottom drawer.

A manly voice was saying "Shhhh."

Shit, I thought to myself. I was sure whoever it was was on his way to the bedroom. One of my brothers, for sure. I could have just gone on cleaning, got my dust rag out and pretended I had been cleaning all this time, now that Armando was paying me to do this, now that I had a legitimate reason for being here, but something about the whispers and the "shhh" spooked me. The pills in my pocket made me feel guilty—why hadn't I put them back where I found them? All of this made me forget that I had permission to be in the guys' room for its weekly cleaning. The only closet had a thick beige curtain hanging from it. I hid behind it, my cleaning supplies—glass cleaner liquid, rags and dust cloth—set next to the chamber pot in a discreet corner.

They were opening the door, girlish giggles now, followed by that same manly "shhhh."

"Are you sure this is OK?" she said.

"Yeah, just so long as we keep it down." It was Octavio. "But I'll lock the door, anyway. Nobody comes in here except my brothers, and it's cool with them."

"I like your bedroom," she said. "It's cozy." She giggled. I didn't recognize her voice. There were so many girls who called Octavio, and I couldn't keep the names straight with the voices anyway.

"The four of you sleep here?" she asked.

"Yeah. Here, make yourself at home," he said. I heard him pat the bed as one would pat a mattress at the store to see how firm it was.

"Oooh, on the bed," she said, again giggling. "Isn't that a little dangerous . . ."

"I don't know about dangerous," he said, "but it could get pretty exciting. Think you can handle that?"

Silence. I heard what sounded like kissing. Some deep sighs. I was sure they were making out, the sound of the bed creaking when someone first sits on it.

I took a look.

Sure enough, they were lying on the bed tangled up in each other, kissing like there was no tomorrow. I didn't know who she was, she didn't look familiar. Good. I didn't want to know who she was. Then I let the curtain fall back, didn't want to see anymore, I felt sinful. Ashamed. I closed my eyes, thinking this might block the whole scene out, the sounds and everything. That feeling came over me again, the same one I felt when Octavio and my sisters and our neighbor Marisa had gone into the culvert and I had caught Octavio kissing Marisa and grabbing at her breasts there in the stinky old culvert.

That's how I was feeling: a sick feeling of something being wrong, ugly wrong.

"No," she said. "Not there. No, I mean it. . . ." I heard the bed creak some more, a lot of bumping or something was going on. Someone moaning deeply, hard. They were in pain, but maybe not. A zipper unzipped, more kissing and moving on the bed. Shoes thumped to the floor. My eyes were shut tight, but not my ears. The sound of clothes being taken off, tossed on the floor.

"No," she said again, her voice sounded muffled. Lots of kissing sounds. "No, not there . . . no . . ." her voice sounded weak and far away. "Oh," she moaned.

"Here, baby," Octavio was saying. "Touch it right here. Yes, that's it. Oh, yes baby, yes, that's it. Just like that. Yeah, just keep it up, baby. . . . Oh . . ." He was moaning. Then I heard something being unwrapped, like a bag of candy being opened. A bag of candy? Pendeja, I thought to myself, could I really be that stupid?

I thought of just jumping out from behind the curtain, revealing myself. But I couldn't move. It was as if my whole body had turned traitor on me, was being a sneaky thing detached from my brain. I was able to close my eyes, but I couldn't move my hands to plug my ears, to open the curtain; I couldn't make myself cough or shout at them, "Stop it! Stop it right now, you two." Nothing, absolutely nothing. My body refused to obey my mind's thoughts and commands. I seemed entranced by the sounds. A perverse fascination.

Then it got worse. The bed was moving in hard, rhythmic bumps and Octavio's moaning was louder, the breathing hard and heavy, and he sounded like he was in deep pain, and I could barely hear her above all his groaning, and he must have been on top of her because her moans sounded muffled. She let out a feeble, feminine gasp every time he pumped her. I couldn't move and yet I wanted to run out of there, disappear into the air or just die and be swallowed up by the earth, be anywhere but there, hearing those sounds. I felt scared. And then a long, hoarse moan from Octavio like he was slowly dying, expiring, and burning in hell.

How long had I been there? I didn't know. I couldn't breathe or think. The fear and the shame seemed to strangle my whole body. For a moment I couldn't think or hear anything, I just had the urge to get on my knees and start praying for him, for her, for myself—for forgiveness or I don't know what.

I heard some crying and at first I thought it was me, but then I realized it was her, weeping. She was crying for a few minutes and I thought maybe Octavio had fainted, or maybe he really had died since he wasn't reacting to her crying. Not consoling her or anything.

Then finally: "Why're you crying?" he asked her.

"I didn't want to go all the way," she said. "You knew that. It hurt me, I told you you were hurting me. . . ."

"Hey, don't give me that bullshit," Octavio said. I'd never

heard him sound that rough and ugly. "You know you wanted it just as much as I did."

"It hurt, Octavio," she said, her voice sounding feeble and defeated.

"It's supposed to hurt the first time," he said. "I just popped your cherry, what do you expect? Didn't your mommy ever tell you about the birds and the bees?"

"It hurt me, Octavio. It hurt me a lot."

"Hey, come on," he said. "Don't make a big deal about it, OK? I'm sorry if it hurt, baby, I didn't mean for it to hurt. I tried to be nice and easy, slip and slide nice and easy, you know. But it's going to hurt a little the first time, see? But next time you'll enjoy it more. I'll see to that, OK baby?"

She was weeping again, muffled. "What if I get pregnant, Octavio, what about that?" She sounded so far away. Lost.

"Don't even think of that," he said. "I used a rubber, remember? Look, see?" I heard something being tossed. "Oops," he said, laughing. "Missed. See that? That's the Sahagún sperm on the desk, nowhere near you, baby, OK? So don't worry. I'll make sure I don't knock you up. What's the fun in that? I want to make love to you and take care of you, teach you how to enjoy it. You'll see, baby, I'm not going to let you down. You're gonna fly high with me."

"I love you, Octavio."

Some kissing sounds.

"Do you love me, Octavio?"

Some more kissing sounds, one of them turning in the bed.

"Do you love me, Octavio?"

"Yeah, of course I love you," he said. "That's a silly question."

Somebody getting up. "We better get you home, baby," he said. "It's getting late."

It took a few minutes after they had left for me to get the courage to come out from behind the closet curtain. My knees were weak and I felt drained, as if I had gone through the whole horrible pain that Octavio's girl must have felt. But when I did finally come out, the first thing I saw was the used rubber on the desk.

Even though my mind wanted to get the hell out of there, even though my lips trembled, threatening to cry, I went through the motions of my job, like some meticulous, obedient robot. I dusted the trophy case, shook out the little bedside rug, emptied the chamber pot, sprayed the mirror with the glass cleaner, tidied up the bedspread, ironing out the wrinkles and bumps with a swipe of my arm, avoiding the desk altogether, avoiding the gooey limp sac waiting for me there.

One time when Chuy was still in high school, he and El Chango executed one of their best pranks. It was the talk of Mar Vista High School for weeks. Chuy and El Chango had been on old lady Crawford's shit list from the beginning of the school year. Neither guy could figure out what they'd done to the old crab. Even the other students couldn't figure out why she had it in for them, so the whole class was rooting for the guys.

Just before English class, Chuy and El Chango had sneaked into the empty classroom and fished out a pile of unused condoms they had hidden in their pockets. Smearing the rubbers with mayonnaise, they then placed the gooey sacs inside the rolled up screen, knowing old maid Crawford was sure to use the overhead projector that day, as she had the whole week, to dissect sentences. Once the students piled in and sat themselves down, old lady Crawford positioned the overhead projector at the front of the class, setting on it her transparencies with diagrammed sentences. Sure enough, with a quick tug on the screen, gooey, milky-like condoms cascaded onto the old maid teacher's head. Chuy claimed one landed quite nicely and snugly on old lady Crawford's little hair bun.

We all found out about it because Chuy and El Chango— who else could've pulled such a great stunt?—were sent straight to Mr. Rindone's office and were promptly suspended from school for the rest of the week. At the time Chuy and El Chango told us about it, going over the details again and again, the look on old lady Crawford's face, the detail about that one gooey rubber landing on her hair bun, we all had shrieked with delight, all us brothers and sisters surrounding the now famous pranksters as they recounted the story.

Everyone talked about it for weeks. Those who'd witnessed the moment said she looked like she'd been attacked by giant killer worms. Others claimed that this was about as close to the sex act as old maid Crawford was ever going to get.

Poor Miss Crawford. Maybe I should quit this cleaning job, I thought, just tell Armando the room was too stinky dirty for me to bother with. 'Do it yourself, you pigs,' maybe I should say to my brothers. 'Clean up after yourselves, why don't you?' giving Octavio, in that moment, a long hard stare full of secret meaning. Coming into their room, snooping around, it wasn't fun anymore. Maybe I was better off not knowing too much about a man's world.

Using Kleenex, I carefully picked the limp, gooey sac up off the desk and dropped it into the trash can, feeling as if some mean trick had just been played on me.

—18

Not a moment to lose. I quickly got on my bike and headed toward the beach, headed to where El Chango worked. I rode down busy Palm Avenue, my heart pumping like crazy, one moment feeling weak and tired, the next feeling powerful and strong. I had never ridden my bike this far away from home. If my parents knew I was riding to the beach area on my bike and alone, they'd have me on the Tres Estrellas de Oro bus first thing tomorrow morning for a lifelong stay in El Grullo's convent, with my grandparents nearby for maximum security surveillance.

El Chango worked at a pool hall a block from the Imperial Beach pier, and even as I pedaled with all my might, I wasn't sure he'd be working at this time. But I had to try, I had to get hold of him somehow, and since I didn't have his home number, this was all I could think of.

There was a lot of traffic, and too late I realized this was the late afternoon rush hour. A finger of the bay was to my right, on my side of the lane, and I remembered how as a child riding the bus to Bayside Elementary, I had always felt afraid that the bus might crazily veer off the road and land in the bay, all of us kids and Ralph the bus driver, too, drowning. Now I pedaled faster, keeping my eyes on Palm Avenue ahead of me, pretending the bay was not a few feet away on my right.

Because the thing was this: I had it figured out, why Chuy was acting so weird. Yes siree, the evidence, the proof was in my pocket—four pills jiggling around as my left thigh pedaled up and down. And I had to tell El Chango, discuss it with him so we could together help Chuy out. El Chango would know what to do. Since he'd been working at that pool hall, he'd made friends with some of the beach bums, the junkies who hung around there. He would understand and know just how to help Chuy.

A part of me felt relieved to know that it was just this, Chuy taking drugs and stuff. I thought to myself, of course it's going to make you act weird, look at Ruben in my American History class, stinking of pot—God knows what other drugs he was doing, all the while his trip making him talk back to the teacher, mumbling incoherent shit to himself, always ending up suspended or with a referral to the boys' VP.

Yes, of course, that was it.

I passed my neighbor's store, John Lawka's Watch Repair Shop, wondering what this solitary Swiss man thought as he walked the four miles to and from his store. Had he, in his loneliness, ever thought of taking drugs, getting high to feel less lonely? Were there war zones even here on the home front that drove people to drugs?

I was now in Imperial Beach proper. There was a small mall on my right side with a Big Bear Market, a yardage shop my mom sometimes went to, while across Palm Avenue on the south side, Palm Theater's marquee announced the present attraction, *Midnight Cowboy.* Not too long ago Mamá had given us sisters permission to see *Romeo & Juliet* at Palm Theater. I'd never seen *Midnight Cowboy,* or *Easy Rider,* for that matter, but in a way I had seen these forbidden movies since everyone at school talked about them. There was always some clever kid from Southwest Junior High who sneaked into the movie and came back to school the next day with the details. So in a sense, I had seen these movies, and they were in no way like the *Romeo & Juliet* movie.

The breeze whipping my hair back grew cooler as I neared the beach. I could see the pier in the distance, and since I didn't know exactly where El Chango worked, I decided I would start with the pool halls on the north end of the pier and work my way down the south side, inquiring about El Chango—or rather, Johnny García, as he was probably known at work.

Once at the pier, I got off my bike and walked with it. Holding to my plan, I made my way north, peering into anything that looked like a bar or a pool hall—I wasn't sure there was a big difference. There were a lot of guys around, just hanging in and out of the bars. It was about 5:30, 6:00 o'clock, growing dusk, growing cold.

In the first bar I peeked in just at the doorway, with my bike in tow. It took a few seconds for me to adjust to the darkness. "Excuse me, please," I called to the shadowy figure at the bar, "but does Johnny García work here?"

"Who?" he called back.

"Johnny García—El Chango."

"Nope, never heard of him." Once my eyes adjusted to the darkness, I realized there were about six guys sitting at the bar.

"Hey, sweet thing, you looking for some action?" One of them called out to me. "I'll be your Johnny García."

I quickly mounted my bike and high-tailed it out of there, suddenly conscious of the fact that I was wearing short shorts and a t-shirt that must've shrunk in the last wash. Damn, why hadn't I changed into some long pants before heading out here? In my rush to talk with El Chango, appropriate attire was the last thing on my mind.

By the time I made it to the next bar, night had set in and creepy-looking guys were everywhere—one was sprawled half lying down, half sitting up on the sidewalk smoking who-knows-what while strumming a warped-looking guitar. His buddy, surely in a deep sleep, sadly thumped on a pair of small bongo drums. None of these beach guys looked anything like Frankie Avalon and his gang of friends. The few girls hanging on to the guys could have taken a few lessons in demeanor from Annette Funicello and Gidget.

Again I inquired, tentatively peering into the bar, clutching the handlebars of my bike in case I needed to make a quick getaway.

"What? Who'd you say," the bartender asked. "Johnny who?"

No luck there, I pedaled my way to the next bar half a block south of the pier. By now I was shivering, feeling completely exhausted, wondering if I had done the right thing in coming here. The pounding sound of the waves breaking made me feel lonely and scared. I stood again at the doorway of another bar, about to weakly call out to the bartender when I suddenly felt someone's hands on my butt, squeezing me, hurting me.

I gasped, startled, and turned to see a guy with the longest beard on Earth and hair that looked like a bramble of knotted rope. He looked like a cross between Father Time and the devil.

"Don't do that," I said weakly, about to crumple to the floor and cry.

"Oh, baby, you're one hot chick," he said in a gruff voice, his eyes not quite focusing on me. He had a strong, hurting grip on my butt. "I just want a little piece of ass, a quick fuck, OK?

I promise I won't hurt you." His words sounded heavy with arousal or with drugs, or both. But what made me react, made me suddenly get angry, were his words. They sounded just like Octavio's when he had seduced that girl in his bedroom. Suddenly I felt a deep and righteous rage, and not stopping to consider the fact that this creep was over six feet tall and I was not even five feet, I swung the front of my bike toward him, slamming him in the legs. He backed away in an unsteady shuffle.

"Leave me alone, you creep!" I screamed, getting ready to push my bike against him and make a run for it.

He started laughing and was just about to lunge at me when some guy grabbed him from behind and pushed him to the ground.

It was El Chango.

"Goddammit, Wayne, get the hell out of here," he said to the disheveled heap on the ground.

"OK, man, OK," he said, slowly picking himself up. "I was just having me a little fun with this cute thing. . . ." He mumbled a few more things to himself and then slowly shuffled away.

"Yoli, are you OK?" El Chango asked, now coming up to me and steadying my bike because I was trembling like crazy. "What are you doing here? Who's with you?"

At first I couldn't say a word. I just stared at him as the tears came silently out. I thought about how close I had come to being molested or something by that creep, how his words and actions reminded me so much of what I had just witnessed in the guys' room. Octavio, my own, protective brother. In those short moments as I stood staring at El Chango, I thought about this Wayne creep's actions. There was no doubt he had been flying high, that the drugs were doing this to him, but what was Octavio's excuse for his behavior? And another frightening thought: what were the drugs doing to Chuy?

"Yoli, are you OK?" El Chango asked. "What's going on?"

"I need to talk to you," I finally said. "It's about Chuy."

"OK, sure," he said. "Hold on a minute." From the doorway he called in. "Hey, Scott, can you cover for me awhile?"

"Yeah," the bartender called out to El Chango, "It's pretty slow tonight, anyway. Go ahead. . . ."

El Chango turned to me and said, "Let's go take a walk on the pier." As we moved in that direction, he said, "Here, take my jacket. It's kinda cold."

I quickly put on his jacket, now feeling safe and protected, what it must feel like when you go on some exotic, dangerous trip and you return home, feeling a great sense of security. Walking next to El Chango, wearing his warm jacket as we made our way down the length of the Imperial Beach pier, the salty air felt refreshing, the rush of the waves sounded familiar and friendly.

I told him about finding the drugs in Chuy's Japanese box, along with the fortune cookies. And putting my hand into my pocket, I pulled out the four pills for his inspection.

He stopped to look at them for a long time, but he didn't say anything.

"This is the reason he's been acting so weird," I said. "So if you and I can figure out how to get him to stop taking this stuff, maybe drug rehabilitation or something like that . . ." My voice trailed off as I realized El Chango wasn't really listening to me.

We had come to the end of the pier, and we stopped. El Chango said nothing, just stared at the dark Pacific Ocean. I waited, looking first at him then at the ocean, wondering what was taking him so long to say anything.

"Yoli," El Chango finally spoke. "It's not the drugs. That's speed you have there. It's not the drugs that've got him this way."

"What do you mean," I said. "It's gotta be the drugs making him act all weird."

"No, Yoli, it isn't," his voice sounded sad, old. "I've been around a lot of druggies, have taken the stuff myself now and then. Chuy's acting weird in a whole different way. It isn't the drugs that're doing it, Yoli."

"But how can you be so sure?" I said. "Maybe he took all sorts of stuff when he was in Vietnam. . . ."

"Yoli, there's something going down with Chuy, and I'm pretty sure it's not his being high. The look on his face, the things he says. There's an anger, or rage, or something in his actions that goes deeper than drugs, Yoli. He's like a time bomb getting ready to explode. I can't explain it real good, but there's something about the way he stares at people, the weird things he says that's way beyond being high on drugs. All I can think of is there must've been some pretty horrible shit going down when he was in Vietnam."

I looked toward the east, back down the length of the pier. It was brightly lit, and I noticed a few solitary fishermen posted at the pier's railing, determined to catch something before returning home. A lovebird couple walked past, arms around each other, the boyfriend saying something, the girl giggling appreciatively. A young woman was pushing an elderly lady in a wheelchair, a drunk was sprawled on a bench, in a deep, rattling sleep.

The moon was up, bright and watchful, preparing for its full splendor in a few days.

"Come on," he said, turning back. "I'll take you home. I think I can fit your bike in my car."

I didn't say anything—couldn't. We walked toward the people, the lights, the town, our backs to the immense black ocean. I hugged myself, shivering, while El Chango, limping next to me, walked my bike, the wheels making an occasional rhythmic clicking sound.

—19

A ghostly silence hung in the air over Palm City, over San Diego, over all of southern California. October 1969. Indian summer in San Diego whispered secrets and hints, purposefully lazy and inattentive, while invisible phantoms scraped the streets with scraggly claws, pretending to be dried, curled up eucalyptus leaves skittering and pushed along by intermittent gusts of air. I knew better. This was rehearsal time for the Santa Ana desert winds from the east. This was also hide-and-seek time.

We all gathered in the middle of Conifer Street—all the neighborhood kids—under October's full moon. Hide-and-seek had become a long-standing street tradition, a kind of block party played a few times a year—whenever we could organize the neighborhood—under a full moon. We looked forward to the game with the same anticipation and excitement as we did Halloween and Christmas. This was the one time we set aside our age differences—twenty-seven-year-old Armando to seven-year-old Luz—and brothers and sisters, neighbors, boyfriends, and girlfriends joined in the game, as if to honor, at least a couple of times a year, the child in us.

For me, there had always been the added intrigue and curiosity of meeting in person my brothers' latest girlfriends, many of whom relentlessly telephoned day and night: "Hello, is Octavio home?" "Can you please tell me when Armando will return?" Even shy Tony had his fan club: "I just called to tell Tony about a Ray Charles concert. Can you tell me what his work hours are this week?"

Their voices sounded at once urgent and hopeful; there was

a tinge of despair when their inquiries were answered in the negative, and I felt compassion for them—these feminine voices—in their desperate attempts to reach one of the handsome Sahagún brothers. I enjoyed being the telephone secretary for the flood of love calls my brothers received, except for the ones coming in for Octavio. When Octavio's girls called, I hated wondering which one—Sherri? Vicky? Cindy? Nadine?—was the one he had taken to the guys' room.

Only Chuy, since his return from Vietnam, received no phone calls. So only my brother Chuy, on that hide-and-seek night, did not have a girlfriend clinging possessively to his arm.

We had a buddy system for this game. Since so many people played—usually about fifteen to twenty people—we paired off when we hid. We set certain boundaries; otherwise poor "It" could spend all night looking for the hiders. People could hide in the front yards of the two houses to the left and right of the utility pole, but the canyon was off limits. We had great hiding places. The empty lot across from our house had an old, thick pepper tree and plenty of bushy shrubs and an abandoned, rickety shed, so when "It" started calling out slowly: "One . . . two . . . three . . ." we scattered in no time flat, like wood elves and fairies in delightful flight.

It was October 25th, the hunter's moon bright and ghostly. Haunting.

How we paired off could be as choosy as picking a date or as random and arbitrary as tapping the kid closest to you when the countdown started. Lydia was always my partner.

"Why'd you wear a yellow sweater," I whispered to her as we shot out to our favorite hiding spot, the pepper tree on the empty lot. "You should've brought dark clothes, tonta."

The sound of scampering, of rushing, of whispered giggles.

". . . five . . . six . . . seven . . ."

Rustling bushes. "Ouch!" Another giggle.

". . . eight . . . nine . . . ten—ready or not here I come!"

Then the eerie stillness. In those moments, I pitied It. The lifeless night was spooky, and I imagined that It must've felt alone, desolate, like a character from *The Twilight Zone,* the only living person on the planet. Not a bush rustled, nor a hint of another human's breath. Conifer Street seemed abandoned by all living things, except for It.

"Uuuuuuuuy, cucuuuuuuy," somebody in the direction of Socorrito's front yard called out, a clue to It, or a challenge?

I held my breath until I thought I was going to burst. It was hard to decide which was more exciting and terrifying—being caught unawares by It (ha, ha, Yolanda and Lydia, gotcha. Eeeek! as we tried to outrun It to the Safe pole) or having to squat uncomfortably here behind the tree trunk for God knows how long while creepy spiders, ants, crickets, hard-bodied unidentifiable bugs crawled all over me until It (hurry It, hurry It, I'm feeling itchy and creepy, hurry up and find me!) found me.

Lydia and I sat hunched and hidden behind the thick trunk of the tree and, too late, I noticed the moon's rays lit upon us as if we were on stage in the spotlight. We didn't move a single muscle or eyelid, tried not to breathe. I closed my eyes tightly. I thought about Tito, who had minutes ago sauntered down the street toward all of us just as It started the countdown, and I was sure he and Ana María would pair off. I had glanced at Octavio who seemed to stiffen when Tito walked up to all of us, Ana María's forbidden love intent on joining in the game. Our brother Octavio was suddenly on alert, even though a girlfriend (was she the same one he had in the guys' room? I wasn't sure), was dreamily, victoriously clutching his arm. With the crowd of people around, Octavio wouldn't dare make a scene, wouldn't dare say something to Tito about staying far away from his sister. In my hiding place next to Lydia, my body quivered as if in anticipation of great things to come. I felt frightened.

The stillness was now and then interrupted by the soft sound of steps—It walking slowly along the street, on gravel, now stepping on crunchy twigs, brushing past a bush. Then the patter of running feet, the victorious shout: "Ollie, ollie oxen free!" as one hider touched Base, made it free.

My hiding time seemed interminable. Should I run? No, Lydia was too slow, we'd never make it. So we waited.

In the stillness, then, is when it happened. One of the girls let out a long, piercing scream, all of us knowing it was a joke, just a ruse to unnerve It. So nobody moved, we all stayed put in our hiding place, some of us suppressing giggles.

Then again a horrifying scream, true and ugly, as if from the demon's pit, and at first, again, nobody moved. We were momentarily frozen with the shock that this was a real scream and something awful was unfolding, something we would never forget, something that in years to come we would recount to our children and grandchildren about the 1969 hide-and-seek game on Conifer Street, so long ago, but yes, it seemed like just yesterday when we heard the girl's scream pierce the night of the hunter's moon, then pierce our guts, and stab the fear deep into us for all the rest of our living days.

The night felt hollow and full of echoes.

Then we came to action, quickly, in a panic, all of us out of our hiding places.

"Who is it?" "Where?" "What's going on?" We walked in circles, looked in bushes, now all of us were "It" trying to find where the screams had come from.

Marisa came stumbling out from behind the shed. She was almost unrecognizable, her face a bloody pulp. The buttons on her blouse were ripped and she fumbled, trying to clutch the front closed. She was sobbing, and, staring at her, I felt like fainting. I couldn't breathe. I didn't want to hear what she was going to say, but I couldn't move and I stood suspended in the thick air, staring at her as did everyone—who could resist staring at such horror?—all of us sensing there was more to come.

"I felt sorry for him," she said between gasps of breaths, sobs. "Nobody wanted to pair off with him, so I did," she said, looking dazed and broken. "I felt sorry for him. . . ."

We all understood whom she meant, no need to waste words pronouncing his name. We all understood.

"He tried to kiss me," she said, slowly, in shock. "I told him not to. Then he started hitting me, slugging me and trying to pull off my blouse. . . ." She started crying again. We girls surrounded her, trying to console her. "It's just that I felt sorry for him. . . ." She sounded far away. Lost. Poor Marisa was a bloody mess.

Tony, shy and reserved his whole life, now seemed endowed with supernatural powers as he seemed to fly over to the shed in a split second's time. We all followed, stumbling, bumping into each other, twenty or so of us all in a stupor, our fear now hypnotizing and leading us.

He was crouched in a corner of the shed, looking scared, then Tony was all over him, punching his head, his face, screaming at him, and Chuy did nothing to defend himself, just sat there receiving his brother's blows.

Somebody shouted, "Get an ambulance." I heard running, someone called out in a weak strained voice to the houses, "Mamá . . . Papá . . ."

Other girls started crying, there were whispers and shouting. "Hey, call the cops." I couldn't move, I couldn't see anything beyond the crouched animal-figure of my favorite brother Chuy as Tony beat him up.

There were sirens, more running, somebody pulling Tony

off Chuy, Tony crying with anger and hurt. "You fucking loony, what did you do to her?" he screamed. "What did you do to her?" Tony's question, his actions, proof of how much he cared for our next-door neighbor Marisa. We all knew it now for sure. "You're so fucked up. Why don't you just get out of our lives, you fucking crazy. Go back to Vietnam and stay there. Get the fuck out of our lives, man. . . ." Somebody held Tony back, he struggling to have another go at Chuy.

I stared at Chuy, my flesh and bones icy cold, my whole body trembling with fear and hurt and I don't know what. In that moment, he had been transformed into a horrible monster terrifying the neighborhood—a werewolf, a blood-sucking vampire, a Frankenstein—a monster created by what?

He slowly got up, a thick stream of blood making its way from his nostril to his mouth, down to his chin, ruby red drops staining his t-shirt. Chuy looked past everyone, hard and absent. A zombie, dead to this world. His face was smeared and marked with bruises and blood as if he were wearing war paint, or a mask, readying himself for the battle ahead.

He staggered toward us, and we quickly backed up, parted a path for him, afraid he might now attack any one of us. He ignored us, staring intently ahead at something. We turned to follow his gaze. There was nothing but night, hollow and black. Then just like that he was gone, disappeared into the night of the hunter's moon.

PART THREE

And the night comes again to the circle-studded sky

The stars settle slowly, in loneliness they lie

Till the universe explodes as a falling star is raised

The planets are paralyzed, the mountains are amazed

But they all glow brighter from the brilliance

of the blaze

With the speed of insanity, then he dies.

—From "Crucifixion," by Phil Ochs

—20

While waiting for Lydia to get here so we could get ready for tonight, I helped Mamá till the soil for the sweet pea seeds, digging a neat trench along the front picket fence. In the next two days, November 1st and 2nd, she would be planting the whole perimeter of the yard with seeds—her annual ritual—in honor of All Saints' Day and the Day of the Dead, in honor of family members who had died. Not that anyone had recently died or anything. I was sure Chuy was still alive, hiding someplace. And Marisa was OK. The ambulance had arrived within minutes and so had the cops. So while the ambulance took off with Marisa, the stupid cops poked around the neighborhood: the canyon, the alleys, everyone's back yard. Shining their big, evil-eye spotlight on every bush and crevice in the neighborhood, they called out his name from their car speakers, the damn fuzz, as if Chuy were some kind of criminal. Marisa had been cool about it, so had everyone else. Even as they put her in the ambulance on a stretcher, she kept saying, "It's not really his fault. He's not well. He's not well." Marisa was like a sister to us, and I was glad she felt we were like family to her, too. She had a broken nose and some broken ribs, was bruised here and there, and real scared. "I know he's not himself," she told all of us brothers and sisters and Mamá and Papá when we went to see her in the hospital. "I don't hold anything against him, because he's not well." She said she felt more sorry for Chuy than for herself.

Tony was with her when the ambulance took her that night and it seemed he hadn't left her side since then. True fucking love, I thought. But we all tried to figure out why Chuy would beat her up like that, tried to figure out what made Chuy tick. She had asked him to pair up with her when she saw he didn't have anyone. Even shy Tony (who really cared for Marisa all this time) had some dingbat girl hanging all over him. So Marisa felt sorry for Chuy, and together they went and hid in the old shed.

What was he thinking that hide-and-seek night? What was he feeling—rejected, lonely, what? I only knew this: If I ever found out where Chuy was hiding, I'd never tell anyone. I'd already stuffed some of my belongings in a backpack and had it hidden in the canyon under the wooden steps and some bushes, ready to take off with him when he came for me.

In the meantime, in these five days he'd been missing, I'd shined the chrome on his motorcycle and bought some special leather conditioner for the seat. Every day after school I'd shine that baby until it looked like new. It was only a matter of time before Chuy came for it and I wanted us to be ready to take off.

Once Lydia arrived, I had permission to leave the gardening chores and go inside to get dressed for Halloween.

"I've got to hand it to your parents," Lydia said as we

walked up to the house. "They sure know how to make a far out garden. They must have magical green thumbs or something. Man, I don't blame Socorrito for being envious."

Like Mamá and Papá, who were rightfully proud of their garden and tended it with meticulous care, I, too, kept an eye on the progress of the sweet peas in the spring. My observations came to this: Once the sweet peas began to grow tall, the gardener had choices—to either let the vines meander any way they wanted, or to set a trellis from which the plant could grow straight and upward. Left alone, the vines crisscrossed, bumping into each other, entangled in a bushy spray of color. Set against a trellis or guiding string, the sweet peas could grow straight, obedient and untangled. Yet nature liked to tease even the most fastidious gardener, creating here and there unruly vines, tendrils refusing to conform to the configurations of the trellis set to guide them. Unruly, rebellious sweet peas. Unruly, rebellious children.

Then Lydia thought of something and added: "Hey, maybe that's why Socorrito's been accusing all of us of stealing her fruit. Envious old biddy. *Wishes* people would want to steal her fruit!"

"Stealing her fruit?" I asked.

"Yeah," Lydia said. "Vieja loca, she's been pestering every kid that comes her way. Just right now, coming over to your house, she asked me if I'd seen Georgie and his punky gang, says they've been stealing her figs. And her guayabas. Ay sí, she wishes," Lydia said, "as if anyone wanted her dinky old fruit."

"Georgie and his gang?"

"Yeah," Lydia said. "She's been bugging the heck out of every kid that comes by, complaining that she's not going to have enough figs to make the mermelada she makes for the neighbors every Christmas. Yuk, who wants that junk anyway?" Lydia said, scrunching her nose in disgust.

I stared at Lydia a moment. She was dressed in one of her brother's hand-me-down grubby jeans with some stupid floral patches on them. Carrying a baseball bat with a cloth bundle hanging from the end of it, Lydia looked like a pathetic imitation of a Hobo.

"You gonna wear that shit for Halloween?" I finally said.

Trick-or-treat, smell my feet, give me something good to eat.
If you don't, I don't care, I'll pull down your underwear.

My face painted a camouflage green with ghoulish white around the eyes, wearing black pants and a sweatshirt, hair ratted stiff with sticky hair spray, I was good and ready for the night. So Halloween crept up on us good and savage. I found a blood-red lipstick sample on top of the girls' dresser and smeared it hard on my lips.

"Let's go over to that old cemetery in Nestor," I told Lydia.

"How're we going to get there?" Lydia asked. "It's kind of far."

"We're going to walk with our patas, stupid," I said.

"Hey, man, you don't have to talk that way to me, Yoli. I'm not some animal or something," Lydia said. "I don't know what's eating you, but cut the bitch crap already."

Lydia the Hobo and I the Ghoul got on our bikes and headed out the three miles to Nestor. We rode out of my street, up Hollister, watching out for cars.

Miniature Frankensteins, space men, ballerinas, and princesses invaded the neighborhood streets, had dominion of the night. I wondered if Chuy might be hiding behind one of the masks, disguised as what?—Dracula, or superman, an astronaut, a Hell's Angel biker, a soldier? I slowed down, now seriously examining the disguised hoodlums, hoping to discover Chuy behind one of the masks. Since the hide-and-seek incident the week before, we hadn't heard anything from him, and I didn't feel like talking to anybody about it, either. Lucky for Lydia, she was smart enough to get the hint and not bug me about it.

The patter of many feet running through the dark streets sounded like the running of a battalion of soldiers. I could hear the rustling of brown grocery bags bumping up against little legs, against scratchy, stiff Batman and Robin costumes from K-Mart, against tulle and gossamer, and glimmering fairy gowns. "Trick-or-treat," echoed down the street, flying up Conifer, down Hollister, over to Palm Avenue and Harris Street. Sudden shots of light from flashlights poked holes in the black tarp sky. Small voices squealed and laughed and giggled with delight at being allowed to wander the streets late at night. There was a perverse festivity to the night, and I was certain La Llorona, the mythical, crazy mother crying and wailing a witch-like shriek as she searched for the children she herself had drowned, hid somewhere amidst these children. I was certain she was preparing to snatch any one of the trick-or-treaters for her own. I pedaled a little faster.

"Hey, not so fast," Lydia called out to me. "Wait for me."

"Yeah, well hurry it up, pendeja," I called back to her, keeping my same speedy pace. "That's what you get for eating so goddamned much, Gordinflona."

She said something back to me, but I was too far ahead of her to hear.

The cemetery was abandoned and, except for a single street light shining dimly at the gate's entrance, perfectly, wonderfully dark. There hadn't been fresh dead bodies for about fifty years or more. The grounds were crowded with crumbling, lonely tombstones, and it seemed nobody ever came out here, not even on Halloween night.

We walked our bikes past the rotting wooden fence, into the cemetery's yard, stumbling over gopher holes, brushing past scratchy tumbleweed.

"What the hell are we doing here, anyway?" Lydia asked, breathless.

"I thought we should do something really spooky, you

know," I said. "Maybe next year we're going to be too old to go trick-or-treating."

"I'm never going to be too old to go trick-or-treating."

"Well, I will," I said. "Next year I'm going to Montgomery High's Halloween dance, even if I have to sneak out of the house to go. Fuck this trick-or-treating anyway." I picked up a rock and threw it at the nearest tombstone.

"Yoli, that's not nice," Lydia said. "It seems kind of disrespectful to the dead. It's probably a sin to do that."

"Fuck the dead," I said. "And fuck you, Lydia, with all your moralizing. Who anointed you my fucking conscience?"

"Yoli, why are you cussing so much?" Lydia asked. "You didn't used to cuss like that. . . ."

"Fuck you, fuck you." I grabbed my bike and ran deep into the cemetery, leaving Lydia behind to talk to herself.

"Yoli, come on. Let's get out of here," she called out to the darkness. Her voice sounded weak and faraway. "Come on, man, we're missing out on all the candy we could've had by now."

I hid behind a tombstone. The night trembled, the air, thin and vaporous, was full of witches preparing to snatch disobedient, cussing teenagers. La Llorona was lurking behind the jacaranda tree.

"Uuuuuuuuuuuy," I called out spookily to Lydia. "Cucuuuuy." I was one of the witches lurking in the cold shadows of the cemetery.

"Yoli, come on," Lydia called out again.

My first thought was to rush Lydia while screaming ghoulish witch screams. I could hit her over the head with a big rock and watch the blood drip all over her.

"Yoli, let's go back," Lydia called out. She sounded light years away, far beyond the world I had discovered.

And I thought, squatting there in the dark behind the tombstone, that then the police would come and take me away, and soon Chuy—wherever he was hiding out, because I was sure he was hiding out nearby—would find out that I had been taken to some mental hospital and so would come out of his hiding place and sneak into the hospital late at night and rescue me. We'd climb out through the window and I'd hop on his Harley, my arms wrapped around his waist, and he'd take me away. Man, we'd just fly with the wind and never come back to stupid old Palm City.

Or would I have to actually kill Lydia? *Then* would they put me in an insane asylum? Would they say it ran in the family, this weird, criminal behavior, some genetic problem that was now revealing itself in the Sahagún family?

"Yoli, if you don't come out now, I'm leaving," Lydia said. "I mean it, man. You're getting too weird."

There was a rock, a big one, right by me. Was this God telling me to do it—or the Devil? I picked it up. I had to use both hands, it was so heavy. I could rush her and then throw it at her, aim it right on her head and bash her brains out.

"OK, that's it," Lydia called out to me. "I don't know how you talked me into coming here. I'm going now."

She didn't make an effort to go, I noticed. She stood, unsure, still holding the bike's handlebars and looking around for me in the black cemetery.

Then I did it, I charged her, running with all my might, screaming a scream to rival all witches' screams. Now *I* was La Llorona, shrieking an ugly shriek and wail.

Lydia saw me charging her from out of the blackness, and she froze, her mouth open as if she were about to say something, but my ghoulish looks and mad charging and wicked shrieks left her cold and paralyzed.

With both hands, I raised the rock, still running toward her, aimed to bash her brains in.

Shocked and confused, she stared at the rock in my hands, and then at me.

I was upon her now, the rock positioned to crush her head. She covered her face and screamed.

Then I lowered my arms and let the rock slowly drop out of my hands to the ground. "Get out of here," I said, vicious and hard. "Get the fuck out of here, pendeja."

I turned and walked back into the blackness.

Where was he right now, anyway, I wondered as I sat against a crumbling tombstone. I could hear Lydia, getting on her bike and crying as she pedaled away, back over to Hollister and Palm City, back over to her house and security and all those little brats begging for stupid candy that was just going to rot their teeth anyway, so who the fuck cared for even one little Almond Joy that would rot your teeth and next thing you know you're at the dentist's and he's yanking out all your teeth. Fuck the Halloween candy. And what if he climbed into my window to rescue me from the mental hospital and the police were waiting for him? What if they just shot him on sight, without a chance to explain what he'd done to Marisa? No, maybe it was better that he just stayed put, hidden wherever he was.

I was suddenly very cold, shivering and with a bad headache, as if I had just tried to bash my own brains out. And I thought that somewhere my favorite brother Chuy was hiding out and maybe he was cold and shivering just like me. Maybe he was terrified, just like me.

—21

We were back to praying the rosary every evening—Lent or no Lent. Things were that bad. After Mamá planted the sweet peas, she stopped working in her garden altogether, while Papá stopped watching TV, even *Bonanza*. Luz and Monica stopped bickering with each other and instead played in hushed, quiet voices with their dolls, so even poor Barbie and Ken and Alan and Midge had to figure out their love problems and complicated lives in whispers. Carolina was thinking of stopping her education for a semester to get ready to marry her man Tom, and Ana María stopped telling me anything more about Tito, so I figured that hot and heavy love affair was over. I stopped listening to my goddamned junior high school teachers—fuck them all!—concentrating, instead, on how to get Francisco Valdivia to fuck me. No sense in being a pure little virgencita and waiting until I was married. With the way things were happening to the Sahagún family, I was afraid I might not live to be the ripe old age my religion and culture dictated to get married and be de-virginized.

Since Halloween, Lydia and I had stopped talking to each other. If we ran into each other in the hallway or the lunch compound, we looked the other way nonchalantly, pretending we hadn't noticed each other. So good riddance to fatso Lydia. She only bugged me anyway, the stupid idiot.

The point is, we all stopped living normal lives; this was a kind of *day the earth stood still* for the Sahagún family. Nobody knew where Chuy was hiding out; the cops were always over to our house asking questions and whether we'd heard from him, had any idea where he might be. They once even questioned me.

"You and he were special to each other," they said to me, sitting in our living room in their police uniforms. You could hear their patrol car out front squawking, the dispatcher saying things, filling the neighborhood with cryptic messages, stupid police talk. The kids on the block hung around the patrol car, like groupies of a rock band, or pretended they were cops and spies themselves, big detectives, the whole fucking lot of them.

"Do you have any idea where he might be hiding?" one asked me in a soft voice. They were probably trying to be all gentle to get my confianza so I'd tell all.

But I didn't know, and if I had, I wouldn't have told. Another bunch of stupid pendejos. Yeah, we're tight, I felt like telling these idiot cops. So tight, man, you think I'm going to tell you anything?

Then one day Socorrito came knocking at our door. "Have you seen them?" she called in at the screen door. "I know it's them."

"What?" Mamá said, coming to the door. I was the only other one around, reading *Hamlet* in my favorite armchair. "Who?" she asked Socorrito.

"I counted fifty-eight guayabas yesterday night and this morning I only had twenty. And the apples, too. They've taken the nicest crop of apples I've ever had."

"What are you talking about?" Mamá said.

"Georgie and his gang," Socorrito said. "They're stealing my fruit. I had a feeling something sneaky was going on. I didn't want to accuse anyone, no, not yet, anyway. I wanted to be sure. So I've been keeping an eye on my trees. I count the fruit and write down the numbers. See?" she said, holding out a scratch piece of paper. "Cincuenta y ocho guayabas, quince manzanas," she read. "That was last night. Now I only have seven apples left. . . ."

"Georgie and his gang, you say?" Mamá said quietly. She looked pale.

"Ay, por favor, Dolores, I wasn't born yesterday," Socorrito said. "Those traviesos have been getting on my nerves for ages. I'm sure those good-for-nothing hoodlum kids have been eyeing my fruit. Everyone in the neighborhood knows I have the best guayaba tree around."

"I'll be sure to keep an eye out for them," Mamá said.

"Those malvados are going to be sorry when I catch up with them," Socorrito said. She walked away, double-checking her before-and-after list of fruit.

Then Mamá turned to me. "You didn't hear this conversation, ¿comprendes?" she said. "Not a word to anyone about this."

I nodded.

I would have ditched school altogether, except that I seemed to be getting somewhere with Francisco. I could tell he was catching on and even responding to my little tactics so well learned from Ana María. But when I mentioned this to Ana María, she didn't seem real interested.

She was lying on the bottom bunk bed listening to the radio, a little spaced out as if she wasn't really there, off dreaming on the moon.

"Hey, Ana," I said. "Guess what? You were right about

the techniques. Francisco's going for it." I sat down at the foot of her bed. "Ana?"

"Oh, yeah, that's good," she said in a dreamy whisper, not even looking at me. She had the transistor radio pressed against her ear on the pillow.

"How're things going for you and Tito?" I asked. "Did you guys break up or something?"

"You know, Yoli," she said, "sometimes you ask too many questions. Leave me alone, OK?"

"I was just trying to help," I said. "You helped me, so if I can help you, you know that's what hermanas are for, OK?"

She didn't say anything; I wasn't even sure she had heard me, but she didn't look happy. It occurred to me that maybe what I thought at first was dreaminess was sadness or something like that. I left the room to give her some peace and quiet.

Carolina had Tom, Luz and Monica had each other, Armando, Octavio, and Tony had each other, so I thought Ana María and I could be each other's partner since she didn't have Tito anymore, I guessed, and I never had Francisco in the first place, and Lydia was sure out of the picture, and now my Chuy was hiding out somewhere eating Socorrito's fruit. I thought Ana María and I could hang around, kind of support each other until Chuy came for me. But at that moment, it seemed Ana María, with her long black tresses on the pillow, her blue eyes looking sad and lonely, just wanted to be alone. Not with anyone and certainly not with her punky younger sister.

I walked across to my canyon to do a little thinking and writing in my diary. It was warm that day, I suddenly noticed. A dry, desert warm. Walking across the street to my sanctuary, I could tell the Santa Ana season was here—the sky was a piercing blue, the air was deathly still. The clarity of the day was too sharp, my vision clean and focused.

By the time I reached the canyon, slid down the ravine over to the wooden steps, the eucalyptus and pepper tree leaves were rustling, the wind was picking up. I sat on a rotting wooden step, my diary in my lap, but I didn't open it. Someone whispered my name. I looked around me, surveying everything. The bushes, the overgrown weeds, the bloated brush, the spiky tumbleweed. Everything around me looked desolate and mean, crazy for a spit of water, a little rain. From where I sat, I had a clear view of the freeway, cars whizzing by. The freeway culvert was within view, too, but again came something that sounded like a whisper. Was it the wind picking up, the leaves of the trees? My arms were full of goose pimples, and I was tempted to just pick myself up and climb back up the ravine as fast as I could. Go straight home. I thought about Ana María lying on the bunk, and then I heard the sound again and felt scared, really scared. What if Chuy was hurt or sick or something? What if he was hiding out here in the canyon?

"Chuy?" I whispered. "Is that you?"

Nothing, just the sound of wind, of the leaves and bushes rustling.

I looked around me, thinking I might find one of Socorrito's half-eaten apples or a rotting guayaba. Nothing. I stood up and climbed farther down the steps into the ravine, but all I could hear now was the swoosh of the cars on the freeway and the wind.

"Chuy?" I called loud enough for anyone in the vicinity to hear. "Chuy, is that you? Where are you?" I left the steps and slid down to the bottom of the canyon, pushing through bushes. Nothing was going to get in my way, not even scratchy tumbleweed.

"Chuy? I'm here, Chuy. Where are you?"

I was now in Kastlungers' field, looking out to the freeway. The wind had picked up, dry desert wind. I could see the mountains out to the east; the crispness of the day seemed to crinkle and crack with an uncommon sharpness. Had last year's desert heat seemed so penetrating? The brilliant blue of the sky made me squint. I checked behind crevices and tall dry grass and overgrown weeds. Nothing. *No thing,* no one, no wonder. I was here alone, stupid Yolanda, I said to myself. How could you have thought Chuy would be here? And waiting for *you?* You have got to be kidding, pendeja, why would he take you along with him?

I tripped, my foot stuck in a gopher hole. "Chuy, where

are you? Godammit, please, Chuy." Then I started crying, first little whimpers, then sobs, loud and angry from deep down in my gut.

The wind gathered strength, puffs of hot desert wind. It seemed to be mocking me, laughing at me. *It* whispered to me.

I slowly hobbled up the ravine, my ankle throbbing, my eyes feeling achy and parched. It wasn't anybody, I told myself. My knee was bleeding, tiny pebbles and dried grass and leaves stuck to the blood. Just wishful thinking. No one was whispering to me. Just the damn wind.

Because I sprained my ankle and Ana María had bad cramps, the two of us didn't have to go to church the next day. Which was a good thing because those days I wasn't feeling real spiritual or anything. I was beginning to hate God for all our heartaches. So it was just as well Ana María and I got to stay home. Maybe we would be partners, after all. They left for nine o'clock mass, feeling sorry for us because we would miss out on the church bazaar afterward. Mamá reminded us that they'd probably be getting back late since she'd be manning the Guadalupana booth most of the day, the ever-popular tacos de carne asada booth. She showed me where she had put the Tupperwared leftovers in the refrigerator. For the first time since the hide-and-seek incident, she even looked a little happy. I felt relieved and reassured her that Ana María and I would make do.

"We'll bring you back some confetti eggs," Luz and Monica promised.

Then they piled into the station wagon and headed for St. Charles.

About an hour after they left, I heard a car out front. Tito was in his maroon-colored Impala, and he was looking over at the house. Waiting.

Ana María ran past me out the door while still putting on her sweater. "If I'm not back before they are," she said, sounding out of breath and looking pale, "tell them I felt better and went over to study with Esther."

"Ana," I called out to her, "where are you really going?"

She was already out the door and at the car. In one swift movement, she flung the door open, slid in and shut it. She and Tito sped away.

I knew there were secrets people sometimes didn't want to tell others. There were times in our life, I supposed, when we hid behind masks and pretenses in an effort to hold onto little intimacies with ourselves, when we delighted in clandestine actions. I would give Ana María that much. But I thought I was more than just a good sister to Ana María, maybe her confidante. So then why was she pushing me away now? What secret of hers was not safe with me?

I was glad my ankle was throbbing and hurting me so much. No way was I about to get a pack of ice and soothe the swelling. The throbbing pain complemented the pity I wanted to wallow in at that moment. I was alone in here, and my favorite brother Chuy, my Knight, who would have taken care of my sprained ankle, who would have applied cool compresses to ease the swelling and the pain, was somewhere out there.

—22

The tick of the clock that was never heard before now seemed annoyingly loud; the barking of neighborhood dogs—had I ever noticed that the alley was filled with a hundred mutts? The swoosh of the freeway cars now sounded like waves rushing in—was the Sahagún Estate a seaside cottage? In that rush of cars I tried to single out the one that I was waiting for, Tito's maroon-colored Impala. I knew, first of all, this was not the usual Ana María-and-Tito rendezvous, of that much I was certain. I sensed something was up, and all I could do was wait: wait for Ana María's return, wait for my family to return, wait for Francisco to make his move on me, wait for Chuy to come for me.

Sitting on the couch, I stared at the image of the Sacred Heart of Jesus, and then over at the picture of the Virgin of Guadalupe, the King and Queen of the Sahagún Estate. I felt ready to ask them a few questions: OK, so how many Hail Marys would it take to get our old Chuy back, I wanted to demand of the Queen. How many Our Fathers would we have to recite on our knees before you, O Your Royal Highness

King, before our bloody, dripping hearts stopped bleeding? How much goddamned penance was it going to take before the earth started spinning normally for my family? Was Chuy the sacrificial lamb? Huh? Answer me that! I wanted to shout at our Heavenly Royal Patrons. But I didn't. The earth would probably swallow me up just in the moment I said it, and while I was burning in hell, Our Royal Highness would, for good measure, go ahead and punish all of California, making Earth fart out of its San Andreas crack, all of California finally out to sea like it'd been promising forever. So was God now punishing me because I wasn't feeling religious these days, was that why Ana María was shutting me out?

I wandered around the house, out to the back. I hadn't been to the guys' room since that incident with Octavio and his girlfriend. I told Armando I was too busy with school and homework and all to clean his room. They'd have to do it themselves. But now I wandered in there, knowing everyone was at the church bazaar and there was nothing else to do.

The first thing I did was open the bottom desk drawer. The Japanese box was still there, and I opened it, figuring I'd read Chuy's fortunes again. Instead, there on the top of the small slips of fortunes was a note on 3-ring binder paper folded over enough times until it fit in the small box. The note read: "Yoli, leave canned vegs in bag in shed. Can opener too. Don't try looking for me. Leave it & go." My face was burning, my whole body ready to faint. I looked around me, my heart beating wildly. I quickly put the note back in the box, placed the box in the drawer and limped-ran out of the room as fast as I could.

How did he know? How did he know I had found his box? I was scared, wishing Ana María would come back already, wishing someone were here. I looked around me, but there was no one. Of course Chuy would know. He must know everything. From wherever he was hiding, he could probably see each of us going about our daily routine, noted the patterns of our lives. Chuy was smarter than any of us, way beyond us, and so he probably saw things we couldn't even imagine. Maybe he noticed my fingerprints on his box or smelled my scent on it. Yes, of course Chuy would know.

I quickly hobbled—my sprained ankle throbbing again—into the kitchen. Searching the cupboards, I pulled out every can of vegetables I could find. No, that wasn't a good idea, I thought, remembering how Socorrito had noticed her supply of fruit gone. I decided I'd take a couple now, and then again the next day, and on and on until he came for me. When was he going to come for me? My hands trembled as I selected a can of sweet corn and barbecued pork n' beans. I had half a package of red licorice vines left in my backpack, so I added them to the stash.

I walked as quickly as I could manage across the street to the shed, looking around me to see if I were being followed or observed. The street was eerily quiet. Everyone in Palm

City must be at the bazaar, I thought.

Since the hide-and-seek incident, nobody played in the shed anymore. The kids in the neighborhood claimed it was haunted; claimed they could still hear Marisa's screams, could see wet blood trickling down the rotting wooden walls every full moon. Chuy must've figured that, that we'd all be too spooked to hang around the shed. Is that where he'd been hiding out?

But when I got there, there was no sign of anyone having been there, no shoe prints, nothing. I set the bag in a corner and ran out and back across the street as fast as I could.

Ana María made it home before the family did. I had been staring at my book, staring out the window, not knowing what to think or do. No way was I going to tell the police. He was just biding his time, I was certain, waiting for everyone to calm down about it. Then he'd reveal himself, he'd go up to Marisa, first and foremost, and apologize to her. I was certain of it.

When Ana María and Tito drove up, slow and easy, the Impala crawling to a stop before the house, I knew something was wrong. Tito jumped out of the driver's side and went and opened the door for Ana María. She got out slowly, not her sprightly self. They walked up to the front door together—which was a first. Tito knew that if our brother Octavio found out about him and Ana María, he'd hang him by the balls, so Tito always rendezvoused with Ana in neutral territory.

I watched from the living room window the way they care-fully walked up to the house, Tito's arm around Ana, like two wobbly old people supporting each other. Ana María had been crying, I could tell from her smeared mascara and puffy eyes and nose. Her eyes were too blue, still teary-eyed. Tito looked pale and hunched over, didn't look like his cocky, sexy self. Just like a viejito, looking about fifty years older in just an afternoon's time.

At the door, he wrapped his arms around Ana María, but not in a sexy way. More like he was consoling a little girl and twenty-five-year-old Tito, now turned into a little old man, was her father or something.

Then he walked back to his car and drove away.

"Ana," I said. "What happened? Did you guys break up?"

"Yoli," she said. "I'm real tired and don't want to talk about it right now, OK?" She went to our bedroom and closed the door.

For a few minutes I just stood where I was. I wanted so badly to talk with Ana María, but I felt scared. She looked sick and pale and sad.

Then I heard her go into the bathroom and shut the door.

I entered the bedroom and sat at the edge of the foot of her bed, waiting for her to come out of the bathroom so we could talk.

I changed the station on the radio, smelled the new perfume samples on the dresser, brushed my hair. It was getting long, down past my shoulder, and Francisco approved. Last Thursday in homeroom he had said "Hi" to me as he walked in and then, "You've got pretty hair, Yolanda." That was it, just that compliment. Then he went and sat down at the back of the classroom as usual. My heart was flying, silver wings attached, and my whole being raised to the clouds and heavens. I had to do everything possible not to grab him right then and there and declare myself to him. Keep cool, Yoli, I kept telling myself all through homeroom period. Just keep cool. Don't forget what Ana María told you: all in due time. She still hadn't come out of the bathroom. Half an hour had gone by.

"Ana," I said, knocking on the bathroom door. "You OK?"

There was no answer. "Ana, are you OK in there?" I said. "Open up, Ana." I shook the handle.

A few seconds later I heard the lock click open. She was sitting on the toilet, pale, her helpless black curls pressed against her sweaty forehead and neck as if she had been in a steam bath for hours. She looked drained as she leaned against the toilet tank, her eyes staring vacantly up at the ceiling. Her jeans, crumpled in a heap next to her, were a deep, purple blue, sopping with blood.

My first thought was to call an ambulance, scream for help. Ana María must have read my thoughts. "No, Yoli," she said. "Don't call anyone, just help me clean up here, OK?"

I couldn't move. I just stared at her, my lips quivering.

"Please, Yoli," she said, sounding feeble and thin, faraway. "Listen to me, OK? Get a plastic bag and put the pants in them and get rid of them. *Now* Yoli, before they get back."

The thought of our family—especially of Mamá and the girls—seeing this bloody mess snapped me out of my shock and into action.

I limped-ran to the kitchen where I found a plastic bag and went back to the bathroom and carefully put the bloody jeans in the bag.

I looked at Ana María who, all the while, sat on the toilet. Now she hunched over with cramps, it seemed. She looked ghastly and ready for the other world.

"Ana," I said in a whisper, afraid to look her in the eyes. "This isn't your period, is it?"

For a moment she didn't say anything, and I felt relieved. I didn't want to know.

Then she said, "Tito's cousin's wife knew of this doctor in Tijuana . . . that's where we were," she said. "Yoli, we didn't have a choice. It was either that or having Papá and Octavio kick the shit out of Tito," she said, starting to cry. "I know they would've killed him, I just know it."

"But Ana," I said. "You guys could've gotten married. You know, eloped or something. Then it'd be all right."

"No, Yoli, it wouldn't've been all right," she said. "You know Papá and the guys and how they guard us like we're part of their harem, like we're their prized horses or something. No, Yoli, they would've shot him first, then asked questions."

I knew she was right, so I didn't say anything more.

She was sobbing now, hunched over herself, holding on to her emptying uterus. I was holding the clear plastic bag with the sopping, bloody jeans, and now the bag itself was stained with blood. I would throw it in one of the big dumpsters out in the alley, I thought, trying to think clearly in that moment, hide it underneath all the other trash.

"I wanted the baby," she said. "God, how I wanted my bebito. . . ." Her black curls hung limply, sadly. For all the years I had thought of Ana María as some wild, untouchable gypsy woman, she now seemed like just a scared and confused sixteen-year-old, just a wobbly, fragile filly.

Ana María was still bleeding a lot, the toilet bowl was maroon red with tissue and gobs of stuff, but she felt the bleeding was less and she could get a pad on and lie down to rest.

Limping along at her side, holding her arm, I guided her to the bottom bunk bed, and she weakly slid in. Then I hobbled quickly to the kitchen and opened up a can of soup. My hands were trembling and it seemed to take forever to get the damn can open. I got a glass of water and a couple of aspirin. While the soup was heating on the stove, I looked out the front window.

It was dusk now, the sharp, clear November sky beginning to turn purple, and I knew that the family would probably get back just after dark, after having dinner at the bazaar—tacos de carne asada, a rich, red pozole, tamales de puerco, agua de jamaica y tamarindo, a glass of horchata. For a moment I imagined I was with them, walking with my sisters and listening to them comment on the cute "mangos," biting into a sugar and cinnamon-coated churro, deep-fried and oh so yummy; playing a couple of rounds of lotería as the Caller called out the cards, reminding us that the moon—"la luna, el farol de los enamorados"—was the lovers' lantern, the Caller taunting the players with "El Diablito"—"do we have a little devil in the crowd?"—eyeing my sister Carolina suspiciously, flirtatiously. How I wanted to be at the church bazaar with all of them—with Ana María and Chuy and all the rest, obliterate this moment, wake up and realize it was just a nightmare. But I needed to stay focused. The soup was now boiling.

With the bowl in my hands, I walked slowly to the bedroom, my hands shaking slightly. I set the plate on the dresser while I propped up the pillows so Ana Maria could lean against them and comfortably have her soup in bed.

She was shivering.

"Are you cold, Ana?" I said. "Here, get under the covers. Come on, mi'ja, move over so I can undo the bed."

She seemed to be in shock or something and could barely lean to the side as I pulled the covers off and then over her. She was still shivering and unable to look at me. Instead, she fixed her eyes on the window. I went back to the dresser and brought her the bowl of warm soup. The bedspread was a design of bulging maroon and purple roses on their thorny stems. Seeing Ana María lying against this dramatic floral backdrop, it seemed to me my once gypsy sister—wild, savvy, indomitable—was just one more fragile blossom, withering and fading quickly.

—23

The dry desert winds swept into San Diego one night in early November, the day after the church bazaar, the day after Ana María's "incident." That's what I was going to call it if ever I mentioned it again, although I swore to her and the Father, Son, and Holy Spirit that I wouldn't mention it again. Erased from my memory, I told myself. But I kept seeing the red-purple jeans in a heap next to the toilet, kept looking at Ana María's own helpless, pale face ready for the other world.

But my chicken noodle soup must've helped her because within minutes after eating it, she had curled up in a secure fetal position under the blankets and fell into a deep sleep. I was afraid she might suddenly go into convulsions or, worse, die in her sleep, so I sat at the foot of the bed and kept watch over her.

What had it been like, I wondered. I knew nothing about abortions, only that they were not allowed by the Catholic religion—my religion, Ana María's religion, and that now she would surely burn in hell for having killed a baby. I'd heard expressions in news magazines, expressions like "back street abortions," "alley abortions," but because this world of unwanted pregnancies had little to do with me and my family, I hadn't given it much thought. The thing I didn't understand was that Ana María and Tito seemed to really love each other, so maybe they could've made it a go. But Ana María's words, her explanation for doing this, made me understand that stronger than her love for Tito and a love child was her fear of our father and brothers. I wasn't sure why this thought made me angry, but it did. I thought about our family's living arrangements, the complete privacy granted my brothers in their bedroom, while we five sisters had to share a hallway-like bedroom that afforded little privacy. The feeling of being trampled, violated. Was Ana María entirely to blame for what she had done, or was it the abortionist who had sinned? Or was it the fear instilled in her by our father and brothers that led Ana María to such a desperate act in some deadly, dangerous back street?

So the desert wind lit upon us with a vengeance, and I embraced it with morbid glee. At school, it seemed as if everyone was in slow motion: slow motion walk to our lockers, slow in getting out our textbooks, notebook binders, chewing gum packs, leftover Halloween candy. Who could concentrate on Algebra or World History when our bodies were in a sweet state of lethargy, trying to carve out our own style of history?

It seemed we students were only interested in getting through the day with as little academic concentration as possible and as much gossip as our ears could absorb.

I usually sat in the lunch compound with some friend or other, now that Lydia and I were no longer buddies. Eating a bologna sandwich, a banana, potato chips, sipping milk from the standard school mini-size carton, I half-listened to Rita yak away about nothing. It didn't seem important to me anymore whether Marisela was angry at Robert because she saw him flirting with Laurie after school by the basketball courts. Was Marisela going to break up with Robert? Who cared, I thought to myself. All of it seemed trivial and childish. There was a larger world out there, and Southwest Junior High was just a tiny pimple on this great cratered, crusty face called Earth. Now Rita was saying that she hoped Marisela would tell him off and break up with him because then she would try for him.

"Rita," I said. "Did I just hear you say you'd try for that two-timing Robert? You want him to do the same to you?"

"It's Marisela's fault, you know," Rita said. "She doesn't know how to take care of her man. He wouldn't be messing around with anyone else if she was satisfying him." She wasn't real bright, this one, but I was starting to get hard up for friends to sit with during lunch since most of my close friends were in the other lunch period. Except for Lydia, but she probably hated my guts because of that scare I gave her over in the cemetery. Oh well, Rita would have to do.

"Man, Rita," I said. "Aren't you learning anything from this Women's Liberation Movement? Why is it always the woman's fault?

"Oh, so now you're the big defender of women, huh?" Rita said. No, she wasn't bright, this one, but she had some bite to her. "Hey, I know how to catch a man *and* keep him, too," she said. "Don't forget about Ernesto. I had him eating out of the palm of my hand, the poor pendejo. Finally felt sorry for the damn fool, and let him go." She started laughing.

How come I had never noticed Rita's packed on make-up and spidery, false eyelashes? How could I have been this desperate?

I looked around and saw Lydia sitting at a table directly across from me at the other side of the compound. Lydia had been cheering me on about Francisco, had advised me, like Ana María, to go slow and pay attention to his rhythms.

"Don't play games with the guy the way Rita does," Lydia had advised me back in September, before Halloween came around, before the cemetery incident. "Be clever, but don't be shrewd and too calculating."

That was damn good advice.

Here I was listening to Rita brag about the games she played with her men, how she caught the guy, as if he were on the ledge of some high rise building and about to jump, and— lo and behold!—there was Rita, ready to catch him, save the poor pendejo.

I say let him jump. I wouldn't catch him.

"See, get them on the rebound," she was saying. "They're all sad and llorones and you stroke their egos so good, they don't know if you're stroking their egos or the other thing, man, it feels so good to them."

"You know, Rita," I said, putting my half-eaten banana back in the lunch bag. "You can be pretty gross sometimes."

"Ay, tú," she said. "What's bugging you? Getting all righteous on me, defending women and all. This is a Man's World, esa, and you got to know how to play their game. Besides, this Women's Liberation is for the birds, just a bunch of crap that's gonna do us in. I don't want to have to pay on a date. And I don't know about you, Miss Woman-Libber-of-the-Month, but I like it when a man opens the door for me. Shit," she said, now chuckling. "I want the pendejo to treat me like a queen, esa, because that's what we are: princesses to our fathers and queens to our men. Besides," she said, "this Women's Liberation Movement is just for Lesbos, man, backed by a bunch of dykes. Didn't you see the picture in the newspaper of that Women's Rally? A bunch of marimachas is what they are. No thanks," she said, now looking in her purse for her compact mirror. "I like things just the way they are, so I don't know what your problem is."

I was so tempted to slap her, to pound some sense into her. No wonder this was a Man's World. With idiotas like her, we women would never get very far, never be able to make fearless decisions for ourselves.

That's when Francisco Valdivia and his friends walked into the compound, and my heart skipped a beat or two, my face red and unprepared for this encounter.

"Hi Yolanda," he said. His friends just checked me out, but kept a respectful silence. They had learned their lesson, I figured.

"Hi," I said.

They walked over to another table.

When they were out of hearing distance, Rita laughed at me. "Man, Yolanda, you're an open book. Why don't you do something with him? Get him out of your system, pobrecita."

"What are you talking about?" I asked.

"Hey, don't get huffy with me," she said. "Everyone knows you've got the hots for Francisco."

"What do you mean 'everyone knows'?"

"Shit, the whole school knows," Rita said, laughing at me.

I felt the urge to rip those spidery things off her lashes and then slug the crimson red lipstick smirk off her face.

"Nobody teases you or even lets on about your big crush on Francisco because of what you and your family must be going through with your brother and stuff," she said. "That's probably the only reason why Francisco even bothers to say 'hi' to you; he probably feels sorry for you, too."

For a moment I saw black, then red, a sharp white blitzed my vision, and I didn't know whether to punch Rita first or just run out of the compound, bawling. But in the moment it took me to gather myself, the bell rang, signaling lunch was over, and now Francisco Valdivia was standing in front of me and asking me if I'd meet him after school at our lockers. Around three or so.

I nodded at him, still too angry at Rita to have his invitation register.

Rita and I watched as he walked away from the lunch compound. I was stunned, but she looked impressed. "Shit, maybe I was wrong," she said. "Suerte, eh?" and she crossed her fingers for me.

I looked over at Lydia who was talking with Concha. How I wished in that moment Lydia and I could be friends again. Man, did I ever need her advice. How was I going to act in front of Francisco? What was I going to say to the love of my life? Damn, I'd never spoken more than three words to him in all the time I'd known him, in all the time he'd been in my most romantic dreams, his name forever gracing the pages of my diary these last few years. But then the horrible, tormenting questions: Was he just being nice because he felt sorry for me, Yolanda Sahagún, sister of the famous local outlaw? Was Rita right—did all of Southwest Junior High know I was in love with Francisco—including Francisco? Would he take advantage of me? Was he mocking me?

Just about everyone had cleared out of the lunch compound, except for me and a few others.

I noticed Lydia glance my way, and maybe it was my imagination or something, but she looked sad and regretful, as if maybe she missed me, too.

The winds had picked up by the end of last period. Leaves and broken dry palm fronds scratched the pavement. We students looked out the windows, anxious to be out of our cells and into the open. I was certain the desert winds had picked up on cue for me: I was about to meet up with Francisco Valdivia, my love and my life; it was only fitting that the desert winds would appropriately sweep onto the scene and heighten the melodrama of my first meeting with my true love.

I ran to the girls' bathroom fifteen minutes before sixth period let out. I checked myself out in the mirror: my pimples were behaving, pretty much out of sight for the time being. Now I checked my teeth for stuff wedged between them. The bit of mascara I had on still looked fresh, and, thinking of Rita and what she looked like, I decided against lipstick. I was wearing jeans. Now that Southwest Junior High allowed us to wear pants, almost every girl at school wore them most of the time. My pink, baby doll blouse gave my complexion a soft, rosy hue. Not too shabby, Miss Yolanda Sahagún, I said to my reflection. Not too shabby. Of course, these were the outer trappings, just the frame of the picture. The real question was what was within the frame. Of what did the painting consist? What was I like inside? And what did others think of me, like

Rita, Francisco and Lydia? If Rita was right and everyone knew I was in love with Francisco, did they think I was a fool? And what did Lydia think of me? Did she think I was an immature, crazy girl? I had a lot of friends, yes. But still. What did these people really think of me? Was I the town fool, a Shakespearean jester, *Hamlet's* Yorick, perhaps? Or did I have some value as a person, as a woman, in the larger scheme of things? Should I join the next Women's Movement rally, or be content to be ignorant and stupid like Rita, playing the game according to men's rules? Was I being hypocritical: wanting freedom of choice and opportunities, not wanting to be treated like a second-class citizen, yet here I was in the girls' bathroom, primping and preening for a guy. Who was Yolanda Sahagún?

Just then three girls came barging into the bathroom. I quickly turned on the faucet, absent-mindedly washing my hands as their high-pitched voices reached never-ending crescendos. I dried my hands with a paper towel and walked out to my world of Junior High.

The locker hall was noisy with the sound of metal doors banging shut, laughter, shouts, whistles, the school bus engines revving up and grumbling to get going and deposit wild, unruly junior high kids to their homes.

"Let's go over by the auditorium, OK?" Francisco asked me.

I nodded. Good, this would give me a little time to gather myself, take a few deep breaths and compose myself. Be cool, Yolanda, be cool.

There was a grassy area out front by the steps leading to our auditorium and a bushy pepper tree with about a hundred gnarled knots on its trunk. Like the nervous knots in my stomach?

We sat under the tree.

"Yolanda," he said right off. "I wanted to know if you would go steady with me."

I could tell you that his eyes were black and so was his hair. I could tell you that he stood about a head taller than me, had an easiness to his stride—not quite the pachuco, tough-guy stride, but sexy enough to make me weak-kneed. What I couldn't tell you is how my feelings and emotions miraculously rose to the occasion. How I, Yolanda Sahagún, danced in step with him; the pauses in our conversation were natural and easy, the beat of my heart kept pace with his, the twinkle in his eyes matched mine, and the perennial smile on our faces made us seem as if we were drunk-happy. No one could tell me this wasn't love, no one could mock my hopeful, fourteen-year-old heart. But say what they wanted to say, I didn't care; I was in the world of love-believers and, for me, there was no going back.

In the distance, on someone's front porch, I heard a wind-chime singing.

"Are you feeling sorry for me like everyone else?" I asked. "Because of Chuy and all?"

"No," he said.

"Because if you are, I don't need your pity or anyone else's," I said. "Everyone thinks we're hiding him or something, and it's not true."

"I know it isn't," he said.

My hair was getting in my face, the wind picking up speed.

"How do you know it's not true?" I asked, brushing it back.

"Because I was talking to Lydia about you."

"Why were you talking to Lydia about me?"

"I wanted to know if she thought you would go around with me," he said.

"Oh, yeah?" I said. "And what did she say?"

"She said 'maybe, maybe not,' but that if you did say 'yes' I better not hurt you or she'd personally kick my butt. She said you had enough things to worry about not knowing anything about Chuy and so you didn't need some 'cabrón'—her word, not mine," he said, laughing, "yeah, she said you didn't need some cabrón hurting you along with everything else."

"When did she say that?" I asked. "When did you talk to her?"

"Yesterday," he said.

"Oh," I said.

"So will you?" he asked.

"Is it true everyone at school knows I like you?" I asked.

"I don't know about that," he said, laughing. "What I know is I'm good at hiding my feelings from everyone so they don't figure out that I like you."

And so there it was: the object of my desire standing before me and in some way or other proclaiming his love for me, and Lydia—ahh, Lydia—my most wonderful, dear friend, ready to kick his butt if the cabrón hurt me. I wondered how far I could fly.

—24

"Your mother and I followed the road of the Caballo Blanco, all the way from Guadalajara to Tijuana, including Ensenada, same as the horse," Papá was saying as he carved the turkey. He was wearing his charro suit, easily over a hundred years old judging from the fading black wool, the slightly tarnished buttons running the length of the pants. The bolero style jacket was frayed and the white trim was yellowing—too many dry cleanings or just plain too old. Dressed in his outfit of days gone by, Papa looked like a cross between a bullfighter and a square-dancer. He was proud of his charro suit, proud he could still get into it.

"What white horse, Papi?" Monica asked, madly in love with horses.

Papá knew this, of course, and counted on at least Monica to be a captivated audience as he sang for the umpteenth time the Mexican ballad of the white horse.

"Ay, mi'ja, how can you so quickly forget the Corrido del

Caballo Blanco?" he said has he poked the serving fork into a delicious dark thigh. Shaking his head, now pausing with fork and thigh in mid air, he shook his head, feigning exasperation, although we knew he was proud of Monica's prompting.

All of us brothers and sisters—including Papa's clever little sidekick Monica—knew the ballad by heart, and only Monica pretended she forgot the corrido so that Papá would sing it again. The rest of us dared not groan out loud or protest in any little way because Papá made it a point of timing the singing of the ballad with carving the turkey, doling out pieces to his listeners—his hungry, captive audience. God forbid, any one of us children should protest—"Ay, Papá, not again! Can't we just have a peaceful all-American Thanksgiving without the white horse galloping in from Jalisco?"—and next thing you know, the complainer's favorite piece of turkey would be given to one of the more attentive, respectful listeners.

Every Thanksgiving, then, Papá sang the ballad of the white horse, a Sahagún family tradition as familiar and expected as the roasted turkey, cranberry sauce, mashed potatoes and gravy, baked glazed yams, and charro suit. Something about celebrating this holiday made our father nostalgic for Mexico, so he chose this American holiday every year to sing the ballad of the white horse who travels the long, arduous route from Guadalajara all the way north to Tijuana.

But this Thanksgiving there was even more reason to recount the ballad with grand pomp and circumstance:

Carolina's Tom was our guest.

"Papi, did the white horse have a name?" Luz asked.

"I suppose he must have, but it's not mentioned in the corrido. Perhaps it wasn't important. Perhaps he was just one of many horses to follow that road."

"Was the horse a kind of Everyhorse?" I asked.

"What?" Luz and Monica said, giggling at me.

"Kind of like an Everyman, but only an Everyhorse," I insisted.

Carolina gave me a cut-the-shit look but she didn't say anything since her honeycito was sitting right next to her and she didn't want to come off seeming like a bitch too soon in their relationship.

Tom smiled and Papá finally plopped the drumstick on my plate, probably hoping to keep me quiet and occupied with my food. Hallelujah, some meat, at last!

The dinner table was made up of four six-foot cafeteria tables we had borrowed from St. Charles Church for just this occasion, and set in a long row. It was rare that we ate all at the same time, but Thanksgiving was one of those rare days. This year, Carolina made sure that the long, skinny twenty-four-foot "table" looked as elegant as possible, almost looked like a traditional American Thanksgiving table right out of *Good Housekeeping*. She bought four white tablecloths that were on sale at K-Mart, and made three harvest-themed centerpieces of miniature colored corn and squash and pomegranate, maple leaves, and a couple of pines, these doodads centered along the length of the tables. I was impressed. I hadn't thought Carolina had artistic, domestic tendencies under all that psychoanalyzing she did in the family. She even bought cloth napkins for just this occasion and was very particular about how the forks and knives—"silver" she called it, though it was only stainless steel—were set. When I offered to bundle and tie the "silverware" and pristine cloth napkins, she didn't even deign to answer me, and instead looked up to the heavens and shook her head, as if asking God for a little bit of patience with the barbaric members of her family.

While he was passing out the wings to Tony and the other drumstick to Ana María, knowing exactly who liked the dark, who the white meat, el Señor Lorenzo Sahagún cleared his throat ceremoniously and, with much pomp and circumstance, once again sang the ballad of the white horse.

Papá seemed to be singing better than usual this time around, more gruffly dramatic, I supposed, for our guest's benefit. This was what I imagined was really going on: a duel was being played out by father and daughter's lover. If Tom could put up with this kind of Sahagún weirdness, then fine, perhaps he could marry Carolina. I was convinced Papá was putting him through a test. Then Tom would be challenged to sing an American folk song—say, "She'll Be Comin' Round the Mountain." The wager: if Papá sang better he would keep his daughter, and if Tom sang better he could have Carolina.

The duel was about to begin.

Just as the White Horse was beginning his trek, leaving Guadalajara and crossing into Nayarit with its green hills and blue sky, the phone rang. Octavio, Ana María, and I simultaneously jumped up to get it, as if we were expecting a call from The Millionaire Man who was about to hand us the million-dollar check. Papá ignored the phone, ignored us three as we ran to get it. He didn't miss a beat now that the White Horse was nearing Culiacán.

Octavio got it first, and Ana María and I stood next to him, listening. "Yeah she's here," he said. "No, you can't," and he hung up. My first thought was that it was Francisco calling me to wish me a happy Thanksgiving. Even though he knew that he shouldn't call the house, especially when Papá might be around, still I thought that was very courageous and romantic of him. I turned to Octavio, angry that he hadn't let me talk to my love, and was about to say something when he said to Ana, "It was for you." He gave her a mean I'm-warning-you look, but Ana María didn't say anything. Just looked him straight in the eye and stood her ground.

"Let's go to the kitchen," he directed Ana. "I need to talk to you."

The kitchen was a ways off, a door separating it from the living room. The Caballo Blanco was just passing through the valley of the Yaqui as Octavio, Ana, and I slipped into the kitchen.

"Not you," he said to me, as he was about to close the kitchen door. "I want to talk with Ana alone."

"What about, big brother?" I asked. "About her and Tito? You gonna tell her she shouldn't be seeing him? He's too old for her, too experienced in the way of seducing women? Is that what you're gonna tell her?"

"Yoli, this isn't any of your business," he said. "So just go back out."

"Oh, but it *is* my business," I said, my voice angry, sarcastic. "Why don't you take this moment to give me some advice as well, loving big brother? Why don't you tell me, too, about the dangers of dating a guy who knows how to seduce a woman, get her into his bedroom, and de-virginize her?"

"What are you talking about?" he said.

"Maybe he'll say something like 'I want to make love to you and take care of you, teach you how to enjoy it,'" I said. "Reassure her, loving big brother, that she's gonna fly high with him."

At first it seemed as if Octavio was going to slug me. But instead my brother studied me, uncertain. He looked pale, shaken by my words.

Ana stared from one to the other of us, confused as to what was going on, or maybe not confused.

"What does it mean, Octavio?" I asked. "Is it your lifelong brotherly mission to keep your sisters virgencitas, meanwhile trying to de-virginize every woman that comes your way and make sluts out of your girlfriends? What's all that shit about?"

"Yoli, you don't understand," he said.

"What don't I understand, big brother?" I asked. "That your sisters are supposed to be virgins and your girlfriends are supposed to be whores? Do you think Carolina's been Tom's whore all this time they've been together?"

"Yoli," he said. "You don't know shit."

"Yeah," I said, nodding, "maybe you're right. Maybe I don't know shit, but I can't help asking myself, hermano, why shouldn't Tito and Tom, Dick and Harry think like you, try to get a piece of ass any chance they can? Pop someone's cherry and promise her she's gonna fly high with him. Why should the next guy be any different from you, Octavio?"

He made as if he was going to slap me, but Ana must have known what was coming. She grabbed his arm before he could strike me.

"Leave her the fuck alone," she said to Octavio, staring at him hard and determined. "Leave all women the fuck alone unless you're going to treat them with respect—the way you'd like to have your sisters be treated."

Octavio looked visibly shaken, shocked. He stared from one sister to the other, speechless.

Ana María and I turned and walked out into the living room together.

In the meantime the White Horse had already passed through Mexicali, feeling as if it were going to die, but pushing itself through the treacherous Rumorosa, finally arriving at Tijuana in the light of day. The deed completed, it decided to continue the trek to Rosarito, not giving up until it had reached Ensenada. I looked at all the people at the table, at my brothers and sisters, Mamá and Papá and Tom, at Octavio who was just getting back to his seat at the other end of the table, stone-quiet with his head bowed—thoughtful? repentant? I wondered. And I thought, how I loved all of these people and wanted them, us, to do the right thing, if only, now glancing at Octavio, we could agree on what was the right thing. El Caballo Blanco, heading out one Sunday from Guadalajara, had now reached its destination, exhausted and spent. What a journey that had been, I thought, feeling oddly exhilarated.

After dinner and pumpkin pies with whipped cream lathered on top, we were asked to leave the living room while Carolina and Tom, Mamá and Papá talked. We sisters scrambled out, all right, to wherever we could get a good view and listening spot for the action about to take place in the living room.

The four of them—Mamá, Papá, Carolina, and Tom—were sitting in the living room while Monica and Luz stood huddled against the bedroom doorway trying to listen in. Ana María and I had gone outside and stood under the living room window, taking turns peeking in. The sofa where Mamá and Papá were sitting was next to our window.

Carolina and Tom announced their plans to get married next April and, miracle of miracles, Papá actually gave his consent. But it wasn't that easy. God forbid Papá should be simple and direct and leave it at that. No, for the first daughter to get married, he wasn't just about to merely nod his head and say, "Yes, well, yes, I give my permission." No, Lorenzo Sahagún took the opportunity to wax philosophical and offer much unsolicited marital advice for good measure.

"First off, you need to know, Tomás," Papá began, "that the woman is always in charge—on top of and under the blankets."

"Lorenzo, por favor," Mamá said.

"No sense in beating around the bush, Dolores," he said. "That's the way it is."

Ana María and I started giggling, uncontrollable gasps of laughter we tried hard to suppress. "He's Polonius," I whispered to Ana María between fits of giggles.

"Who?" Ana María said.

"Polonius, *Hamlet's* Polonius."

Yes, indeed, Papá had now become good ol' Polonius, the pompously bumbling fool in *Hamlet*. Like Polonius, Papá wasted no time in dishing out a litany of unsolicited advice and dichos on marriage: Entre marido y mujer, nadie se debe meter. No one should meddle in the affairs between husband and wife, he said to his oldest daughter and his future son-in-law.

Then Mamá spoke: "Don't have children too soon," she said. "Wait a while."

Papá looked at her, surprised. "Why wait, Dolores?" he asked. "Let them have children immediately. Caramba, I want grandchildren right away."

"Which reminds me," Papá continued, "a good thing to keep in mind when finding a place to live: Do not live too near either set of in-laws, although it is quite appropriate to live nearer your wife's family than the husband's."

Carolina and Tom dared not say a word. They seemed to be holding their breaths.

Then turning to his wife: "But why not children immediately, Dolores?" Papá said. "We had Armando immediately, followed eleven months later by Octavio. See," he said now turning to Carolina and Tom, who listened quietly and attentively on the orange vinyl love seat, probably just wanting to somehow get through this session without making waves. "See, this way you get them out of the way, see them all grown up—hechos y derechos—and you still have some life left in you, like your mom and me here, eh Dolores?"

Mamá didn't say a word.

Children all grown up, well raised and on their way, was that what Papá had just said?

Why had Mamá advised them to wait on children? Did she regret having so many children of her own? Did she regret having children at all? The idea of Mamá regretting having us made me feel sad, scared. Was there a whole world of parents and children I knew nothing about? Aside from Chuy, had we children given her grief? Is that why she was now advising her daughter to take her time in having children? Was there something big and significant behind her advice? I recalled the time she defended Chuy for taking off on a motorcycle, the way she defended him against Socorrito's criticism. "Do you know how many times I've dreamed of just getting up and going?" she had said to Socorrito. "Leaving all my kids behind and just hopping on a motorcycle of my own. . . ." At the time she had said this to Socorrito, months ago, I had felt pleased—yes, even proud of my mother. She was, after all, defending Chuy. But now, listening to her advice to Carolina about waiting on having children, I wondered if she really had felt like hopping on a motorcycle and leaving us kids behind—I wondered if she really might still. It seemed to me I had a lot to learn about Mamá and Papá, their lives as husband and wife, as father and mother. There was a whole other dimension to Mamá, I thought sadly, that I could not yet know.

Her silence seemed to disorient Papá, and he forgot what he was advising "Tomás" and Carolina.

"Well, anyway," he said, getting up from the green velvet armchair and shaking hands with Tom. He glanced uneasily at Dolores, who remained quiet, too quiet. "I've got things to do," he said. "No sense in wasting time with idle chitchat."

And he was out the door.

Luckily, Mamá had Carolina's wedding preparations to keep her from thinking about Chuy. It was the respite we all needed. The earth seemed to be revolving again.

Luz and Monica were delirious over the fact that they were going to be junior bridesmaids; Ana María and I would be regular bridesmaids. Armando, Octavio, and Tony would be ushers. It was just November, and the wedding wasn't until April, but we were too excited not to plan immediately. I sensed, too, we needed something to get us moving, something not to remind us of Chuy's disappearance.

During breakfast, lunch, and dinner, during car rides to church and the stores and market, on our way to catechism and school, the talk was of invitations, guest lists, bouquets, bride's dress, appliqués and taffeta, bridesmaid dresses, ring bearer, waxed azahares made by cousins in Guadalajara, the bride's headpiece, and wedding colors.

"Pink," said Monica.

"No," said Luz, "aqua blue and yellow."

"How about purple with black stripes?" I said.

My little sisters ignored me; they were getting too wise for their own good.

"Don't forget Chuy," Luz told Carolina. "He's going to be an usher too, isn't he?"

"Oh mi'ja," Carolina said, brushing Luz's hair away from her face. "Yes, of course, if he returns by then."

If he returns, Carolina said, as if there were any doubt. Four weeks had passed since the hide-and-seek incident, and meanwhile, I delivered the bag of canned goods to the shed, buying the cans with the money I'd saved from cleaning the guys' room, always adding an extra goodie—an Almond Joy, Bazooka Joe gum, Snickers, something sweet. I was tempted to leave him a note in the bag, asking him when he was coming for me, but I didn't think it was a safe thing to do, just in case somebody got to the bag before Chuy did. Incriminating evidence. And every day, when it seemed safe, I'd sneak into my brothers' room and check the box, hoping to find another note from Chuy. But there was none.

I knew he'd be back, though. God, he *had* to come back for me. He was biding his time, that's all. Waiting for things to calm down, waiting for the neighborhood to calm down. Absence would mend the hurt, he must have reasoned, make everyone more forgiving and contemplative.

While I waited for him, I was happy to be occupied with thoughts of my new boyfriend and with plans for Carolina's wedding. Even though the wedding wasn't until the spring—"Oh, yes, a spring wedding is so romantic," we sisters approved, sighing dreamily—it was never too soon to start making arrangements. Spring was just around the corner.

Only Ana María didn't seem genuinely excited about the wedding. Since her incident, she had become a pale reflection of herself, no longer sassy and daring. She was more inward and quiet.

"What's with Ana?" Carolina had recently asked me. "She's been pretty quiet and seems to follow you like your shadow."

It was true. Since that day, she always offered to go with me to the store, the market. She listened for hours on end to my yakking away about Francisco, and only when I asked her for boyfriend advice did she liven up and offer wise counsel. And Tito?

She didn't want to talk about Tito right now or any time soon, it seemed. "We're taking some time off from each other," was all she shared.

My life was in full swing now that Francisco and I were going around. My younger sisters knew about him but were sworn to secrecy. "You keep this from Mamá and Papá and our brothers, and when it's your turn," I said to Luz and Monica, "I'll do the same for you." Ana and Carolina didn't have to swear, since I had already proven my loyalty and discretion to them.

And what did this "going around" consist of? It meant we had lunch together a few times a week in the lunch compound, and it meant he would walk me halfway home after school.

"Just walk me up to Hollister Street," I told him on our first going-around day, "because once we get to Citrus and Conifer streets there's just a bola de chismosas—gossipy old biddies—all over the place."

Francisco laughed. "OK," he said.

Now that I had a boyfriend, it did seem that overnight the world had filled with gossipy people, spies lurking behind every telephone pole and tree trunk. If Papá and Mamá knew I had a boyfriend, they would surely send me straight away to the convent in El Grullo for the rest of my life. I was being extra cautious.

Since Ana María was my most trustworthy advisor, I listened carefully to her advice. I wasn't letting Francisco hold hands with me yet. Ana had advised me to go slow, *real* slow. I couldn't help wondering if she would have given me the same advice if the incident hadn't occurred.

But I wasn't going to pretend that I didn't want to hold hands with him. I wanted more, so much more, and only my diary knew this for sure. I wanted him to hold my hand, then caress my arm, moving up and down and everywhere. I wanted the ecstasy of heaving and breathing and sweating. And so I thought to myself, slow down Yolanda, whoa, easy does it. All in due time, mujer. Because Francisco was my true love, of that I was certain. And I had the feeling he felt pretty much the same about me.

This is what I was thinking as I sat in the canyon, ready to spill my passion onto the pages of my diary. It was one of those brilliant November days—bright and dry and windy. I had a bad case of cramps and this month my period was heavy and clotty. I was sitting on the wooden steps, pen in hand and ready to confess my sexual longings to Dear Diary, when I got the first whiff of smoke. The sky was bright blue, clear and clean, but the smell of smoke meant that somewhere, probably in east San Diego, in the back country, there was a brush fire going on. We southern Californians were used to them: the Santa Ana desert winds, followed by brush fires, a kind of "season" of its own, only this season seemed to start out later than usual. It was already the end of November.

I wrote down my thoughts quickly. The cramps were hurting too much for me to do my usual Saturday daydreaming in the canyon. My pondering and fantasizing would have to wait. I hadn't written in my diary all week so this was catch-up time, and now that I had a boyfriend—had I already mentioned this?—there was much to write in my diary.

About half an hour later, when I looked up again from my mad writing, the day was dark. The blue of the sky had been wiped away and in a matter of thirty minutes or less, the heavens had turned ashen gray with smoke.

I jotted down one last finishing line in my diary: *"I pray that my love for Francisco will grow in wonderful ways, Dear Diary. Francisco, my love and my life, my dear, dear boyfriend. . . ."* I finished with a drawing of a little heart at the end of the sentence, for good measure. As I put my pen away and was about to close my notebook, a flake of ash drifted my way and landed on the page.

25

The newscasters were predicting that this was going to be the worst fire season on record in San Diego. East San Diego County was fast being consumed by flames, houses and vegetation wiped out in seconds. The skies were swollen with smoke, and every day the San Diego newspaper headlines and TV broadcasts detailed some new devastation and horrific scene. We were mesmerized by the live, on-location shots of blackened and crumbled homes. The fires and desert winds seemed to sound an apocalyptic warning.

Who could sleep at night, who could talk lightly and laugh and joke? The world—our world—spoke of nothing but the fires, the blistered sky, the suffocation. December had arrived, but even the Christmas decorations and carols at the markets and stores seemed a cruel joke. Insulting. Who could imagine joy to the world, silent nights, the jingle of jolly bells, and Santa Claus when we were in the midst of smoldering landscapes and ruin? San Diego had become a wasteland in December, and our wintry snowflakes were nothing more than flakes of ash.

The air felt mute and ragged, and a pall covered all of Palm City, all of San Diego and southern California. We held our breath and waited for this to pass, huddled near the TV for news that the worst was over, that the fires had been contained.

We waited to be told we could now dust off the ash on our cars and sweep our sidewalks and get back to the usual business of living. When would the moment come to pick up the blackened remains of our communal devastation? The fires, edging aggressively closer toward us, brought helicopters and small twin-engine planes to join in the battle against the flames. Churches and temples were full these days, and my family prayed the rosary every evening in the living room with a new fervor and a new anguish—where was our Chuy in all of this?

That evening, with the constant rumble of planes and helicopters overhead, feeling as if I were in the midst of a World War, I made my way down the canyon into the field, past collapsed barbed wire, the skeletal remains of a rusty car, a twisted bicycle, warped tires, and a tin can riddled with bullet holes. What drew me to the culvert under the freeway that evening, I don't know for sure. It was as if the ash and smoke, the heavy oppression itself, allowed me a new intuition, a heightened survival instinct. As when a death comes to your family, suddenly you see the world and your life with new eyes, you see something with a singular, momentary clarity. So I trudged on, stumbling over gopher holes, brushing against thorny tumbleweed. By the time I reached the culvert, the sun had disappeared beyond the blistered slice of the horizon. The desert winds had quieted. I was out of breath, feeling icy cold one minute then burning hot the next as I neared the tunnel's entrance.

When had I been here before—was it a few months ago? How old was I then—fourteen? And how old was I now as I once again entered the tunnel—fifty? sixty? Surely I could not still be fourteen! Back then it had seemed an adventure to go into the forbidden tunnel with Octavio and my sisters. It had been a spooky thrill, and for a moment I stood thinking I should just turn around and run home now, this very instant, not go in.

All this time I had been waiting for him to come to me, to take me away, not realizing, until now, it was *I* who had to go to him. I knew Chuy was there waiting for me.

I took a deep, uncertain breath and stumbled into the tunnel.

He was there. Chuy sat huddled in a heap in the middle of the culvert. It was too dark to see him clearly; I could only see the shadowy form of his person, his trembling bulk.

"Chuy, it's me," I called out to him in a weak whisper. "It's me, Chuy, Yoli."

Only the drone of the cars and the rumble of the fire fighting planes overhead could be heard.

The air felt brittle and callused.

I made my way into the rubble and stench, feeling deathly frightened and uncertain. What if it wasn't Chuy? What if it was an evil spirit drawing me in? Had I taken the wrong road—a road full of slime and muck and blackness that would taint me forever with its evilness?

"Hey, Chuy, it's me, Yoli," I whispered, as much to myself as to him. "Chuy, can you see me?"

When I reached him, I saw that his face was still smeared with the dried blood of weeks before, crusts of snot. All over, there was the smell of vomit and shit and rot.

"Fucking gooks, man, get the fucking gooks outta here," he was mumbling. He had his arms wrapped around himself as if he would unravel if he loosened his grip.

I shivered. My thin blouse and shorts suddenly felt skimpy, made me feel vulnerable and unprotected. I backed up, knelt down a few feet from him.

"Chuy," I said. "It's me, Yoli. I'm going to take care of you now, OK mi'jo?"

"Fucking gooks," he screamed. "Get the fuck away from me, you gook bitch. Shit in your face if you don't get the fuck away," he shouted, but he didn't make a move to untangle himself from his embrace.

"Chuy, please, mi'jo, it's me, Yoli." I edged closer to him in my kneeling position. The sharp gravel was digging at my bare knees, stinging me, but I didn't dare make a sudden move to get up, just inched my way closer. Slowly, very slowly.

Another fire helicopter could be heard, its rumble deafening; it sounded as if it were hovering just above our heads like some monster mosquito about to suck the blood out of us.

"Oh God, not another fucking gook!" he screamed, rocking himself back and forth. "Jesus Fucking Christ, Charlies all over the place, man."

"Mi'jo," I whispered. "It's me, Yoli. It's OK, Chuy,

really, it's OK. You're not over there anymore, mi'jo. You're at home, Chuy."

"Get away from me, bitch," he screamed, hiding his face in his crossed arms, not seeing me, not recognizing me. "You get any closer and I'll kill the fucking daylights outta you, you gook bitch!" He screamed the scream of a demented witch, a ghoul.

I froze.

His cries were wails of a ghostly past, a past I could not fathom. Not knowing exactly in words what his darkness was, I became enveloped in it; it wrapped itself around me and claimed me for its own.

I started trembling, my whole body shaking uncontrollably. Icy, blade-like air stung my face and my eyes, entered my bones. My whole body shook with such traitorous abandon that I couldn't breathe. The cars overhead sounded like waves crashing down on us, overtaking us. I felt as if I had plunged into black glacial waters, murky and slimy, and I was trying to come up for air, my lungs about to explode. Inside my head a thousand pieces of rusty metal were clanging, coming after me and laughing at me, mocking me. My whole being was reverberating, and I thought I could hear myself wince or whimper, a small cry being crushed by the grating noises in my head. I tried again to cry out, to get ahold of myself, to stop the violent trembling, but I couldn't, and I thought that if I hugged myself, I would be OK, but my body and my arms wouldn't move. I was drowning, drowning, and so I did the only thing I could think of to do in that moment of chaos and death: I came up behind Chuy and cautiously, slowly, wrapped my thin, trembling arms as best I could around his own trembling body, hugging my brother. I rested my head against his back, pretending we were on his motorcycle and that this was just one more wild ride. Immediately he stopped screaming and swearing and yes, now I was back up at the surface, reaching for air. I was breathing again, desperate gulps of air from somewhere and the clanging and screeching in my head had subsided.

"Mi'jo," I whispered to Chuy, "it's going to be all right now. Sí, mi'jo, shhhh. . . ."

He was sobbing in my arms now, his shoulders heaving, his whole body feeling shattered and defeated.

I tried rocking him in my arms, but my knees were stinging as the gravel and dirt dug in, and Chuy was too large for me to move and I didn't want to disturb his quiet.

From behind, I kissed him on his temple—salty, sweaty hot skin. I ran my fingers through his hair, smoothing down the coarse grimy strands, now gently massaging his head. His muffled sobs came from deep inside. I could feel his body's tremors, as if his every nerve was electrified, and then a long heave and shudder, as if he were slowly being extinguished. I stroked his forehead, grimy and sticky, now his cheeks. I smoothed his crusty eyebrows, then traced the bridge of his nose, dipping into the groove on his upper lip, which was wet with snot. I wiped it clean with my finger.

"Shhh, mi'jo," I whispered to my Chuy in the most soothing tone I could muster. "It's going to be OK, mi'jo." I kissed his temple again, feeling his rapid pulse.

"Hush, little baby, don't say a word," I recited in a singing whisper the only song I could think of in that moment. *"Papá's gonna buy you a mockingbird. . . ."*

He was now moaning in rhythmic waves, as might a disturbed child in his fretful sleep, in nightmares too dark and bloody for me to penetrate.

The reverberating roar of the freeway had subsided. The planes could be heard from a long distance, retreating, and the night was finally still. How long had we been in here? Ten minutes? Ten years? It felt as if our planet Earth had paused a moment in respectful silence for Chuy and me, and in the cold entrails of the concrete tunnel, then, my brother and I held on for dear life.

—26

"Before we begin the evening's celebration of Our Lady of Guadalupe," Father Stadler announced to the jam-packed congregation, "I would like for everyone to join us in a special prayer for the Sahagún family." He paused, head now bowed. "Let us pray that Our Lord will give the Sahagún family the strength needed to get through this difficult time, and let us say a special prayer that Chuy will soon be sitting here with us again. This we ask you through Christ, our Lord, Amen."

I could tell people were glancing over at us, at me. I looked straight ahead at the giant Crucifix, and all I could think of was, yes, please dear God, let Chuy be my old Chuy again and be let out of the VA hospital and back to us. That was where he was now, in the Veteran's Hospital, and we were assured by the VA that they were taking care of him, taking tests and giving him the proper medication. It seemed Chuy wasn't the only Vietnam vet that had come back that way, truly messed up.

That evening in the tunnel I had known I had to get help, I knew it the moment I saw him and put my arms around him. I would've wanted to take care of him myself, but when he didn't even recognize me, his favorite sister, I knew it was more than I could handle. So I had left him in the tunnel and run for home as though both our lives depended on it.

Mamá was sitting on the couch mending a pair of pants when I burst in on her.

"He's in the tunnel," I said to her, heaving and gulping for air. Then I started to cry, deep throaty sobs. I was probably stinking real bad, too, with the smell of the culvert and Chuy.

She quietly set her sewing things on the couch and got up and hugged me for a long time, without saying anything, smoothing my hair like I'd smoothed Chuy's.

"Sí, Corazón," she finally said. "Now we can all take care of him."

About five police cars arrived, and as soon as the police ran down into the culvert and got a look at the moaning heap that was Chuy, they radioed for more backup and an ambulance.

He surrendered himself without a struggle. The whole world was out there standing at the edge of the canyon where the Kastlunger field began, watching as the police led Chuy, handcuffed, back up to Conifer Street. We parted a path for him, people on both sides. He didn't look up, his head hanging, staring down at his bare feet, mumbling something incoherent to himself. I was glad Mamá had held me then, her arm around me, protecting me, because if she hadn't, I might've run up to Chuy and pulled him from the police. "Hurry, Chuy, let's do it. Let's get the hell outta here. Quick, your chopper's just over there. . . ." Instead, I said a Hail Mary.

■ ■ ■ ■ ■

Prayer and the Virgin of Guadalupe had become my family's salve—or maybe it always had been, and I hadn't realized it until now. Neither rain nor snow, fires nor earthquakes could keep us from celebrating the novena for Our Lady of Guadalupe. The fires had died down, our world now a blanket of ashes from under which we were slowly coming out. We had resumed our usual business of living. St. Charles

Church was packed with more devotees than I'd ever seen on twelfth of Decembers past. Even el loco Raimundo, the hippie pachuco from Citrus Street, Palm City's notorious atheist—who for years tried to get the neighborhood to see that the Virgen de Guadalupe story was just a tactic on the part of the Catholic Church to convert the Mexican Indians; who for years claimed that the Church invented the dark-skinned, Indian-looking Virgin of Guadalupe who appeared to the humble Indian Juan Diego; who said the story was invented to convert and pacify the Indian masses and make good, submissive, oppressed Indian subjects for the Catholic Church—yes, even el loco hippie pachuco Raimundo showed up wearing a tie with his Pendleton jacket to pay homage to Our Lady. His appearance would have been the talk of the night were it not for the fact that there were so many new faces jam-packed in the church that December twelfth evening. We regulars were turning our heads every which way with wonder as we spotted another convert, singing in clear robust voices:

Juan Dieguito, la Virgen le dijo,
Juan Dieguito, la Virgen le dijo:
Este cerro elijo, este cerro elijo
Este cerro elijo para ser mi altar.

I sang with gusto all the while looking this way and that.

It was difficult to concentrate on the Hail Marys and Our Fathers, what with the fun commotion of new faces in church. Luckily, I could recite the prayers backward if I had to. After praying the rosary and singing the songs about the story of Our Lady and how she appeared to Juan Dieguito, the priest conducted mass.

I spotted Lydia a few pews down sitting with her family. She looked my way at the same time, and we quickly looked away, back at the altar, pretending to be concentrating on Mass.

After mass, we all piled into the hall for the potluck banquet. Red, white and green tissue paper cuts hung the length of the hall, looking like festive articles of clothing on a clothesline. Pots of poinsettia graced each banquet table amidst the food. I saw Lydia talking to her brother, her brother laughing at something she was saying. Lydia could be pretty funny sometimes, I remembered. We still hadn't spoken to each other since the cemetery thing, almost two months before, and I missed her so much and wanted to be her best friend again, but I didn't think she'd want to have anything to do with me. Yeah, she'd put in a good word for me with Francisco, but it didn't mean she missed me. I didn't have the courage to approach her and risk being rejected.

There was so much to eat and choose from, I didn't know where to go first—should I have the sweet tamales, just in case they ran out before I got to them, or should I have some tacos de carne asada, or the pozole? The salads looked yummy, too, but those probably wouldn't run out so I could take my time on them. I couldn't make up my mind, and while everyone was already in line at their favorite food, the hubbub of laughter and hugs and music in the distance, I stood in the middle of the hall just looking like a boba.

"Go for the tamales first," Lydia said, now standing next to me. "Then go for the rest of the stuff."

"Lydia, I'm really sorry about Halloween and all," I said.

"I know you are. It's OK, but you better get in line for the tamales," she said. "Get me a chicken one while you're at it. I'll get us seats by the entrance."

While I stood in line, the mariachi started up, first with "Las Mañanitas" to honor Our Lady of Guadalupe on her day and all Guadalupes in the world. Then, with their trumpets and guitars, the musicians broke into a string of traditional Mexican songs I had grown up with. I looked around, expecting to spot Socorrito hightailing it to the center of the room and kicking up her legs in fiery passion. Poor vieja chismosa made me laugh.

I filled my plate and went over to where Lydia was saving me a seat. She had a knack for picking the best places to sit. We had an unobstructed view of the hall and the piles of people streaming in and out the door next to us.

"Did you see him?" she asked.

"Who?"

"What do you mean, 'who'?" she said. "Your love, that's who."

"Francisco's here?" I couldn't believe it. He lived way over in San Ysidro and his family went to Mount Carmel Church. What was he doing here?

"What are you looking so surprised for, man?" she said, laughing. "Pendeja, stick those eyeballs back into their sockets. He's been staring at you for the last half hour. When I tell you to, real easy, you're going to turn your head slowly to the right as if you're just casually looking around, in no big hurry," she said. "But wait, not yet. Before you catch his eye and take off with him to the moon or something, I just want to tell you one thing and then ask you a favor, OK?"

Before I could answer, she went on: "Yoli, I just want to tell you I'm sorry about Chuy having to be in the hospital and all, but you did the right thing when you told the police where he was. I know you guys are close, and I know you probably thought maybe you could help him on your own. You did good, Yoli. And everyone's praying for him, and I know you're hurting, and you've been hurt and angry for a long time now, so I don't take it personally, OK?" Lydia said.

I couldn't say anything, the words tangled and bumping into each other in my throat. I was blinking a lot to keep my eyes from getting watery.

"And this is the favor I'm going to ask you," she continued. "I probably don't have to ask you this, but I want to make sure you get it right: You've got to give me the whole scoop when Francisco kisses you and all. I want a detailed description like only you know how to give. Make it real romantic so that I can dream about the day it happens to me, all right, cabrona?" she said.

"Man, Lydia," I said, laughing. "Since when do you start calling your best friend 'cabrona'?"

"Like right now, pinche cabrona," she said. "And remember, when you guys make out, think of all us women with our virginal lips and do it right, man." She got up. "I'm going for the pozole now. I'll cover for you if anyone asks for you. Orale, cabrona, make me proud."

"Thank you, Lydia," I said.

She nodded and was soon off to the pozole table.

We met in the courtyard between the church and the social hall. A brick and stucco ledge enclosed the square-shaped patio and also served as a sitting area. Behind this a trim hedge of hibiscus ran along the perimeter of the patio. Just beyond the patio along the walk leading to the social hall stood a cluster of tall roses, roses which Father Stadler always alluded to in some symbolic way in his sermons when talking about the paths we should and shouldn't take. The velvety red ones were my favorite; they had a pretty smell and thick, mean-looking thorns.

Francisco and I sat next to each other on the ledge, not saying anything. The sky was a clean black, as if all the smoke and burning of the last week had given it a new skin, soft and healing. The speckles of stars looked like granules of sugar ready for me to lick.

"Yoli," Francisco said, "how long have we been going around now?" His voice was soft and smooth, and I wondered if he could hear my heart pounding; I wondered if he felt as breathless and ready as I did.

"About a month," I said. Actually, it was twenty-three days, seven hours and—if I were to glance at my watch—about forty minutes, but I needed to keep cool here. Just remember Ana María's wise words: go slow.

We were silent. The night was too perfect to talk. In the distance the mariachi started up with "Sabor A Mi"—one of my favorite songs, and you could hear people clapping with approval, a few off-key voices unabashedly singing along.

Francisco gently moved my face to his and kissed me, and in the background the singers sang of not knowing whether there was love in Eternity. He now had his arm around me, and I rested my head against his shoulder.

Let the world stop right this moment, I was thinking. Let Eternity be this. I breathed in slowly, wanting to drink the night and the stars, hold on to this moment. It seemed a miracle that no one walked by, that we had the lovely courtyard all to ourselves on this December night. I was certain, gratefully certain, Our Lady of Guadalupe was allowing me to share this day with her, allowing me this special moment with my love.

It could have gone further. Leaning against his shoulder, I was sure I could hear his irregular breathing, his heart in a race with mine. The temptation to surrender myself completely to him was powerful. I remembered Lydia's request. Yes, I would describe it all in lovely details. And my diary awaited word, too. Already I had so much to report. And so I wanted to savor every little bit of what awaited me in the future: First, the holding hands—so many pages of my diary filled with precious details of his hand, the soft creases of his palm, the strong slender fingers, the dips and grooves, soft here, knobby there. Our hands interlocked, our hearts embracing in a cumbia, a cha-cha-cha, the twist, swirling and twirling and giddy.

And our kiss.

I looked up at the black night, searching for the moon, but it was nowhere to be seen.

Aha! A new moon. It made perfect sense to me. Its meaning was true and brilliant, and I shivered with the discovery of it, for I was certain now of what this night of my first kiss meant. It meant my life would reveal itself in phases like the moon's: first a new moon, the sky clean and alone and waiting; then slowly the peek of a silver sickle, preparing itself for the harvest that lay ahead; patiently growing—all in due time— now the half moon, a crisp white boat bobbing gently and tranquilly in a sea of infinite nights and possibilities. Little by little, then, the moon would reveal itself, until finally, slowly, ever so slowly—making a grand entrance as befits Her Majesty—the full moon, regal and victorious and ripe.

The night felt healing and full of promise.

27

"Where the hell are the boutonnieres? Did you take them out of the refrigerator? Are the guys wearing them?" Carolina asked, not really directing the question at any of us sisters, more at the air or the mirror or the closet. It was hard to tell whom she was talking to, and it didn't matter. She was in her slip and white stockings and bra, and because this was her wedding day, she was being obeyed by all of us, her humble subjects, as she directed us this way and that. Four lime green chiffon dresses lay draped from the top bunk bed down, making a canopy of the bottom bunk, a kind of curtain to the joyful backstage hysteria going on in the girls' room in preparation for the performance. On the single bed, four bouquets of pink and white carnations surrounded a triangular flowing bride's bouquet of white roses.

"Who the hell left these bouquets on the bed?" Carolina was beside herself now, near tears. "They belong in the refrigerator, for God's sake. Man, they're going to wilt any minute, don't you see?" Now spotting little Luz who was sitting on the floor carefully lining up the four pairs of lime green satiny high heels, Carolina said: "You there, take these bouquets and put them in the refrigerator."

Luz giggled at her, understanding that it was OK for her big sister to be hysterical and bossy. After all, it was her wedding day! She quickly got up from the floor and obediently carried the box of bouquets to the kitchen.

I was putting on my nylons, these new-fangled pantyhose, while at the same time being careful not to disturb the hair-do of gajos, a hair spray–sticky cluster of curls nesting on my head.

"My mascara," Ana María was calling out. "Who's got the mascara?"

"You mean to say you don't even have your make-up on!" Carolina seemed ready to burst. "Do you know that the wedding is in less than two hours and you don't even have your make-up on? Do you realize that?" Her voice was on the verge of hysteria. "What are the guys doing? Are they ready? Do they have their tuxes on?"

"They're outside putting the flowers on the cars," Monica reported.

"They don't fit in the refrigerator," Luz said, returning with the box of bouquets. "Mamá said to just leave them on the bed until it's time to go."

I now carefully slipped my dress on from the bottom up.

I looked around me, the girls' room a flurry of lime green chiffon, of wax orange blossoms for the lazo, of white tulle for the veil, of delicate pearls and appliqués on the bride's head piece, a crown for the Queen—the room itself looking like a bridal bouquet, bright and full of the promise of love and sweet perfume and satiny ribbons, the promise of being Queen for more than just a day.

"What about Chuy?" Carolina said, now getting into her wedding gown. "Is he ready?"

"He's fine," I said. "I'm going to go get him. Simmer down, mujer. It's just your wedding day, don't have a cow."

Carolina stared at me a moment. She wore her dark brown hair to her shoulder, soft and gentle. And her blue eyes looked excited and scared and anxious and probably a whole lot of other emotions I couldn't understand. After all, it was her wedding day, not mine.

"God, Carolina," I said. "You look absolutely beautiful."

Everyone stopped what they were doing and looked up— Ana María, with the just-found mascara poised in mid-application; Monica playing with her new dangling earrings; and Luz hugging a stack of *Bride's* magazines—and we all stared at our oldest sister for a moment.

Then Ana María went over to Carolina and hugged her, and I came up and hugged them and then the little ones came up to hug us, too. We didn't say anything, just held each other in a circle of five, a sisterly totem pole.

And Carolina, who had all morning been on the verge of hysteria, now seemed peaceful and still. "Thank you, hermanitas," she whispered to us.

I went outside, heading for the guys' room. Armando, Tony and Octavio were out front decorating the cars with strings of white Kleenex flowers we had made the night before. They were dressed in their tuxedos and yes, they had on their boutonnieres.

I lightly knocked on the door. "Chuy, it's me, Yoli," I said.

No answer. I slowly opened the door.

He was seated on the chair, facing the desk. The room was dark and so I turned on the reading lamp.

"I found the nail clippers, Chuy," I said. "Let me cut your fingernails now, OK?"

He quietly placed his hands on the desk, palms down. His nails were brittle and yellowing with a fungal disease, looking like hard, crusty tortoise shells. He looked out the window, his mind far away in another world, another dimension, branches and leaves and vines a tangle of knots in his head. The clip-clip of my actions was the only sound in the still room. So I joined Chuy in his meandering.

In my mind I had an image of the perfect sweet pea vines: During the day these delicate green tendrils made their way up—up, up, up—toward the sun. But in the night, when everyone was asleep in private dreams, the vines sneaked up to the moon, a crescent moon, and spun themselves around, entwined themselves in the nocturnal glow, catching the halo of the waiting, tranquil moon, a playful tangle of looping and curving. The moon laughed—tickled, delighted.

I looked up at Chuy, who had been silent this whole time and who was now staring at his nails as I clipped them. For a moment, I thought of taking his hand in mine, turning it over, palm side up and trying to read the creases, trying to decipher his future and mine. It didn't really matter, though. For wherever I might be—in the guys' room clipping Chuy's nails, in the girls' room applying a dab of perfume before the dresser's mirror, at a college dorm cramming for a Bio midterm, or in my lover's apartment, now about to make love or war (could anyone really know for sure?)—I would look up at our cielo, both heaven and sky, and see Chuy straddled comfortably on his chopper, on the curve of the crescent moon. His legs would be dangling as if he were a wild cowboy riding bareback on a loco horse. He'd wave to me, a playful salute. Up and down the curve of the moon—yahooo! whoopee! ahuwa!—he'd be riding his motorcycle. He'd wink and wave to me, both of us knowing he was feeling the freedom.

Then he'd do a simple thing: he'd toss me a translucent sweet pea blossom. As it fluttered down, I'd hold my breath and wait, hoping it wouldn't crumple or disintegrate in its descent. I'd run after it as it drifted through Conifer Street, as it whispered a greeting to the eucalyptus trees, for a moment disappearing behind the pepper tree trunk. It'd gracefully slip through the diamond pattern of the chain link fence. Swiftly it'd swoop down the canyon and sneak into the culvert under the freeway where I could no longer see it.

I was out of breath now, I didn't want to be teased; I didn't want to be hopeful and then disappointed. What if the blossom perished? What would it all mean? What would it all be for? My hands were cupped and turned upward toward the heavens—a prayer? a surrendering? a humble plea for its safe landing?

In the distance I could hear a car honk, a door slam, some talking and laughter out front where our brothers were prettying up the cars with Kleenex flowers.

Then it reappeared, this teasing, unpredictable sweet pea blossom as it drifted gently toward me. It dipped one last time in a curtsey.

There! I caught it, whole and undamaged.

More honking out front, somebody was calling our names.

"Come on, Chuy," I said. "It's time to get Carolina married."

We walked out of the guys' room toward the front yard where everyone was waiting. He shuffled a bit, groggy and lethargic from the medication. I lightly touched his arm to guide him.

Once out front, everyone in the universe seemed to be there waiting for us: Carolina in her magnificent gown, waving frantically; Papá, in his tuxedo looking guapo like all the men in my family, motioning for us to hurry it up, tapping his watch. Yes, yes, we're coming, my nod said. Mamá was beaming, wearing a beige brocade suit she had made herself. Even Don Epifranio was all decked out for the wedding, wearing some pinstriped suit about a hundred years old like himself, looking like our very own neighborhood Mafia viejito. Tony was letting Marisa into the passenger's side of his car, she looking pretty in a soft lavender dress. The rest of the guys were already in the Pontiac LeMans, revving up the engine, ready to get the show on the road.

We were now walking down the front sidewalk, me in my lime green chiffon gown and Chuy in his black tuxedo, looking ourselves like a tentative bride and groom. Someone handed me my bridesmaid bouquet. Hurry up, hurry up, everyone seemed to be saying, though no one spoke. There was a respectful silence as we made our way down the front walk.

Socorrito, dressed in a lacey blue dress and wearing blue high heel shoes and not her tired old fluffy blue mules, stood at her fence. And there was El Chango, limping toward us down the street, in a suit and tie, all formalito and distinguished-looking. The whole neighborhood was out on the street, and it occurred to me that they were here to greet Chuy, really, knowing he only had a day-pass for this event, not knowing when they might see him again.

Walking past our front fence laden with sweet pea flowers, on impulse I reached over and picked one, tucking it in my bouquet.

"I knew you were going to do that," he said, and for the first time in months, Chuy smiled.

■ ■ ■ ■ ■

—Acknowledgments

Many thanks to my editor Elizabeth Hadas for believing in my book and gently guiding me through the process. I am grateful to Alejandro Morales and the University of California Irvine Chicano/ Latino Literary Contest for twice giving me the initial, encouraging nod—a nod so valuable and deeply appreciated. Rudolfo Anaya, mentor and generous supporter of writers, mil gracias.

The following friends and writers offered me thoughtful and valuable suggestions for my novel: The Flower Hill Writers—John Dacapias, Tom Larson, Cory Meacham, Rava Villon, Lana Witt, and Bonnie ZoBell. A thank you to Annette Bostrom for suggesting I make my short story a novel. To Mark Avery, Mike Harberson, and Francisco X. Stork for their encouragement. Thank you to Julie Cárdenas for insightful comments, as well.

I am forever—and happily—indebted to the following for their friendship and guidance over the years: Dolores Nims, Eve Lill, and Yolanda Guerrero for showing me what an empowered woman can be; Joel and Birte Wise, for delicious dinners and nourishing conversations; Patti Kingston and Locke Epsten, my sophisticated L.A. Book Festival cohorts; Marta Sánchez and Paul Espinosa, for enduring friendship; Laurie Sanders-Cannon, for offering a peaceful retreat in her home and in her heart; Gayla Brown, for giving me much-needed grounding at the highly dramatic moments of my life; Sylvia Mendoza, for inspiring me with her admirable discipline as a writer; and Julie and Ezequiel Cárdenas, for exquisite friendship and moral support throughout the years.

Thank you to my brothers-in-law and sisters-in-law—Richard Larive, Hector Hernández, Victor Espíritu, Henry Soriano,

Alma Alicia Lepe, Lucy Angulo, and Patty Santana—for patience and good humor amidst the inevitable craziness and complexity that is sometimes part of life with the Santanas.

To the memory of Hymie and Sidonie Lowenkron—exemplary human beings—for understanding and loving me unconditionally.

To Bob Zamba, who has taught me valuable lessons in kindness and forgiveness, and who makes my heart dance in ways I never thought possible.

To my dear friend Cathy Anthony Tkach—role model and mother extraordinaire—who has shared wonderful walks with me through the eucalyptus groves of Scripps Ranch, all the while leading me towards clarity and self-knowledge.

Para Guadalupe, Teresa, y Cecilia Rosas—queridas tías, amigas, y madres—con todo mi cariño y aprecio por guiarnos y por ser mujeres ejemplares.

My love and gratitude to my son and resident technical expert, Isaac Manuel, who patiently helped me with an endless stream of computer questions, and who humored me by listening to dinner-time readings of my manuscript.

My love and gratitude to my daughter, Deborah Victoria, for reading draft after draft of the novel, offering important suggestions and insights and, in the process, allowing me valuable peeks into her own beautiful young woman's heart.

To the memory of my mother, Victoria Rosas, and my father, Manuel Santana, the sun and the moon of who I am.

And finally to my brothers and sisters—Victor, Oscar, Jorge, Sergio, Gloria, Delia, Irma, and Beatriz—whose spirit and love guided me in the telling of this story.

■ ■ ■ ■